The Book of Christmas Joy

A Rev. Thomas Book Mystery

Darrow Woods

RELUCTANT SLEUTH
LIVING IN A NOT ALWAYS SO COZY MYSTERY

Reluctant Sleuth Press

This book is fiction. The characters and events portrayed exist only in the author's imagination.

ISBN-978-1-7390508-2-5

Chapter heading tree graphic by: flatart on Freepik

Cover Art by: Max Vanderheide

Cover Design by: Grace Enns

Author Photo by: Lexie Chamberlain

Published by Reluctant Sleuth Press

Reluctant Sleuth Press has a physical office on the shore of Lake Erie. We gratefully acknowledge the Three Fires Confederacy (Ojibwe, Potawatomie and Odawa) and the traditional ancestral, unceded territory of our neighbours, the Caldwell First Nation. We recognize and respect the First Nations who have cared for the land and waters of Turtle Island since time immemorial.

Created in Canada

**This book is dedicated to my family,
and to the generous folks who support and encourage my writing.**

"joy is the intersection between the human and the divine, and that's why at some points, when you experience joy you throw your hands in the air, you laugh, you dance, but at other times you experience joy you cry, and you like release in this other way, and it's the same thing, and its coming from this place of letting go..."

MICHAEL FRANTI

Foreword

Sharpe Street United Church does not exist outside of the author's imagination. Sun Parlour is a made up town, that may look a little like an actual community on the shore of Lake Erie, in Southwestern Ontario.

In the real Essex County there is a massive agricultural industry, much of it greenhouse-based, that employs tens of thousands of temporary foreign workers. Most greenhouse operators, and other farm owners are law-abiding and fair employers.

The references to human trafficking, undocumented workers, disappeared people, and to an underground economy catering to greenhouse workers are all based on articles from credible news sources.

The Christmas Tree Farm in the story is a very real, and absolutely wonderful place where we get our tree every year.

Chapter 1

Tuesday Evening (11 days to Christmas)

Hope said, “Uh, Dad… the Christmas tree fell over, and it’s bleeding.”

The heavy oak door at the church’s main entrance slammed shut behind Tom, but not before allowing in a final wintry gust. It sent a shiver through him as he sped to catch up with his daughter. The only light in the dark foyer was an eerie red glow from the exit sign above the door.

Hope had halted between the swinging doors that opened saloon-style into the shadowy sanctuary. Zeke, a large sable-coated German shepherd was beside her, poised stiff as a pointer dog tracking a fallen duck.

“Zeke’s acting weird. He’s like aimed at the tree, and just staring at it.”

Tom said, “I’ve seen this before. He’s picked up a scent, and he’s telling us he wants to work the scene.”

Tom remembered the search dog’s intense stance from the day he’d first met Zeke and his handler Annika. They’d been brought in by a reality TV show for a video shoot at Tom’s previous church. Filming had ended when Zeke sniffed out a dead body in the basement.

Tom could see Hope was shivering.

Before heading over to the church she’d pulled on Tom’s Timberland hikers, which were three sizes too big, but hadn’t bothered grabbing a jacket. Hope’s long blonde hair, falling loose down the back of her over-sized sweatshirt, reminded Tom of his daughter as a little girl. He took off his barn coat and draped it over her shoulders.

"Thanks Dad."

Tom fingered the cellophane bag in his cardigan pocket for a cube of freeze-dried beef liver. The treats and instructions about when they were needed, were part of the K-9 care package Annika had left with him before he brought her to the airport.

They'd agreed to take a break, and she was spending Christmas in Holland with relatives.

Zeke's ears went up at the crinkle of the treat bag. He turned his big head back towards Tom. The search dog issued a short sharp bark, then resumed his straight arrow posture, pointing towards the downed tree.

"Easy, Zeke. You're a good dog."

Zeke's head turned toward the voice. His long pink tongue lolled out to lick the morsel from Tom's open palm.

"Good boy, Zeke. Stand down."

Zeke squatted on his haunches, his frame relaxed.

Powerful outdoor security lights blazed bright, activated by their dash across the snowy yard from the parsonage to the church. The hulking Victorian brick structures were built within a stone's throw of each other, not that anyone would be allowed to throw a stone, or anything else in the shared yard.

A harsh white glare pushed through the tall leaded glass windows to illumine the twenty-foot artificial tree, which had toppled from the chancel platform. Branches had jammed upward, bent and broken as they were crammed between the oak pews on both sides of the centre aisle.

Tom pushed open the swinging door to his right and felt along the sanctuary wall for the switch to activate the pendant lamps that hung down from the ceiling. The additional light glinted on shards of broken glass ornaments, scattered under the pews. Tom thought a few had survived intact, but he expected there'd be hell to pay over the smashing of those cherished relics.

The angel tree topper, in a lacy gown like a wedding dress, had flown off to one side of the crown of the fallen Christmas tree. White frilly fabric was stained a ruddy brown, as it absorbed the dark viscous fluid that flowed out from under greenery.

Hope was right. It looked like the tree was bleeding.

Chapter 2

Late Tuesday Evening (11 Days to Christmas)

Hope's Journal

I'm starting the journal I need to keep over the Christmas break for my Contemporary Spirituality course, because right now I really need something to do.

Professor Barbour taught us about the Examen in the very first lecture, back in September. He reminded us of that last week as he spread index cards out on a table in front of us.

He said, "I asked you to take 5 minutes at the end of your day to record when you noticed feeling something.

"Were they sensual moments, like when you bit into a fresh strawberry?"

"Were they moments of frustration, like when you step in something left on the driveway by the neighbour's dog?"

"What did those experiences evoke in you? Did they put you in touch, give you a glimpse of something deeper?"

We were each to turn over an index card and pay attention to our inner responses to the word written on it. Our final assignment would be to write something based on a word that spoke to us.

He said, "This is not about spouting words back to prove you read the syllabus. I want you to go deep and show me something real about you."

I was glad he didn't say anything about keeping the first card you touched.

My first one said Guilt. Nope.

The second was Hope. Not doing that.

Then I pulled Joy.

There's this song by Bruce Cockburn my Dad loves.

When Mom was dying, I repeated the chorus over and over, as a prayer.

"As longing becomes love. As night turns to day. Everything changes. Joy will find a way."

I'll write my book of joy, not just to get the assignment done, but to try to get at the inkling, this vague sense I have, that there actually is something deeper than the good and bad of the day, the pluses and minuses. My goal is to see if it's possible to recognize a deeper joy that persists even when you've just stepped in the neighbour dog's crap.

It's after midnight, and Dad's still over at the church. This feels too much like before. He found a body in his last church, and we were both almost killed, and he ended up in hospital.

Tonight was going so great. We were each plunked down in one of our big leather lazy boys. Mom bought them before I was born, when she started making real money as a nurse. Laying back in mine always makes feel held by her. I had Gran's quilt on top of me.

We'd just got to the part of the movie "It's a Wonderful Life" where Donna Reed and Jimmy Stewart began their honeymoon in the broken-down old house she bought without telling him. It was the old Grenville house. Earlier in the movie we learned kids in that town would make a wish and throw a stone at the house. If they broke a window, they'd get their wish.

There's a lot in that movie about how sad it is when dreams don't come true.

It blew me away how much the house in the movie looks like the parsonage. High peaked roofs and tall windows, and all that old brick.

The furniture at Dad's is less sketchy than the stuff in the movie. It's a weird mix of things he brought here, and pieces that came with the place.

Gran told me in the old days church-provided houses usually came furnished. She said many ministers couldn't afford their own furniture on what the church paid, and it was cheaper to move them when the time came, if all they had was a few boxes and some luggage.

It looks to me like this also gave church folks a place to dump stuff they didn't want anymore and feel good about it. If she were here, Gran would probably say I was being "most uncharitable" then wink and tell me I was bang on. I miss her, the way she was before dementia took away her spark, and everything else.

I pushed things around in the parlour to make room for the Christmas tree, which we'll set up one night this week. Then I'll tackle the moving boxes that Dad still has in every room, even though he's been here for like a year and a half.

Back in Bedford Falls, Jimmy and Donna were getting romantic in that hokey old movie way that was too cringey to watch with my father.

I got up to zap more popcorn. Looking out the window, I saw a weird glow bouncing around inside the church next door.

Zeke picked up that something was going on.

We all went next door to the church. Zeke's a big German Shepherd who can look scary if you don't know him, so he's a good friend to have when you walk into an old building that's supposed to be empty but might not be.

Zeke's a search and rescue dog, who's also been trained to sniff out corpses, blood, and body parts. He's with us for the holidays.

Zeke belongs to Annika, who is lovely. My Dad met her when she and Zeke were hired for a video shoot at Dad's old church. That's literally a whole other story.

Dad and Annika hit it off and started something that seems to be kind of on hold for now. The fact that he moved away from Oakville after Gran died makes it harder.

But back to tonight, and why I need something to keep me occupied.

I played so much flashlight hide and seek in youth group it kind of feels normal to walk into a dark church, but... this church is never locked. My Dad doesn't even have keys for the outside doors. So anyone can walk in and do whatever, to whoever.

As Zeke and I entered the sanctuary, the light through the big windows was enough that I saw that the ginormous artificial tree had been knocked over. The broken branches and smashed ornaments weren't the worst of it.

Dad came in pretty quick behind us, which I was glad about, because Zeke had switched into search mode and was letting us know there was something bad.

Dad hit the lights, and we stepped close enough to see the fallen tree, and a lot of blood on the floor. He raised his hand and waved me off with some words about not disturbing the scene, which made me think he'd already noticed something.

Dad leaned in and felt around under the twisted branches with his hands. He paused with one hand deep under the fake greenery, but was shaking his head as he pulled it back.

"It's too late. There's no pulse, and she's cold to the touch."

He saw that I hadn't moved, and I saw fear, and something else, in his eyes.

I don't think he was totally aware of his actions. Dad waved me off again, and this time, thick drops of dark red blood flew off his fingertips.

He wiped his hands on his pants, then dialed 911 and sent Zeke and I back to the parsonage.

Even though I didn't like leaving Dad on his own, I was glad to get out of there.

All that blood. And the smell. Like dirty old pennies, and the freshly filled diapers I remember from walking the hall to Gran's room on the memory care ward.

I don't know how my Auntie Gwen does it. She's a funeral director and has told me about some of the dead people she's helped to clean and fix up, well the best they could.

In the midst of all this cruelty, sadness and death there was a good thing.

As Zeke and I left the church Dad's phone blared the beginning of the 1960's Batman theme, the ring tone I set up for Michael Powers.

Michael and Dad met when his mom and mine were in hospice. He's a police detective. For a while my Auntie Gwen (who's not really my aunt) thought he was a bad influence, dragging Dad along as Robin to his Batman, into things a pastor had no business messing with. She's mellowed about that, so now it's more like a tease.

Dad had probably left a message, and this was Michael calling back. But maybe not. Michael has this way of showing up when Dad needs help. When things hit the fan last time, we found out that he was still connected to the cops, even though most people thought he was retired.

I'm glad Dad has Michael to talk to about what we saw tonight, and I also worry about what happens next. Dad kind of fell apart after Gran died.

Chapter 3

Early Wednesday Morning (10 Days to Christmas)

Tom was deep into one of his early morning dreams. This one was like seeing himself in an old black and white movie. He was played by a young Jimmy Stewart, decked out in a dark wool suit with an English vicar's clerical collar, bright white all the way round like a halo.

The Reverend Jimmy/Tom stood at one end of a board room panelled in dark wood, arms outstretched like Jesus standing in the prow of boat, attempting to calm a storm. Around a long oak table warped and cracked by age, people Tom didn't recognize leaned forward from captain's chairs to yell at him.

The sheer volume of their conflicting voices washed any sense out of their words. The air was electric and heavy like lightning would soon strike. Tom felt the room rock violently, like he was in a very small boat in a large turbulent sea.

At the other end of the table, the most angry of the strangers stood, balancing both hands on the table against the motion of the waves. Tom felt their eyes drill into him but couldn't make out the face. Heavy mist obscured his sight. A voice thundered through the cloud.

"At your last church the senior pastor was killed, and you got their biggest giver arrested for murder. You come here, and see what happens?"

His dream morphed the way they do. Now Tom looked more like himself, but as a boy. It was the day he'd first stood his ground to shield his little brother from his father's drunken rage.

Ten-year-old Tom assumed the ready stance Master Choi taught him at Taekwondo. Feet straight, shoulder width apart, arms up in front with his fists closed and eyes fixed on the threat.

He couldn't make out his father's face, but he heard him roar.

"Get out of my way! Life would have been so different if you hadn't come along. I wish you'd never been born!"

Tom wanted his younger self to say, "Yeah, and you made me wish that too."

Before that line could be delivered Tom was back in his upstairs bedroom in the parsonage, being roused from the murky depths by the jaunty guitar intro of "Wondering Where the Lions Are".

Tom reached towards the nightstand, fumbling to find his phone. Uncovered, his bare arm felt the frigid air beyond the comfort of the thick duvet.

Bruce Cockburn sang out through the phone speaker about the sun being up, and the world having survived into another day, but Tom wasn't ready to confirm either claim.

The night before, the fire crew had been first to leave, and then EMS, after they'd confirmed what he already knew.

He'd stayed on scene with the local cops late into the night. When he finally dragged himself back across the yard to the parsonage, Hope was sitting in the front parlour. She had all the lights blazing so he couldn't miss her, waiting to hear what took him so long.

Sleep had not come easily, after all of it.

The clip from the Cockburn song was his ringtone for unknown callers. It has a line about "wondering where the lions are" that reminds Tom to listen with care, and a degree of caution.

Bruce had sung about the sun being up, but the only light in Tom's bedroom glared bright and sharp from the cellphone screen, which told him it was 7:16 am, and the incoming call was from the Sunny Shores Credit Union.

"Good morning, this is Tom Book."

"Reverend Tom, Sorry to call so early. I trust you don't mind..."

Tom knew the voice. Penny Oltmann-Potter, the credit union manager, church treasurer, and second soprano in the choir.

"Uh, good morning, Penny. What... I mean, how can I..."

The week before, Tom had arrived late to the church hall for the choir's Christmas social. He'd noticed Penny sitting alone at the far end of the long dining table, with empty seats on either side of her. At the other end, Liza Testardo was telling a loud story, to the apparent amusement of the rest of the choir.

Tom had stopped at the buffet to fill his plate, then headed towards Penny, but she'd risen to leave before he could get there. She'd barely touched the food on the plate she left behind.

Penny's dramatic sigh came through Tom's phone, and then she said, "After I heard about poor Gloria, I just couldn't sleep..."

Tom began, "I... uh, I'm not sure..."

"It's okay, Reverend Tom, I already know. My uh... close friend Kelly Halligan is the deputy fire chief. He told me all about what happened to poor, poor Gloria!"

Tom sat up in bed, touched the lamp switch, careful to close his eyes before the light could hit them. He cracked one eyelid, then the other.

Penny seemed to get a charge from referring to Gloria Sharpe, born into one of the county's "fine old families" as poor.

"I can't really talk about that Penny. The police..."

"Oh, I understand Reverend. I'm sure you're as discreet as I am. Working in financial services, I uphold a high standard of confidentiality..."

Tom was awake enough to be cautious of someone who signaled their own virtue.

"Then you'll understand that I need to..."

"It can be such a burden, can't it, keeping a secret? Kelly knows my lips are sealed, and he needed to talk. He said it was terrible. He's known poor Gloria his whole life, and to see her that way..."

Her words roused images of the police constables lifting the middle section of the big artificial tree, revealing Gloria Sharpe, sprawled on the polished hardwood, arms at wrong angles.

Her grey hair was matted to the floor by blood from a deep bash to the back of her skull.

The fingers of her right hand still clutched the strap of her open handbag, which had spilled a sheaf of hundred-dollar bills onto the floor, now thickly painted with congealing blood.

Tom had chastised himself at the time for thinking all that cash had done nothing to protect Gloria from such a violent ending.

“I don’t believe the police have confirmed the identity of the person found in the church, Penny. They have a certain protocol. We really can’t...”

“I couldn’t sleep, thinking about poor Gloria’s head caved in, and the poor dear’s money all over the bloody floor. I decided to come in early to the office. It’s a good thing I did!”

“I’m not following, Penny. What are you...”

“You’re aware most of the church’s budget is covered by the Sharpe Trust?”

As relieved as he was to leave the topic of Gloria’s corpse, it felt odd to shift so quickly to money matters.

“Well... yes.”

At his hiring interview, Tom had been told about the congregation’s finances. He’d never heard anything like it. They didn’t fundraise, and didn’t rely on the minimal donations that came in.

“It’s the church’s current account,” Penny explained. “All scheduled withdrawals come out of it. Utilities, insurance, payroll, things like that. Gloria deposits a set amount every month.”

“Okay...”

“I’ve urged her to leave a larger balance, but she wouldn’t have it. Told me she’d rather keep the money working as long as possible before it was needed.”

“This really sounds like something for the executive committee, Penny.”

"The Credit Union loses money on current accounts, so we don't pay interest. I see her point, or I did... the poor thing. But the money never came in."

"What are you saying?"

"The current account balance is well below what's needed to cover December. And since it was never an issue, the church doesn't have overdraft protection."

"So, the church has no money?"

"Gloria dribbled in just enough each month to cover expenses. Except this month she didn't."

"What do we do?"

"Reverend Tom, my next call will be to Jesse King. It's up to him as chair to call an emergency executive meeting. I thought you deserved a heads up. With poor Gloria... being dead, and all, there's going to be a problem."

Tom tossed back the covers and got up from his bed. The cold floor was a shock to his bare feet, and a chill ran through him. He reached for his robe and searched his mind for a way out of this conversation.

"Penny, you can't keep saying Gloria's dead. We have to wait for the police to release information when they can. As to the church's financial... situation, can't someone else transfer funds from the endowment?"

As he said it, Tom realized Penny had maneuvered him into confirming Gloria's death.

"That I wouldn't know, Reverend Tom. Have a good morning, now. I have other calls to make."

Chapter 4

Mid Wednesday Morning (10 Days to Christmas)

Barbara Palmieri said, "You okay, Tom? You look a little... Well, you look like crap. Lawrence, what do you think? How does he look?"

Tom had first met the Detective Sergeant during a murder investigation at his former church in Oakville. She exuded a confident physicality Tom believed came from her practice of martial arts whose names he couldn't remember.

Barbara's long auburn hair was pulled away from her face in a loose ponytail. On this morning, the intense green eyes Tom remembered were behind cat's eyeglasses fitted with the yellow lenses favoured by hackers.

Tom sat solo on one side of a booth at the Wagon Wheel diner. It was framed in stained pine.

Barbara was on the opposite bench, beside her work partner, Detective Staff Sergeant Lawrence Kitchen. He'd be in charge of the investigation at Saint Mungo's Church in Oakville.

Sharing the bench seat allowed them to peer at the laptop that filled the space between their breakfast choices.

Lawrence spooned yogurt and raisins into a steaming bowl of steel-cut oatmeal.

"How does Tom look? Like any of us might when they've seen a terrible thing."

Tom said, "I'm, okay... mostly. It was a rugged night."

Barbara poured ketchup between the link sausages and home-fries of her Hungry Rancher's Special.

The viscous red fluid reminded Tom of the gory scene in the sanctuary. He focused instead on the large copper carafe left by the server.

Tom said, "Can I warm your coffees?"

"No, I'm good," Barbara said. "Sorry, Tom. I need to remember you knew the vic... I mean, Ms. Sharpe."

"Sure, I'll take a little more," Lawrence said. "Don't mind my partner. She's one of these modern crime-fighters who spend more time with search engines than humans."

Tom set down the carafe to tend to his own breakfast. He crunched away at crisp bacon while taking fork and knife to his buttermilk pancakes, quickly reducing the tall stack to bite-size chunks.

At the Wagon Wheel, pancakes came with a stone-ware jug of maple syrup. Tom hefted the jug over his plate and watched the amber syrup soak into the mound.

"To be honest, after countless conversations with Gloria about committees, schedules and the placement of tables at church functions, I don't feel like I knew anything real about her."

Lawrence said, "Which may not make it any less sad, or stressful."

Lawrence had the vibe of a high school English teacher, right down to the hints of grey in his unkempt brown hair, and the cashmere sweater pulled over his collared shirt. There was kindness in his hazel eyes, and he had a gift for seeing into the hearts and minds of those he looked at.

Tom said, "I could have gone without finding Gloria... like that, and having Hope see all that blood. I didn't get much sleep and today started with a bad phone call. Then I was all set to drive over here, and she'd done it again..."

He paused as two servers passed by, each carrying two loaded breakfast plates.

The servers both wore blue jeans and western shirts, topped with red and white gingham check aprons. The younger of the two sported streaks of Christmas red and green in her blonde hair.

The pair tracked across well-worn carpet, halting at a table in the middle of the room.

Four women Tom recognized from the church walking group looked up with eager smiles at the arrival of their Hungry Rancher Specials.

Barbara said, "Sorry, who did what to who?"

Hoping his voice hadn't carried, Tom listened to the clinking of cutlery on plates, the chatter of other diners, the sizzle of the grill and the ringing of the order up bell. Under it all, Mel Torme sang about chestnuts and an open fire.

There was a loud whoosh of air, and jingling bells as the front door opened, then Tom continued in a subdued tone.

"Every few weeks the church secretary parks her Smart car right behind me. She noses it in, so the passenger side lines up with the Range Rover's rear bumper."

Lawrence said, "This in the church parking lot?"

"No." Tom said, "That's the big lot across the back alley. I'm talking about a parking strip right behind the parsonage. There's a spot for me, and one for church staff, but it's narrow, so we have to park lengthwise."

Barbara hit a few laptop keys, and said, "I see it. We're tapped into the church's security camera. Her car is still tucked behind yours. There's a work truck in the other spot."

Tom said, "Yeah, that was something else. Liza complained I didn't tell her the guys were coming to check the boiler. Why would I know that? She gave them her spot and slotted her car behind mine. Good thing my reverse warning works."

Lawrence angled the screen for a better view.

It must be Barbara's computer. Tom doubted Lawrence had a Bat-Signal decal on his work laptop.

Tom said, "Sorry to be crabbing."

Lawrence said, "If she parked in the big lot, it might mean a dozen more steps to the back entrance. Right now, there's only two vehicles over there."

"One's the red Buick registered to Gloria Sharpe, which will be towed to Leamington before we finish breakfast."

"The other is a silver Hyundai Santa Fe. It has a big crate in the back, looks like a travel kennel."

Tom said, "The Hyundai belongs to my friend Annika."

Barbara spiked peameal bacon with her fork.

"The K-9 handler. We like her. But what's the secretary's deal?"

"I'm the first minister to live next to the church since Covid. She says she got used to parking behind the parsonage. I think it's her way of reminding me I'm temporary."

Barbara said, "And Lawrence wonders why I'd rather work with data."

Like every recruit, Barbara started in uniform. She'd found her niche in data management and research, and earned a master's degree in library and information science during her first years on the job.

Tom said, "I was surprised your guys let anyone in the building this morning."

Lawrence said, "The local Crime Bureau got orders to release everything except the sanctuary, and the scene of crime team was fast-tracked, but given a very narrow brief. The building is to be cleared by end of today, regardless."

Tom said, "Regardless of what?"

Barbara said, "Protocol, forensic findings, or any reservations we might have."

Tom refilled his mug, and offered the carafe to Lawrence and Barbara. They both shook their heads.

Lawrence said, "Michael wasn't pleased. He pulled strings to get us here, because of your involvement, and because... Well, we'll get to that later."

Michael Powers ran the special team Lawrence and Barbara joined when they badged over to the OPP from the Halton Regional Police in Oakville.

Tom said, "I already thought we'd have to cancel this coming Sunday, but maybe be back in the building for Christmas Eve. Why the rush?"

Barbara said, "Notifying next of kin was handled a couple pay grades up, because it meant calling Robert Sharpe, the victim's brother. He's not just a Member of Parliament, he's a rising star in the governing party."

"It didn't take long for a call to be made to someone even higher on the Sunshine List."

"Word came down fast, that we're not to interfere with your church services, especially not Ms. Sharpe's funeral, which may already be scheduled."

Barbara said that last bit with a grin, then crunched down on some very crisp bacon.

Tom wasn't smiling.

"Won't there be a postmortem?"

Lawrence said, "Happening as we speak."

"Isn't that..."

Barbara said, "Yeah, crazy fast."

Tom said, "I'm not a detective like you two..."

Lawrence said, "You were a big help, last time."

Barbara said, "Better let him finish, Staff Sergeant. I think he's on to us."

Tom said, "You've been very free with details... and you just said Michael wanted this case. It's day one of what I'd guess is a high-profile investigation. You wouldn't have time for a leisurely breakfast, unless..."

Lawrence said, "Michael said you talked to him last night."

"I talked to 911, then I called him."

Tom and Michael met at the Oakville Hospice, and bonded over late nights of too much coffee and a jigsaw puzzle they never finished. When Michael's mother died, Tom presided at her funeral. Soon after Tom's wife died, Michael joined Tom's church.

Barbara said, "And Michael called us. We were already in London on a related matter."

When bodies started dropping back in Oakville, Michael confided to Tom he'd been recruited out of retirement for a special intelligence unit.

Lawrence said, "We're here to liaise between an ongoing organized crime investigation, and the investigation of Ms. Sharpe's death."

Tom said, "And you're reading me in because..."

"You're a good pastor," Lawrence said. "You bring a calming presence. Your congregation will need you to keep doing what you do."

Barbara said, "You picked up good intel on the Saint Mungo's case."

Lawrence said, "You're good at reading people. As Michael says, see what you see. We do what we do, and we can compare notes."

Tom was drawn to the sense of connection to their team. He also remembered the painful and sleepless night in hospital after his car was rammed by a murder suspect with a snowplow truck.

"Last time my amateur sleuthing almost got Hope and I killed. Michael rolled in to save the day like he does, and the two of you were great, but..."

Barbara said, "You saw what was done to Gloria, and that's scary. But your proximity to the crime, and to our unknown subject, is the same whether or not you work with us. If we check in with each other, you'll be tuned in. We'll have your back, Tom."

"I believe that, Barbara. I haven't forgotten how your team watched Hope while I was in hospital. But..."

Lawrence said, "There's something else. Michael said to save it for last."

Tom looked at Barbara.

"Is this the finishing blow?"

Barbara smiled. "In karate it's Tegatana. The knifehand. There are ties between Gloria Sharpe's family, and the Kazinskis."

Tom said, "Uh huh."

He had a physical memory of Brad Kazinski's hand pressing down hard on his shoulder.

From an office in the back of a payday loan store down the block from Tom's former church in Oakville, Brad Kazinski controlled a chunk of the illicit drug trade from Mississauga to Niagara Falls. He was also reforming the family image by muscling into legitimate enterprises.

Lawrence said, "We've not forgotten your previous interactions with Mr. Kazinski."

Tom helped uncover a scheme involving the senior pastor. Kazinski threatened Tom and his daughter. At the time, there'd been no way to hold Kazinski accountable without jeopardizing a larger investigation.

Tom felt an urge rising, less virtuous than his instinct to protect Hope. He closed his eyes and practiced what his late wife Carrie called square breathing. Breathe in on a four count. Hold. Breathe out on four. Hold. Repeat as needed.

Lawrence said, “What is it, Tom?”

“Barbara’s right. I worry there could be a killer out there. But what scares me more, is what working in your world brings up in me.”

Lawrence put down his spoon and pushed away the oatmeal bowl. He seemed to study the scratches in the orange Formica table top, as if looking for a pattern.

“I won’t pretend it gets easier. We see the aftermath of people doing very bad things.”

Bells jingled as the diner's front door opened, allowing in a rush of cold air.

Barbara nodded.

“What he said.”

Tom said, “I used to think I was a pacifist. But now there’s a growing edge in me, that feels people who do very bad things should be stopped.”

Barbara lifted her coffee cup.

“So is that a yes or a no?”

Chapter 5

Later Wednesday Morning (10 Days to Christmas)

"I was in school with him, all the way up from kindergarten," Jesse King said. "Johnny Friendly. We were even... close for a brief time, in high school. But he's being a jerk."

Tom sat in a padded chair he'd pulled over from the mahogany dining table that dominated the arrangements room, which doubled as Jesse's office. They often met there with families to work out funeral details.

Jesse sat at his workspace; a roll-top desk set against the back wall. He'd rotated his desk chair to face Tom.

"Sorry Tom, you're not here to listen to me complain..."

In the original layout of the large Victorian house this had been the dining room. The high ceiling was finished in tin plate tiles, and the walls featured dense floral print wallpaper, elaborate crown moulding and ornate brass wall sconces.

The only departure from the original elegance was a large portrait over Jesse's desk of Elvis Presley, looking eternally young in a black leather jumpsuit.

The recessed fixtures that normally lit up Jesse's idol were switched off.

Tom said, "I'm guessing this Johnny Friendly guy has something to do with the plans for Gloria's funeral."

Jesse was the thirty-something managing director of the Aird and Bower Funeral Home. He had a full head of jet-black hair, light olive skin, and piercing blue eyes, which at this moment glinted with anger.

Jesse said, "Yes. He pushed hard to get me to schedule Gloria's service for Friday. He strongly suggested we postpone Sylvie's visitation and service. He said his office would compensate the family."

Sylvie Gauthier had been killed the previous week, in a snowmobile accident up north. She'd been a classroom aide at the primary school, and a support worker at the Community Living group home.

Tom said, "Seriously? He'd bribe a grieving family, like they were being bumped from an over-booked flight?"

"Thank you," Jesse said. "That's exactly how I heard it, and I told him it wasn't going to happen."

Just a few days before, sitting at the long table in this room, Sylvie's widower, Albert had confided that she'd been two months pregnant. This would have been their first child.

Tom said, "Sylvie's funeral isn't just for her family, it's for the whole town. The kids and the other staff at the school adored her, and so did the folks at the group home."

Jesse said, "I'm worried about Albert. He was driving the snowmobile when it happened. He wouldn't say it when you were here, but he told me later he was going too fast. They were on a trail cut through crown land, came around a bend and hit a fallen tree. He held on, but she was thrown off and broke her neck."

"So, he blames himself, on top of losing Sylvie, and the baby," Tom said. "Complicated grief. And your friend thinks he can slip him a few bucks and shift the funeral."

Jesse said, "Not exactly my friend. But I'll get to that. I'm worried Albert might still be charged. On top of everything else. The poor guy."

Tom said, "After we met with Albert last week, I wondered the same thing. I talked to a friend who's high up in the OPP. He says there'll be no charges. It'd be different if other people were hurt, or he'd been impaired."

"That's something, anyway," Jesse said.

Tom said, "My friend talked to his guy up there. Within reason, that detachment tends towards selective enforcement with the winter tourists. The motels and restaurants need the trade, and the municipality depends on the tax base. They talk about the cost of doing business with people from down south who have more horsepower than brains. Not that I'd say any of this to Albert."

"I know you wouldn't," Jesse said. "The whole thing is hard, for everyone. I know Sylvie's family. I went to school with her sister."

"You went to school with everybody's sister."

Jesse said, "It's one of the best, and worst things about life in a small town. And that stuff about what's good and bad for business happens here too. Money talks, and big money hushes things up. The grow lights in those greenhouses turn the sky disco colours every night, despite the laws about light pollution. Sorry, I'm complaining again."

"It's all good, Jesse," Tom smiled. "You need to blow off some steam."

"It's the hypocrisy, Tom. Johnny Friendly argued Gloria deserved special treatment because she's from a leading family. He's schooling me about civic responsibility and I'm thinking to myself, Gloria's family is tight with the big greenhouse growers."

Jesse wore his usual work suit, a sombre three-piece in charcoal wool with the faintest chalk line pinstripe. It could be argued his magenta silk tie and pocket square were a bit flamboyant, but Jesse said the shade matched the flashing purple lights on the funeral home cars.

The silk accessories reminded Tom of the sweat-soaked scarves Jesse gifted with great ceremony to swooning audience members in his side gig as an award-winning Elvis tribute artist.

"Who is this guy?" Tom said. "And is his name really Johnny Friendly?"

"He's Robert Sharpe's personal assistant."

Tom said, "Is he the one who called me? He didn't give his name; just said he was The Member's aide. He told me The Member would only require 15 minutes for the eulogy and wanted me to tell his son Bobby that he would not be invited to speak."

"That sounds like him," Jesse said. "His real name is John Freund, but at Sun Parlour High School we called him Johnny Friendly."

Tom said, "How did any of us survive high school?"

"Johnny weaseled his way up from stamp licking campaign volunteer to being Sharpe's right-hand man. I tried to tell him there was no point trying to rush Gloria's funeral, because we'd have to wait on the coroner."

Tom said, "Exactly. Her death looks suspicious, and they'll need to cover all the bases."

"Johnny said, and I'm quoting him exactly here, 'don't get your sequined jumpsuit all sweaty, Jesse, it's all been sorted.' "

That might explain why Jesse turned off the lights over Elvis.

Tom said, "It sounds like strings are being pulled from way up there on Parliament Hill. So, what's the plan?"

Jesse said, "I asked John to pass on to Mr. Sharpe that while we have a long and valued history with his family, we'd understand if they turned to another funeral home. I suggested Harrison's in Leamington."

Tom said, "What did he say?"

"It would be bad optics to move the event out of town. Who talks like that about a funeral?"

Tom said, "You saved me having to say no. I'm not about to postpone Sylvie's funeral."

"We're on the same page Tom. I also talked to Mrs. Bower, and she backed me one hundred percent. She also said if we couldn't use the church, the family could have the use of our chapel at no charge."

Tom wasn't surprised. Andrea Bower, widow of the third generation of Bowers in Aird and Bower and current owner, was a big Jesse fan.

"So, Sylvie's visitation Thursday, and funeral Friday. How about the Blue Christmas Concert? Are we still on for Saturday?"

Mrs. Bower sponsored Blue Christmas with Elvis every December. It was held at the church, as close as possible to the Winter Solstice. It was a time to gather grieving families, especially those who'd lost loved ones in the past year.

"We are absolutely still on," Jesse said. "The guys in the Takin' Care of Business Band turned down other gigs to be there, and the concert is a big fundraiser for Community Living. We won't mess with that, especially since Sylvie worked there."

Tom said, "I'm glad, Jesse." He opened his phone's calendar.

"Are you thinking visitation for Sylvie tomorrow, her service here Friday, then Gloria's visitation Saturday and Sunday, and her service at the church on Monday?"

"Does that work for you? You okay giving up your day off, with your daughter home for the holidays?"

"She grew up as a preacher's kid, Jesse. It comes with the territory. We compensate by taking time off when no one's looking."

"I figured you'd say that. I'll call Johnny... John and tell him what we're prepared to offer."

"Remind him we're on hold until the police officially release the sanctuary. The forensics team is still working the scene. After that we'll need something more than light housekeeping."

"Johnny said not to worry. The sanctuary will be released by the end of today, and Mr. Sharpe will foot the bill for trauma cleaners."

Jesse raised his eyebrows. "He guaranteed they'd make it like it never happened."

Tom said, "What a tragic and insensitive thing to say... I mean, please thank The Member for his generosity."

Tom checked the time on his phone, then said, "Jesse, I better get going. I've got work to do before Bible Study tonight. Are we still good to meet here?"

Jesse spun his chair back to his desk, and retrieved a letter-sized white envelope, with the official church crest and return address.

"Yeah, of course, ... but can we talk about one more thing, while I've got you?"

Tom spotted the envelope, but said, "Tomorrow night's meeting?"

As board chair, Jesse had called an emergency meeting of the church executive. It would have to be in the arrangements room during the visitation for Sylvie Gauthier, since Jesse, Tom and the rest of the members all wanted to pay their respects.

Jesse said, "It's church business, but probably won't come up tomorrow night, with the other things we have to deal with. I just wanted to give you a heads up."

Tom closed his eyes, but the image of the white envelope persisted in his mind. One of his colleagues said a minister was only ever ninety days' notice away from unemployment. If a congregation decided you were gone, there wasn't much actual recourse.

Tom wondered how he'd feel about being let go. He'd only accepted a short-term appointment because the maternity leave he'd been covering for a Windsor hospital chaplain ended, and his friend Paul Bennett suggested the congregation needed his help.

He wasn't sure he actually felt a call to serve long term at Sharpe Street United.

"Tom?"

"Sorry, Jesse," Tom said, "Just thinking."

Jesse passed him the envelope.

"Read it at your leisure. The gist of it is, the executive talked it over, and consulted with a lot of the membership, and we want you to stay."

Tom exhaled.

"I appreciate that, Jesse. It's a real honour, and a compliment... and I agree, we have more pressing issues before we talk about this. I'm not going anywhere for the short term, and I'm guessing this was decided before Penny's declaration of the congregation's financial ruin."

"You sound skeptical."

Tom said, "I haven't had the opportunity to get to know her..."

Jesse said, "Is there an and or a but coming?"

Tom said, "I was uncomfortable with how fast she went from the violent death of someone she knew, to talking about a cashflow problem as if it was the end of the world. And there was a note of something like... glee, as she delivered the bad news."

"I felt the same way," Jesse said. "I did my best to get her to turn it down a few notches."

Chapter 6

Early Wed Evening (10 days to Christmas)

"Hope, you doin' alright up there?"

Tom tried to keep his tone light. He craned his neck to peer up at his only child. Hope had one foot on the highest rung of a 6-foot aluminum step ladder. The ball of her other foot was balanced on the top cap, which bore the manufacturer's "not to be used as a step" warning in caution tape yellow.

He'd set up the ladder in the parlour, close to the front bay window.

Hope stretched her arm towards a spot on the ceiling directly above the place she chose for the Christmas tree.

If the ladder tipped, would she land on Tom, or crash through the bay window?

Tom gripped the side rails and kept his feet squarely planted to brace the ladder against tilting. The century-old hardwood floor was uneven.

"Hope?"

He wondered if she could hear him over Rosie O'Donnell and Elmo belting out "Do You Hear What I Hear?".

The Rosie Christmas CD had been his late wife's favourite.

"I'm fine, Dad," she said. "I've got this."

The ladder wobbled as Hope strained for just a little more reach. What was with the Victorians and their high ceilings?

"I just want to stick this tape… right… here."

Tom knew this wasn't the time to say she could've extended her reach with a yardstick and stood a rung or two lower. Working together on the tree was a way to move past their supper-time squabble.

The disagreement had been sparked by the moving boxes Hope saw in every room on the main floor. She'd kicked at one tucked under the kitchen table.

"You've been here eighteen months. When are you planning to move in?"

They'd had to shift some boxes to the basement to make room for the Christmas tree, and the ladder.

The ladder wobbled, again. Tom imagined catching Hope or at least cushioning her landing.

"I want the other line to hang down a bit to the left," Hope said. "They're different lengths, so each will have its own space to fly."

She'd made two origami angels in her art elective. The first, in Mardi Gras purple, green and gold was for her mother, who'd loved New Orleans. The other she folded from a page out of a historical atlas edited by her Gran.

Hope's wish was to suspend both angels over the Christmas tree with lengths of dental floss.

Tom's wish was that Hope would not raise her other foot to the ladder's top cap.

"I know what you're thinking, Dad, but I'm fine."

"I'm thinking your mom would love your use of floss," Tom said. "That's how she hung all our pictures."

Rosie's duet with Elmo gave way to one with Gloria Estefan. They sang "Gonna Eat For Christmas".

Hope said, "I'm almost done up here."

Tom said, "I'm sorry I have to go out again, but it seemed like a good idea to still do Bible Study tonight."

Hope said, "It might help folks to have something normal."

Tom said, "That's what Jesse said."

Hope said, "You like him. That's cool. After what happened at your last church, it's got to be hard to know who to trust."

"Even people with good qualities are capable of doing terrible things," Tom said. "There usually aren't clear villains or heroes."

"It's too bad you don't have time for a movie tonight."

Tom said, "Maybe something short, if it's not too late when I get back. What do you have in mind?"

"Heroes and villains. I downloaded a Batman cartoon."

"I thought we were doing seasonal movies."

"It's Christmas with the Joker," Hope said. "Robin wants to kick back and watch *It's a Wonderful Life*, but Batman says criminals don't take a holiday."

Tom said, "Pretty hard to argue with that, especially after last night. Here we are again. Another holiday, another church, another... How are you doing with it all? We haven't really talked about..."

Hope looked down at Tom, even as her voice rose.

"Will you take a holiday, Dad? I don't mean from church work, I mean from playing detective. Or are you already digging into what happened to that poor old lady?"

Tom heard layers in her tone, in her questions. He hadn't told her about the possible connection between Gloria's death and the crime family that threatened them in Oakville, or about the invitation from Lawrence to be an unofficial part of the team.

"Right now, I wonder what other movies you have in mind. Classics from your childhood like Christopher the Christmas Tree, and Bucky the Christmas Beaver?"

Hope said, "More like Die Hard and Christmas Vacation."

"And Home Alone?"

"Dad, you know I hate that movie. The idea a family could fly off to Europe and forget their little boy makes me sick. We don't forget people, ever!"

"Which is why we'll have your angels flying above the tree. Are you coming down now?"

"Yeah, I'm done, and I think they look great, but Dad?"

Zeke padded into the parlour and stood beside Tom. His big head was turned to one side like he was thinking hard, and his ears were fully peaked upwards.

"Hope?"

"Look out the window. I'm seeing those weird lights flitting around in the church again."

Tom felt the sides of the ladder shifting in his grip as Hope stepped down.

She rubbed between the German shepherd's ears.

"Hey Zeke! Finish your nap?"

Tom lifted the ladder to one side and stepped close to the window to peer out. Zeke joined him, pressing his nose to the glass.

Hope said, "Do you think we should go over there?"

Chapter 7

Early Wednesday Evening (10 Days to Christmas)

As Tom entered the space that doubled as the arrangements room and Jesse's office, he heard a deep baritone voice singing.

"Decorations of red, on a green Christmas tree..."

The room was lit in the main by the warm glow from the antique brass wall sconces.

Jesse was perched on a stool, with the casual cool of a rock star. He strummed a large body acoustic guitar with a sunburst finish. Tom remembered seeing him play it at last year's Blue Christmas concert.

"Won't be the same dear..."

From the painting on the wall, softly lit in red and green, Elvis seemed to look down with approval.

Tom said, "It's always good to hear you play."

Jesse grinned, and said, "Thank you... thank you very much."

He was in character, despite the pinstripe work suit. He'd loosened the silk tie.

Tom's phone buzzed. A text from Barbara Palmieri relayed the report she'd had back from the officers who checked out the church.

"All clear, but we'll keep a watchful eye."

Tom forwarded her message to Hope, adding that he'd locked the door behind him when he left for bible study.

Jesse shifted from the stool to the chair in front of his roll top desk. Tom pulled a chair over from the end of the conference table.

"Sorry to be on my phone. Just checking in with Hope."

Tom didn't want to further burden Jesse, who'd asked him to come over ahead of the Bible study.

A hard-shell instrument case lay open on the carpeted floor. The plush burgundy lining suggested comfort and rest. It also brought to mind a high-end casket, which was a sign it had been a long day.

Jesse'd used the word urgent when he texted.

"It's nice to have a preview," Tom said. "I talked to Lianne at Community Living today. She thinks the concert will probably sell out."

"That's good. I've worried that Gloria's death, and the church parking lot full of cop cars might scare people off."

"There were some calls asking if we were still on, but no one wants their money back."

"I'm glad," Jesse said. He gently set the guitar in its case.

"Elvis sang a special number at the end of his '68 comeback special. His country was still reeling from the deaths of Martin Luther King and Robert F. Kennedy. There's a line that says as long as a man has the strength to dream he can redeem his soul and fly."

"Will you do that one on Saturday?"

"I was thinking I might," Jesse said. "Is it a little much, connecting Gloria's death to MLK and RFK?"

"I'd go easy on that. But it's fitting to talk about not giving up, especially when times are hard. This concert was your dream, and you make it happen every year."

"Not without a lot of help, but thanks for that," Jesse said.

"Is that why you texted? I wondered if there'd been more drama from The Member's office."

"No, that's been sorted. Mrs. Bower was sitting where you are when I called Johnny back. She taught both of us grade nine math. When he started in about civic duty, and how the Sharpe family should have priority, I put the phone on speaker."

Tom said. "Uh huh."

"Mrs. Bower set him straight." Jesse smiled. "Well not straight, but she said we didn't want their business on those terms, and he and his boss should be ashamed of themselves. She used her teacher voice. It was a beautiful thing."

Tom laughed. "I shouldn't take pleasure in that, but I do."

Tom saw a stack of study bibles, a pile of scratch pads and a box of pens on Jesse's desk. There was also a tiny terra cotta creche. Mary, Joseph and the other figures were thimble sized, and delicately painted.

Tom nodded towards the desk.

"The nativity is a nice touch. Thanks for loaning us space for the class. I got word we could have used the church, but that feels a little too soon."

"It's no problem. I was here anyway. Mrs. Bower treated me to supper."

Tom said, "She sounds like a good boss."

"She's one of the coolest eighty-year-olds I know," Jesse said, "I wish she could talk some sense into Penny."

"What's going on?"

"The phone rang all day with people asking about the church."

Tom said, "Was it about the police presence? No one's called me."

"They wouldn't, you're still the new guy. It wasn't about the cop cars. It's been all about the money."

Tom said, "So Penny's been sounding the alarm?"

"She's been soliciting donations from businesses, service organizations, and a bunch of the groups that meet at the church. Telling everyone the church is broke, and saying Gloria mismanaged the Sharpe Trust."

Tom said, "Even if there are grounds to suspect wrongdoing, which we haven't seen, that's not the way to handle it."

"She started a GoFundMe Page called 'Save our Church'. It says without an emergency influx of cash our final service will be Christmas Eve."

"Like I said this morning, there's nothing to gain by climbing on the panic bus."

"Well, she's driving that bus all over town, blocking traffic, flashing the lights, and blowing her big horn. Why couldn't she at least wait for the executive meeting?"

Tom said, "It's like the guy who volunteers to do a eulogy on behalf of the family, but all he talks about is where he was, and what he was doing when he heard Uncle Fred died. Some people can't help making everything about them."

Jesse said, "I have to say, after fielding calls all day from worried people, their anxiety kind of rubbed off on me."

"But this crisis, if it is one, isn't yours to fix on your own, any more than it's Penny's."

"Yeah, you're right. But she said we can't cover payroll. We can put off other bills, but paying our people comes first."

Tom felt gratitude for Jesse, and his commitment to doing right by the staff.

"There may be help available from the wider church, to get us through short term. I emailed you contacts for some people at the regional office. I don't think they'll leave us hanging, but this close to Christmas we may not hear back right away."

"I got those, thanks. I sent some emails and left a few voice mails, but there's something else."

Tom said, "What is it, Jesse?"

"This morning, I was excited to tell you we want you to stay on as our pastor. But what does that even mean if we can't pay you?"

Tom said, "Between you and me, I'm okay. I like getting paid, of course, but I don't exactly live from cheque to cheque."

"Your daughter's school is in the states. That can't be cheap. I talked to Mrs. Bower, and we could put something together, like a loan, if you need it."

Tom took a beat to absorb what Jesse had said and to clear the lump in his throat.

"Jesse... I really appreciate it, and please thank Mrs. Bower, but we're fine. My late wife was very good with finances. She started putting money aside for Hope's education before she was out of diapers. We're good."

"You sure?"

"Jesse, I'm grateful for the offer, and I won't forget it. But I also don't think it'll come to that.

"Okay."

"Should we set out the books and pads for the class? And that beautiful little nativity? People will likely be rolling in soon."

Chapter 8

Late Wednesday Evening (10 days to Christmas)

"I left them in the parlour," Tom said into his phone. "Hope was nestled into her recliner, under her grandmother's quilt, with her Mac Book in her lap, and Zeke snoozing at her feet. It was good to see them at peace. I'm worried about what she saw at the church.

"She'll talk about it when she's ready."

"Yeah, that's what I'm hoping. I kissed her goodnight, rubbed between Zeke's ears, then took a photo. I'm sending it now."

"Got it. The twinkle of tree lights, the warm glow of her laptop, and the fuzzy edge of your finger in the top left corner."

Annika chuckled.

"It's good to hear you laugh... I've missed you."

Annika said, "I miss you too."

Tom cleared his throat.

"Why did we think this break was a good idea?"

"Yeah, good question. Are you up this late just to talk to me, or because you can't sleep."

"I did want to talk, and yes, the monkeys are making their presence known. But how are you doing?"

At a retreat, Tom and Annika had heard a meditation teacher liken the unsettled mind to a tree full of monkeys, who clamor for attention with yowling, jumping and the liberal tossing of fresh feces.

"I'm good. Just waking up. It's just after seven here. I'm hoping for a quiet day. We spent yesterday strolling around Christmas markets. I'm going to put you on speaker so I can get changed."

Tom propped another pillow behind him and adjusted the duvet. He said, "So, what are you wearing now?"

Annika laughed.

"That would be a totally different kind of call, which I'm not having in a guest room at my cousins' house."

"So how's it going with them?"

"They're lovely, and I've realized again how introverted I am. Nothing like life in a small cottage with three gregarious relatives to make me miss my quiet country house."

"It sounds like they enjoy sharing their world with you. Do they also ask about you, and your life?"

"They do. They're good hosts, and their interest seems genuine. It's just a lot, at times."

"I'm glad they're trying to get to know you. But I get it. Sometimes we just need solitude. I adore Hope, and her being here also changes the feel of the house."

"And now you also have a great big, spoiled German shepherd in your space. I hope Zeke's not being a bother."

"I can hear them both coming up the stairs right now. He's taken to sleeping beside Hope's bed."

Tom stopped himself from asking Hope if she'd checked the doors.

"He's probably picked up she's feeling vulnerable. He's very attached to her."

"I'm good with that. He at least looks like a guard dog."

Annika said, "If he had to, he'd launch himself between her and anyone trying to do harm. But are you worried?"

"It helps the police are basically across the street. Michael's sent Lawrence and Barbara. She says hi."

"Will you work with the police, like you did at Saint Mungo's?"

"Lawrence asked. I'm thinking about it. I want them to find Gloria's killer. I want the church to feel safe again. I like feeling part of a team, but...I also worry about putting Hope in danger."

"The danger's real as long as the killer is at large, even if you don't help."

Tom shivered, even though he was under a thick duvet. "That's what Barbara said."

"Zeke and I worked a search with her for a missing child. She had to deliver hard news to the family. She's like a few nurses I worked with. Tough, but also protective of those under their care."

Tom said, "She said if we work together, I'll at least know what's going on."

"So, you worry the killer's still out there and you wonder if Hope's been traumatized. What are the other monkeys going on about?"

Tom heard Hope close the door to the upstairs bathroom, then turn on a faucet. The water would have to run for a while. In that big old house, it took time for the hot water to reach the top floor.

"I'm worried..." Tom said, lowering his voice. "And I think Hope is worried, that Gloria's death could send me spiraling, and I'll end up like I was after my mom died."

Annika said, "I remember how you were then. You sound tired tonight, but not... vacant, like you were becoming then. Are you still talking to Paul? What does he think?"

Paul Bennett was Tom's supervisor when he'd been a student minister, and they'd kept a good connection in the years since then. In retirement he'd established a retreat centre in Essex County called the Quiet Centre. Tom had a standing appointment to visit Paul weekly.

"I'll see him Friday. He'd likely say I'm feeling what I'm feeling, and for the most part, not trying to avoid the hard things."

"Does he tell you should trust yourself?"

Tom smiled.

"It's come up."

"Okay, then. What else is keeping you awake?"

"I think I'm winding down. I took a melatonin after I brushed my teeth. Maybe it's kicking in."

"Is that true, or are you just saving the hardest stuff for last? Because I can smell the cousins' coffee brewing."

"Hope and I argued over supper tonight. It started out about all the moving boxes in the house, but it was really her being frustrated with me."

Annika said, "Hard to imagine."

Tom heard soft steps of slippered feet and canine pads on the hardwood in the hall, then the click of Hope's door.

"She's annoyed with me about us. She wants to know what we're doing. Or maybe it's more she wants us to know what we're doing. At one point she said she'd tell us her plan for our future, if that would help."

"I can guess what she'd say."

"Yeah, me too." Tom said.

The cousins are making just enough kitchen noise to let me know it's time for breakfast. Anything else?"

"One last monkey. He's kind of a cute little fella."

"What's he saying?"

"He wants you to get on a plane and fly back here. Spend Christmas with us. With me."

"Are you asking me to come back early?"

"Well... I know it's a big ask."

"Tom... Just tell me what you want."

"Then yes, I really want you here."

"Then yes... I'd love to. If your little monkey friend hadn't mentioned it, I was going to bring it up."

Chapter 9

Early Thursday Morning (9 days to Christmas)

Just ten minutes into his early morning treadmill run, and Tom already felt like he was trudging through sand.

Since they'd found the body, sleep had been shallow and scarce. His late-night conversation with Annika calmed Tom's racing mind, but he'd had weird dreams and woke up feeling like he'd been swimming through high waves.

He'd forced himself to get up and move. He knew he'd be talking to Michael, and wanted to be able to say he got his run in.

Tom exchanged nods with the front desk attendant and a few familiar faces at Move It Or Lose It. The largest gym in Sun Parlour was in the strip mall at the newer end of Main Street, beside The Trough, which boasted the biggest all-you-can-eat buffet in the county.

The early morning regulars were at their preferred spots under the bright lights and overhead fans on treadmill row. Tom's go-to was in front of the television the staff tuned to CBC Windsor.

An ad featuring a large talking carrot gave way to the 7:00 a.m. news. Gloria's photo loomed large behind the reporter at the anchor desk. She bore an unsettling resemblance to Tom's deceased mother. It might have been the glasses.

The scrolling headline ticker at the bottom of the screen declared, "Sun Parlour MP to speak at beloved sister's funeral."

Tom didn't bother with his earbuds. He didn't need to hear The Member's spin on Gloria's death.

Salty drops dripped into his eyes, making him wish he'd worn a headband. He brushed away sweat and caught a glimpse of the display throbbing blood red on his watch. His pulse was above his optimal training rate.

A mechanical whine drew Tom's attention to the right. Lori Gregoire was raising the incline on the treadmill next to him. The fire-fighter pounded up and down simulated hills, her muscled legs and arms pumping and ginger ponytail bobbing. Tom offered a thumbs up, which she acknowledged with a bright smile.

Lori was on the rescue truck dispatched to the church on Tuesday night. She and Deputy Chief Kelly Halligan had been there when the paramedic confirmed Gloria's death but were called away to a motor vehicle accident before the cops lifted sections of the big tree, to expose her corpse.

Tom was glad she and Kelly had been spared seeing the worst of it.

The image rose unbidden of Gloria lying motionless in a pool of her own blood.

How much Hope had seen before Tom told her to take Zeke back to the parsonage?

Why on earth did violent death seem to follow him?

He felt a spike of pain from his left ankle. It reminded him as he started every workout it had been wrenched the wrong way and then snapped when a murder suspect's pickup rammed Tom's car.

Hope had made it out of their car just before the truck hit.

Tom pushed through his ankle's objections, even though it felt like there were weights strapped to his feet. He lowered the incline, and reduced the speed, but kept going.

His workouts were part of the pact Tom had made with Michael almost two years before, right before he left Oakville.

"Partner," Michael said, "What you've been going through, since your mom died... I get it, and I'm here for you."

Michael had appeared as he often did, when Tom was in trouble. They wound up sitting in the front seat of Michael's unmarked, parked a few blocks from Tom's house. Red and blue emergency lights from a marked cruiser washed over them, as well as half the block.

Michael said, "The copper who pulled you over knew your name from that bad business at the church. We go way back, so he made a call. Used his personal phone, so it didn't go out over the radio. His road sergeant called me, and here we are..."

Tom stared straight out the front windshield. It was easier to look at the taillights on the Halton Regional Police cruiser than meet his friend's eyes. He said, "I'm sorry about this."

Michael said, "I told him you would be. My guy says you weren't speeding or driving reckless. He was two cars back when you failed to stop before turning right at a stop sign.

"It's a slow night, so he pulled you over. He says you've been compliant and have no priors. He was prepared to give you a verbal warning, but you made it complicated when you told him you'd had a strong cider before heading out for groceries."

"You passed the field sobriety test. His sergeant called me because the officer said you seemed shook up."

Tom said, "That's... I'd never ask for special treatment. I broke the law."

Michael shrugged.

"He writes you up, it's a fine. Demerits for the fail to stop. He knows, and I know how little that deters the ones we really want off the road."

Tom turned to face his friend.

"But there should be consequences."

Michael powered down the driver's side window and waved at the cruiser parked in front of them. The cop signaled, pulled out, and drove away.

"Oh, there will be, partner. But before we get to that, I want to hear what's been going on."

Tom poured it all out to Michael that night, sitting in the front seat of the unmarked Ford Taurus.

He'd been winding things down at Saint Mungo's. It was a tough place to be. He'd helped secure the confession of a well-loved board member who'd killed the senior pastor. Perhaps worse, he'd raised serious allegations against the church's largest giver. Church people he'd grown to like told him they were counting the days until he was gone.

Every afternoon for months, he'd gone from the church to the Alzheimer's floor of the seniors' residence to sit with his mother, who was mostly not there.

"Then it was sitting with her at the hospice every night, until the end."

After his mother's funeral, Tom put his daughter on a plane back to Atlanta to salvage her semester at Emory. He'd isolated himself, and pushed Annika away before things with her could get any more serious.

Tom wasn't sleeping well and fell into grabbing a mixed six-pack of craft beers and ciders at the grocery store on his way home from work. He chose cans with cartoon labels and jovial names and told himself he wasn't really drinking. Some of the stuff tasted like Kool-Aid.

He also told himself he was nothing like his father, who'd crush three cans in the parking lot after every shift at the Ford plant, and down three more with supper.

"But I'm becoming just like him, and I hate it."

Michael laid a hand on Tom's shoulder. "You're not like your dad, but the way you're going, you could end up flushing your life down the toilet. But I have a different idea."

Tom said, "What?"

Michael called it the Three Outs.

"You cut out the drinking. Anything you have left goes down the drain when we get you home tonight."

Tom nodded.

He pictured the five colourfully labelled cans left in the door shelf of his fridge, and realized what it meant that he knew exactly where they were, and how many were left.

"You talk out what's happening inside you, at least once a week with Paul Bennett."

Paul had been a mentor going back to when he'd supervised Tom for his year as a student pastor.

"I'm not sure if I want Paul..."

"I called him on the way here, and he's already on board."

"Yeah, of course you did, and of course he'd be."

Tom let out a breath he didn't know he was holding.

"Okay."

"Paul agreed that as an introvert, you're way more likely to talk with him than go to twelve-step meetings like I do."

"Yeah, you're both right about that. What else? You said three outs."

"Third thing is you sweat it out. At least an hour at the gym, three times a week. Half your workout should be cardio."

"I used to run, but it's been a long time."

"I remember," Michael said. "You told me you ran a few half-marathons before Hope was born."

"Hope."

"Yeah, Hope. And Annika. And Paul. And me."

"Okay, I hear you. Three times a week at the gym."

"I can set you up with a trainer or show you some stuff with machines and free weights for the rest."

Tom asked, "You think this will work?"

Michael said, "I think it will work if you do the work."

Lori, the pony-tailed firefighter on the treadmill next to Tom had finished her run and was wiping down her machine.

Tom gave her another thumbs up, and said, "See you Saturday?"

Lori said, "I'll see you here in the morning, but Stan's mom will have to bring the girls to the Sunday School Christmas party later. We're both working."

Lori's mother-in-law was Andrea Bower, Jesse's boss at the funeral home.

Tom nodded and waved as Lori left, then grabbed his water bottle for a quick swallow.

He stowed the bottle on the treadmill console and pushed the button to up his speed.

He'd do the work.

Chapter 10

Lunchtime, Thursday (9 days to Christmas)

Tom thought it likely Bobby Sharpe was the guy slouched down in the back booth of Sports Legends, the sports bar and restaurant at Caesar's Windsor Casino. His face matched the photo Michael Powers had sent, and he was the only patron under seventy.

The walls were panelled with flat screen televisions, showing all manner of athletic events. Sportscaster banter competed with the whoops and bells of the video slot and poker games.

Tom closed in on the man, who wore a designer tracksuit that made him think of pineapples. The jacket featured an image of a large parrot. Brilliant yellow, red, and blue feathers popped against green foliage.

"Mr. Sharpe?"

Jungle suit guy sat up. His belly rippled the leafy front of his jacket. The parrot looked ready to take flight.

"Hey... Call me Bobby," he said with a quick smile. "Everybody does."

"I'm Tom Book."

"Book, hunh? Great name. I'd lay a bet with a guy called Book. Speaking of..."

He raised his drink towards the screen over the booth. Tom guessed it was a Caesar. A gnawed celery stalk poked out of the tall glass.

"...you got action on this game? It's the Fenway Bowl. Cardinals are kicking the crap out of my Cincinnati Bearcats."

Tom shook his head.

"I'm not really..."

"What's your pleasure? I'm putting together a table up in the poker room later, coupla guys in from Indiana or Iowa, somethin' like that."

"Thanks, but that's not my thing, Bobby. I'm here about your Aunt Gloria. I was her pastor."

"Sorry, Rev!" Bobby sunk back into his seat and gestured for Tom to join him. "Thought you were maybe looking for a game."

Tom couldn't be sure, with him slumped down, but Bobby might be as tall as his own six feet, but he carried more weight. It showed around his middle, and in the folds in his neck. His coffee black hair was combed over to cover his pale scalp.

"You're the one who called. I shoulda remembered."

Tom sat opposite Bobby.

"You've got a lot going on."

Bobby's eyes were brown, with pupils shrunk to tiny dots. His face was pasty, which Tom knew could mean a lot of things.

"Yeah," Bobby expelled a breath. "I feel like I do."

Bobby reached his hand under the track suit's open collar to retrieve a tiny gold cross on a delicate chain.

"I grew up around Sharpe Street. My aunt loved that place."

Bobby rubbed the cross between thumb and forefinger.

"She gave me this when I was confirmed. And a bible in a nice box."

"I'm sorry for your loss Bobby. It seemed like the church meant a lot to her."

"She gave it all she had. I can't tell you how many nights she dragged me there for meetings. I had a little hiding spot so I wouldn't have to make nice with the church ladies. I'd pass the time with a deck of cards, playing all the hands in games of five-card stud."

Bobby let the cross drop to his chest. He stared into his drink, stirring the icy dregs with the ragged-edged celery stalk.

"But hey Rev, I do more praying here, watching college football, than I ever did there."

Tom laughed.

"That's a good line."

Bobby brightened. He liked an audience.

"You should see this place on Sundays. Pilgrims are dropped off by the bus load, bringing their offerings. If they come in the front way, and the wind is right, they get a little spray off the fountain and waterfalls. A blessed sprinkle of the holy water, no extra charge."

"Uh huh."

Tom didn't say holy water was a Catholic thing. It might break Bobby's flow.

"Then they come in and... what you call it, render unto Caesars. Hah, I just thought of that! They're believers, Rev. You can tell them the odds are stacked against them, but it doesn't matter."

Bobby paused to be sure he still had Tom's attention.

"They stick their loyalty cards in the machines, and slide in the twenties, sure the miracle could happen with the next spin. They could be the one with the luck, the special blessing."

Tom wondered how often Bobby dealt this patter.

"I've never heard a casino talked about like that, Bobby. Very poetic."

"Uh, thanks."

"Can I ask you something?"

"Sure, I guess."

"Does..." Tom swiveled his head. "all of this help you right now, as you deal with your aunt's death?"

Bobby flushed, which improved his pallor.

"Want the honest truth?"

"As honest as you care to be."

"I'm fronting. Inside, I'm all tore up."

Bobby blew his nose into a cocktail napkin, then balled it up, unsure what to do with it.

Tom pulled out a tissue, wrapped the napkin, and tucked it in his pocket.

Bobby nodded thanks.

"I want to say a few words at her service. That John guy from Dad's office says that won't be happening..."

Tom felt guilty relief he wouldn't have to deliver that message.

"He says I lack decorum. Who talks like that? Aunt Gloria was like a mother to me. More of a parent than he ever was. I feel orphaned. Is that a feeling, Rev?

Tom remembered his father arriving late to his mother's funeral and leaving before the rest of the mourners got to their cars for the ride to the crematorium.

"Bobby, you can call me Tom."

"Okay... Tom. Do you get what I'm saying about feeling like an orphan?"

"You feel what you feel, Bobby. If you'd like, I can include your words, some memories of your aunt in what I say."

"That's kind of you, Rev... uh, Tom. A lot of people found it hard to like my aunt. She didn't make it easy."

Bobby was watching something behind Tom. He slapped his palms flat on the table.

"You okay, Bobby?"

Looking over Tom's shoulder, Bobby said, "Sorry, I just... You want some lunch? I'll get it."

"You don't have to buy my lunch."

Bobby met Tom's eyes, conjured a smile, and swept an arm like he was revealing the big prize on a game show.

"I get like, an entertainment allowance. I can't be on the payroll, 'cause then I couldn't gamble here... but hey, don't spread that round, okay? It's not exactly above-board."

"I won't say a word."

"It's the kind of hustle gets under my dad's skin. Says I don't live up to the proud family name."

Bobby's gaze shifted again to somewhere behind Tom.

"But my dad has no idea what it takes to survive in my world."

Tom broke in.

"Everything all right, Bobby? Or as all right as it can be, right now?"

Bobby switched on the smile again.

"They're famous here for their Reubens. I like onion rings, but you get your choice of sides. Sweet potato fries are good, or maybe salad. You look like a salad guy to me."

"Sounds good, Bobby. Make it a house salad."

"You won't regret it. This sandwich is a real work of art. I ever go back to cooking; I'm stealing their recipe."

"You like to cook?"

"Best job I ever had was working the grill at the Wagon Wheel."

With effort, Bobby pushed himself up out of the booth.

"I'll put in our order. You wanna drink?"

Tom called after Bobby.

"Diet coke?"

He moved faster than Tom expected. Something had spooked him.

Tom thought back to his morning call to Michael Powers.

"You're my undercover expert. How do I dress to meet a grieving nephew at the casino?"

"Your guy is Robert Sharpe Junior, only child of the local MP. Goes by Bobby. He lives there when he's not in Reno, Vegas or Atlantic City."

"You know all that off the top of your head?"

"With a suspicious death, we look at the whole family. Turns out Bobby's got some sketchy acquaintances."

"Should I be worried?"

"Where are you meeting?"

"Sports Legends. Says it's kind of his office."

"You'll be fine. Caesars has top-notch security. Lots of cameras, lots of people in plainclothes out on the floor. We also have a dedicated presence there."

"I was serious before... what should I wear?"

"You're thinking, not the place for a clerical collar, but I should look competent."

"Exactly."

"You'll see buddies in blue jeans and Harley t-shirts walking by dudes in suits that cost more than my car. Follow the middle path. Pressed khakis, high-end golf shirt. Casual shoes but not runners."

"Thanks."

"Anytime, partner. Call me when you're heading home."

"Thought you weren't worried."

Bobby approached the booth with a plated sandwich in each hand, and a server in tow, with drinks on a round platter.

"Thanks, Debra."

"You got it Bobby. Let us know if you need anything else."

Bobby set the plates on the table and slid into his side of the booth.

The server turned on her heel to leave, but stopped short. She made a little "yip", as her tray clattered to the floor.

Debra sidestepped and bent to retrieve the serving platter. Her path was blocked by a woman not much over four feet tall.

"Sorry, ma'am. I didn't see you there."

The woman's spiky hair was crimson red, and a dead-on match for her over-sized sunglasses and painted nails. She'd picked the same colour for her lipstick, lending a glossy intensity to her words.

"Don't worry yourself, my dear. I'll just have a word..."

Before hearing that confident husky voice, Tom would have pictured her shuffling off a shuttle from one of the nearby retirement buildings. Now he could see her pulling up in a blood-red convertible and tossing the keys at the valet without breaking her stride.

"Actually, just a few more words with Mr. Sharpe here."

Debra turned back to the booth.

"Bobby... anything else you need?"

Bobby handed her a twenty.

"We're good, Deb. I got this."

The crimson-haired woman watched Debra slip away, then shuffled close to Bobby's side of the booth.

"Not a good time, Val," Bobby said. "I'm havin' a bite with the reverend here."

Tom recognized high-end cruise wear for women of a certain age. She sported a lightweight sage green polyester pantsuit, with a fern-patterned scarf.

With one palm flat on the table for balance, Val leaned in close enough to leave a smear of blood red lipstick on Bobby's ear.

Looking paler than before, Bobby said, “Like I told you, Val. I got it handled.”

Val stood straight and dropped a fifty on the table. The red bill went with her colour scheme.

“Lunch is on me, Bobby.”

She left without looking back.

Tom knew what it was like to be dealt with by formidable older women. Bobby might need a minute.

He gave full attention to his meal. The Reuben sandwich lived up to Bobby’s hype. Toasted rye bread shiny with butter, stacked high with corned beef, and dripping melted Swiss cheese and sauerkraut.

There was no sign of the house salad, but Tom didn’t feel short-changed.

“Bobby, this is great. What’s the dressing on the side?”

“Thousand Island. Some places use Russian. This is better, trust me.”

Tom said, “I’ve been warned to watch out for guys who say to trust them.”

“Yeah, you’ve got a point.”

Bobby pushed a huge onion ring into his mouth and raised a finger like he was calling for time out while he chewed.

Tom sipped his Diet Coke. He could wait to see what Bobby wanted.

“Rev... I mean, Tom. Can I trust you?”

“What does your gut tell you?”

“Right now, two things. One is it’d be sinful to let this food get cold.”

“What else?”

“That I could use someone to talk to. I’m in a lotta trouble.”

“Has it got to do with that woman Val?”

“Don’t let her looks fool you, Rev, she’s a scary lady.”

Chapter 11

Mid Thursday Afternoon (9 days to Christmas)

"How you doing partner?"

Michael's deep voice rumbled through the many high-end speakers of the Range Rover.

Two years earlier, Tom's car had been totaled while he'd been running a special errand for the Quiet Centre. After that, Paul Bennett had put one of the retreat centre vehicles on permanent loan to him.

"Good, except I'm being followed."

"Who's on your tail?

"Two guys in a black Cadillac Escalade. I noticed them following me out of Sun Parlour, and now they're back."

"What caught your attention?"

"No front license plate, and it's got one of those heavy-duty wraparound push bumpers."

"Give me your current location. We'll also ping your phone."

Tom named the street he was driving on, and the last intersection he'd passed.

"Okay, we've got you. Take Walker Road to the EC Row Expressway. Stay on it as it turns into county road 22. We need you out of Windsor, and back in OPP jurisdiction."

Tom followed Michael's cues.

"The Escalade's staying with me."

"That's what we want. We're setting something up between Tecumseh and Belle River. I'll let you know where in a minute."

Tom heard his voice pitch high with nerves.

"What do you need me to do?"

Michael chuckled.

"You're doing great partner. We got this... but what is it with you and black trucks?"

In the midst of the mess at Saint Mungo's, Tom had parked his car and was about to cross a freshly salted street when a black pickup barreled through the intersection, roaring towards him at speed. He'd thrown himself back on the sidewalk and just managed to duck behind a light pole.

At the last second the truck veered off to avoid colliding with a transformer box on the same corner, half hidden by snow.

There'd been no proof, but Michael and Lawrence were convinced the driver was part of Brad Kazinski's crew. They drove similar vehicles in neighbourhoods where they wanted their presence known.

Tom said, "What's the connection between Kazinski and the Sharpe family? I mean, other than me."

"Sounds like you're on the case. Lawrence will be pleased."

"You both knew I'd say yes. I want to help Bobby. He's like a lost little boy who just wants to go home. Gloria, with all her quirks, was all he had. He's grieving, and he's scared."

"We saw who put the fear in him. We had eyes on your lunch."

"You that worried about me?"

"We have a unit in Caesar's basement, wired into their cameras, like we do in every casino in Ontario. That wasn't a sweet nothing she whispered in his ear."

Traffic slowed as Tom approached the left turn for the ramp for the westbound expressway. He looked over at the pure white doric columns that defined the entrance to the Hellenic Cultural Centre. They felt genuine. The faux Ancient Roman style of Caesar's Windsor hadn't sat well with him.

"Bobby didn't say much about Val except that she's scary and represents people who hold his marker."

"We piggy-backed on the casino's facial recognition system. Her name is Valerie Kazinski. Also known as Big Val, or Bloody Val. She's Brad's aunt."

"So, the connection between Bobby's family and the Kazinski's, whatever it is, isn't working out so well for him."

"We've got the edge pieces, but there's a lot in the middle of this puzzle, we don't know what fits where."

"Like what does a Vegas poker player have to do with a drug dealer from Oakville?"

"We'll talk more about that later, Tom. You're five klicks from the traffic circle where we're set up. Is the Escalade still on your tail?"

"I'm in the right lane. He's in the left, hanging back a bit."

"In your blind spot?"

"Pretty much. I had to adjust the driver's side mirror to be sure they were there."

"Okay. So they know that you know."

"They haven't been subtle."

"Keep your speed a little over 70."

"It's 60 along here. Am I going to get a ticket?"

"Our cruiser needs a reason to pull them over. Pick it up a little more."

"You got it."

"Is he staying with you?"

"He's behind me again, not as tight as before. He's leaving a couple of car lengths now."

"Perfect. You're two kilometres from the traffic circle. Step a little heavier on the gas. I want to get your shadow to do 75."

"Yeah, I'm there, and he's keeping pace."

"Good. The cruiser was waiting on the side road you just passed. She should be hitting her lights right about now."

Sure enough, Tom heard the wail of a siren, and glimpsed red and blue lights coming up fast behind the Escalade.

"Okay, we've got them on radar and on the dash cam. We're trying to run the rear plate. Go through the roundabout where 22 meets Old Tecumseh

Road. Once you're clear, we'll seal off the traffic circle and have a little talk with those guys."

The siren behind him got louder. He slowed the Range Rover.

He rolled up to the traffic circle, which was clear of vehicles. Looking ahead and left, Tom saw marked cruisers ready to pull into the roundabout.

As he reduced speed to round the curve, there was a slight bump to his side of the Range Rover.

He felt the vehicle slide out of his control. Had he hit black ice?

Tom lifted his foot off the gas pedal and tried to correct the skid. Turning the steering wheel had no effect.

Tom panicked as the Range Rover spun 180 degrees, until it faced the oncoming Escalade.

Tom's heart pounded in his ears as he watched the large black Cadillac roar towards him.

He had no control over the Range Rover, which was now skidding sideways towards the snow-covered island in the middle of the traffic circle.

Tom feared his skid would not save him from a head on collision with the Escalade. He gripped the steering wheel with both hands; certain he'd press permanent prints into its soft covering.

He opened his mouth... to what? Scream? He had no breath, and no time.

His vision focused on the front of the big Cadillac. The strange little emblem on the grille. What was that thing?

At the last possible moment, it seemed to Tom, the vehicle swerved around him and roared away.

Before Tom could even think of being grateful, his world turned sideways. The passenger side wheels of the Range Rover met the base of the centre island of the traffic circle, and the remaining momentum caused it to tip over, and crash hard.

Tom was held tight by the seat and shoulder restraints. Would the airbags engage? He remembered reading they were expensive to replace.

He didn't want to tell Paul he'd totaled his car.

Chapter 12

Late Thursday Afternoon (9 days to Christmas)

Tom wondered if the cops considered discomfort an interrogation tool. His chair was like the others stacked in the corner of the interview room. Chrome frames supporting turquoise vinyl seats and backs with no discernible padding.

He was sitting across a scarred wood veneer table from Lawrence Kitchen, who'd asked for a minute to set up a Microsoft Teams meeting, and who didn't seem any more comfortable in his chair.

Tom said, "Kind of a weird vibe."

Lawrence looked up from his laptop. "You mean out there in the crime bureau?"

The Essex County crime bureau was a large open office, with high windows that added very little natural light to the harsh glow of ceiling fluorescents. Detectives in plain clothes, an equal mix of men and women, worked at grey metal desks lined up along three pale yellow walls. The fourth wall had doors for the interview room and the bureau commander's office.

The round white-faced wall clock could have come from Tom's grade nine home room.

As Tom was walked through, and pointed toward the interview room, all conversation had stopped cold. He felt a dozen sets of eyes give looks that were at once piercing and dismissive.

"I felt like the vice principal walking through a high school cafeteria."

Lawrence laughed.

"That's about right. The squad room is one of the few places cops can let down their guard. They don't like strangers in their house."

"It's not just because I'm a civilian?"

"No, they aren't thrilled about any of us. Cops are territorial, and wary of variations to routine. Barbara and I were parachuted in to their investigation. They likely think we were sent because they can't handle the case."

"It sounds very... human."

Lawrence nodded as he stood and pulled his chair to Tom's side of the beat-up table.

"Can you slide the laptop over, and point the screen this way? Barbara's joining us from the Forensic Pathology Unit in London. Michael's in a car. Someone else is driving."

Barbara's face appeared in a box on the screen.

"Must be one of the perks of being a superintendent."

Michael's voice boomed out of the laptop speaker.

"I thought you two took turns at the wheel."

Barbara said, "Speaking of driving... you doing okay Tom? I hear your car got pitted."

Manuela Ortiz, the uniformed officer who drove Tom to this meeting had explained the PIT manoeuvre. She'd been tasked to do the traffic stop on the vehicle that had followed him, and her dashcam caught the whole thing.

"Precision immobilization technique. If normal methods failed, and we needed to stop that brown Accord ahead of us, I could match their speed, and pull up close on one side of them..."

Manuela demonstrated, moving to the outside lane to line up her cruiser's right front bumper with the left rear wheel well of the Honda.

"Don't worry Tom, I'm just showing you how I'd set it up."

"I'm glad. I wouldn't wish that on anybody."

"If authorized, which would have to be an extreme situation, all I'd need to do is give a little side nudge with my bumper. It doesn't take much for the rear tires to break contact with the road. The target vehicle goes into a spin, I steer around it, and they come to an abrupt halt."

"Abrupt is right."

Manuela said, "You handled it well. Too bad about your car."

"Thanks for stopping to help me. Sorry they got away."

"No way we'd leave you to chase them. We had to control the scene, and make sure you were okay. They probably counted on that."

The constable had waited while the paramedics checked out Tom, and while he called first his daughter Hope, then Paul Bennett, who owned the Range Rover. She'd arranged with a tow service for a flatbed to haul it to the Land Rover dealership. Then her sergeant told her to buy him a coffee and take him to the County Detachment.

As they waited their turn in the Tim Horton's drive-thru lane she'd reached into a pocket on the front of her protective vest and offered him ibuprofen.

"When the shock wears off," Manuela said. "and the adrenaline is burned out of your system, you're going to be sore."

She was right, Tom thought. I should have taken the pills.

"Tom!" Michael's voice cut through Tom's memory of the incident. "You still with us?"

"Sorry."

Michael said, "The officer on scene said you kept your cool. If you'd panicked, and hit the gas, it could have been worse."

"For me," Tom said, "or the car? I'm worried it's a write-off."

Michael smiled.

"They make new cars every day, partner. Just glad you're okay."

"Thanks Michael. Does the PIT manoeuvre tell you anything about those guys?"

Lawrence reached over, then seemed to think better of patting Tom on the back.

He said, "Thinking like a detective, Tom."

"The rear plate was bogus," Michael said. "But a pretty good fake, from what we saw. That tells us something, as does the driver's proficiency with the PIT."

Tom said. "Since I'm not actually a detective, can you spell it out?"

Michael said, "Barbara, what's your read? Did you see the footage?"

"It's cheaper and easier to steal a license plate than acquire a good fake. PIT skills suggest a law enforcement background, or special training in tactical driving. Both point to major money in play. Maybe private security at a level used to acting above or outside the law."

Lawrence said, "So who'd task elite security to tail Tom in such a brazen way?"

Michael said, "That relates to my first question. Were they tracking Tom, or making it look like they were?"

Tom said, "Like to scare me? What makes me that interesting?"

Michael said, "That's my second question. An obvious answer is this connects somehow with Gloria Sharpe's death, which I hope Barbara can tell us more about. If it's not that, what else is Tom adjacent?"

In his box on the computer screen, Michael's fingers made air quotes as he said the last two words.

Lawrence said, "Tom, we look at all possible angles. Anything going on with the church, or Hope, or Annika, or the Quiet Centre we should know about?""

Tom was thrown by the mention of Paul's retreat centre.

"Nothing I can think of with the church. But as I learned at Saint Mungo's, they don't tell the pastor everything. As far as Hope and I... I'd say that our lives are, pardon the pun, open books."

That rated a deep chuckle from Michael, and polite smiles from Lawrence and Barbara.

"I expect the same is true of Annika, and Paul prefers not to offer programs or have guests during Advent and Christmas. It's literally quiet at the centre."

"I get that you're protective of your friend," Michael said, making air quotes again as he said, "and the more under the radar aspects of his work."

Tom was aware of Lawrence and Barbara's silence during this exchange.

"I'll see Paul tomorrow. I'll ask if there's anything happening that I don't know about. We'll have to talk about the Range Rover anyway."

"Thanks for that, Tom," Michael said. "Barbara, can you give us the basics from the postmortem exam?"

"First off, the coroner was surprised, and not in a good way, by the rush order. She wondered if you'd put the fix in."

Lawrence said, "I heard similar remarks in the briefing here this morning. The local crime guys blame us for the quick release of the crime scene."

"Not the first time we've put local noses out of joint. I'll talk to the bureau commander, and the coroner, if you think it's needed, Barbara."

"As you've taught us, it doesn't hurt to at least to try to play nice. Shall I go on?"

Michael nodded his head.

"Please."

"Tom," Barbara said, "I should have asked earlier. Are you okay hearing this stuff?"

"Is it worse than seeing it?"

"Good point. I'll skip most of the forensic jargon.

"The first, and most obvious finding is that the tree didn't kill Gloria. It was toppled over, and on to her prone form after she'd already hit the floor."

"Gloria was struck from behind, resulting in severe blunt force trauma to the back of her head and causing almost immediate loss of consciousness. The base of her skull was fractured, and the occipital bone was shattered. The impact was powerful enough to cause cracks to spread forward on both sides of her skull. Her scalp was torn and severely bruised."

"As we know from the scene, there was heavy bleeding. The actual cause of death was catastrophic blood loss. Coroner says it would have been quick."

Lawrence said, "No surprises there. Did the coroner have any thoughts about the murder weapon?"

"Something heavy enough to deliver a lot of force, but with a small point of impact. She was reminded of a case where someone was whacked from behind with a nine iron. She said an overhead swing could generate sufficient force."

Lawrence said, "The viciousness of the attack feels like anger."

"Barbara, thanks for that," Michael said. "Let's shift gears. Tom, can you summarize what you learned from Bobby Sharpe?"

Tom said, "He's scared."

Lawrence said, "We've seen the footage from the casino. Did he tell you what Big Val whispered in his ear?"

"He just said it made no sense to him, which made it all the more frightening."

Barbara said, "What else did he tell you?"

Tom said, "Gloria was trying to get him out of a jam. He seemed embarrassed and didn't want to tell me how it happened, but he owes serious money to the wrong people."

Michael said, "That's where the Kazinskis come in. Maybe they bankrolled him, or he made a bad bet, and they own his debt."

"He's afraid someone killed Gloria to send him a message. People in Las Vegas knew about her. Apparently, she'd staked him before, but he'd always been able to pay her back, and as he said, 'pass on a little taste of the action'."

Michael said, "Tom, thanks for that. Lawrence, have you looked at Gloria's finances, and the Sharpe Family Trust?"

"Financial Crime got me a look at her personal accounts. It won't be as easy to get access to the records of the trust, which is under the umbrella of the family business. Most of that money is offshore, in banks not famous for cooperating with law enforcement."

"Gloria moved a lot of money out of her own accounts recently, and we can't tell where it went. Before that, there was a regular pattern of monthly deposits into one of her accounts, which she passed on, like clockwork, to the church. That did not happen for December."

Tom said, "Maybe she died before she had the chance."

Lawrence said, "The money came in the first week of every month, and Gloria would relay it to the church midway through the second week. She died on the Tuesday of the third week, without completing the transfer."

"That might explain why the treasurer's saying the church is broke. She's also accused Gloria of mismanaging the family trust."

Lawrence said, "I don't see how she could have. She was basically a go-between."

"The other thing I want to say is I don't see Bobby as a suspect. Gloria basically raised him after his mother died. His father buried himself in managing the family business, and more recently, his political career. Robert Senior has written him off as a disappointing political liability. Gloria was really all the family Bobby had."

Michael said, "That matches the profiles we're building. But as Lawrence said, we look at all possible angles."

Chapter 13

Early Thursday Evening (9 days to Christmas)

Tom felt guilty his clerical collar gained him a pass on the long line of those waiting to pass by Sylvie Gauthier's casket, to pay their respects to her family. He told himself he deserved a break because his chest still hurt from the Range Rover's shoulder belt.

He made his way to the front of the chapel, had a quiet moment with Sylvie's widowed husband Albert, then slipped out the side door.

Jesse King had invited the church executive to meet at the funeral home, so the members could also drop in at the visitation.

Tom pushed open the three-panelled, carved oak door to the arrangements room.

He heard a deep, resonant woman's voice proclaim, "The man always puts himself first. He's disgusting!"

It sounded like Liza Testardo, the church secretary. But who was she talking about?

Tom paused with one hand on the door frame. He leaned into the room, which also served as the Jesse's office.

Liza seemed to have Jesse backed up against his antique roll-top desk. Elvis looked down from the portrait on the wall above them.

In her thick-soled winter boots, Liza was very near Jesse's six-foot height. Her short black hair was spiked up with static. Tom thought it likely she'd just removed the toque she waved like a red woolen flag with each expressive hand gesture.

Jesse stepped with care around Liza. Beckoning towards the open door, he said, "Tom! C'mon in. Liza was just ..."

"I was just saying," Liza said, "Robert Sharpe is out there working the crowd. You should stop him politicking in the funeral home."

Jesse rolled his desk chair over to the head of the large mahogany dining table that dominated the room. He pointed to a place on his right, and said, "Liza, there's a seat right next to Marco. Please, make yourself comfortable. We'll start when Penny arrives."

Liza slipped her winter coat over the back of the chair and settled in beside her husband.

"Of course she'd keep us waiting. That one likes to make an entrance. Have you heard what she's saying around town about Gloria? She's just as bad that crook out there!"

Marco leaned in towards Liza and rumbled something in his deep voice.

She said, "Don't you tell me to be quiet, with that slimy hypocrite out there using Sylvie's death as a campaign opportunity!"

Marco Testardo chaired the church property committee. His callused hands and barrel chest were the result of decades as a builder and bricklayer. His face was ruddy from outdoor work. His thick, muscled neck strained against the pale blue dress shirt and tie he'd worn for the visitation.

Marco and Liza lived in the basement suite of Gloria Sharpe's lake-front century home. Marco maintained Gloria's properties, and Liza ran her household.

Tom hadn't considered what Gloria's death would mean to the couple. He wanted to be patient with Liza, despite his annoyance over her passive-aggressive parking campaign.

Tom nodded greetings to Liza and Marco, then sat directly across the wide table from them.

Beside Tom was Shelley Tinsel-Smith, new chair of the community life committee.

She said, "Isn't that what we all do at these things? Shake hands and try to make conversation?"

Her bright eyes exuded warmth, which Tom thought must have served her well in hotel management. She and her husband Steve joined the church not long after retiring early to take over her parents' Christmas tree farm. She wore a pine-green hoodie embroidered with the sparkly Christmas tree logo for Tinsel Acres.

Liza said, "Shelley you're new, you're sweet, and you don't have a clue. Robert's only here because Albert is on the constituency executive."

Tom thought Liza underestimated Shelley.

He said, "I'm glad people from that part of Albert's life are showing support."

Liza rose from her seat to lean across the table towards Tom. In that moment he appreciated the size and heft of the table between them. She was quite a presence.

She said, "Robert's here to gain support, not show it. He's like the bully pup of the litter, always nosing in for more. When I came through the visitation line, he was yipping on about the importance of old-fashioned values. We're in here trying to figure out how to go on out without his only sister, and nobody I know remembers the last time he set foot in the church. The roof might fall in if he did. What does someone like him know about family and faith?"

Tom remembered the bone weariness he'd felt when he'd had stand for hours to receive visitors at his mother's visitation. It had lifted him to have Hope and Annika on either side, and to see the faces of good friends nearby.

He eased out a breath, met Liza's gaze, and said in a soft voice, "We all need our families. There are times..."

Liza nodded, shrugged, and settled back into the well-upholstered chair.

She said, "There are times to hold your tongue."

Tom wondered who she meant. He said, "Liza..."

She finger-combed her hair with both hands and sighed. Her short-cropped black hair, showing silver at the roots, framed her round face in a way that drew focus to dark eyes, now glistening with tears.

Liza said, "It just breaks my heart. He's barking on about family values while his own son was cornered at the coffee station, with slick little Johnny Friendly pointing a manicured finger in his face."

Tom said, "I didn't see Bobby when I came through."

"It's a disgrace," Liza said. "Mr. Big Dog pranced off to join the pack in Ottawa, leaving Bobby to be raised by Gloria. I should know..."

Liza turned her gaze to her husband, who at that moment seemed absorbed in examining the terracotta miniature nativity set Jesse had set out for the previous evening's bible study. Joseph, Mary and the others seemed tiny and vulnerable in Marco's huge hands.

Liza said, "Marco and I, we've been with her through it all, and now..."

Tom said, "This has to be hard for you both."

Jesse said, "Excuse me. I hate to break in, but I've just had a text from Penny, saying she's on her way, and asking us to not start without her."

Liza said, "She's another one, always needs everything to be about her... but like I was saying, that Robert only appears when he wants something. I don't think he even talked to her the night she died."

Tom said, "I had the impression Robert Sharpe came down from Ottawa after Gloria died."

"Gloria had to go out that night," Liza said. "She was meeting someone over at the church. I was wiping down the counters and putting the supper things away. Robert trots in like he owns the place, which he doesn't. He had some story about papers Gloria was supposed to sign. He thought they might be in her study. Good luck with that, I said, the study's locked, and I don't have a key. It's the only room in that house I never go in."

Tom said, "Did he find what he needed?"

Baring her teeth for a grin, Liza said, "Judging by the snit he was in when he left, I doubt it."

Jesse's cellphone rang. He held it to his ear, spoke a few quiet words before pocketing the phone.

He said, "That was Penny, saying she's almost here. Maybe we can cover some other ground while we wait."

Chapter 14

Thursday Evening (9 days to Christmas)

Hope settled into a leather recliner in the parlour, with her Gran's loon quilt layered between her and the MacBook on her lap.

She'd asked the music app for quiet Christmas tunes for studying.

The first on the playlist was a modern setting of 'O Magnum Mysterium" by Morten Lauridsen, sung by the Kings College Singers at Cambridge.

The music was not Hope's usual vibe. She wondered if the almost-hypnotic lilt would lull her to sleep, especially with the gas fire radiating warmth, and a big German shepherd at her feet, leaning in against her shins.

It was good though; the music helped her slip into a calm zone. The casual way her father told her about totalling Paul's Range Rover had ticked her off. He didn't always seem to get that she worried about losing him.

Zeke's breathing seemed in rhythm with the singer's voices, and the twinkling of the tiny white lights on the Christmas tree.

Hope opened a text file for the journal she'd decided to call 'The Book of Christmas Joy'.

Mom was always into the spiritual, mystical aspects of life, but in the weeks leading up to her move into hospice, it was almost all she talked about.

She said that for her, part of preparing to die was coming to see there's only a very thin boundary, she called it a membrane, between where we live, and where we go when we leave our bodies.

I couldn't have cared less about membranes. I didn't want to hear her talk about leaving her body. Leaving me.

I didn't understand her decision to refuse treatment, and if I'm being honest, which I wasn't being back then, I was angry. But how can you be angry with someone who's dying?

I didn't want her to die. So when she'd start in about how death wasn't so much an end, but a transition to something else, I tuned her out.

Wow, there are a lot of "I's" in those last few paragraphs. How would I, rather, how does one avoid this, when trying to get their thoughts out? No idea.

There's lots I don't know.

I didn't know much back then, either, when Mom was dying, except that I was scared and didn't want to lose her.

Zeke shifted against her legs as he rose to stand. The movement brought Hope back into the warm room with the good dog.

She wondered if Zeke was somehow responding to her mood, until he made a low sound that was almost a growl, padded across the room, and nosed in beside the Christmas tree to look out the big bay window.

"Somebody walking by the house, Zeke? It's okay."

In the middle of a thought, and those deep feelings, Hope was keen to get back into her journal entry.

I felt guilty I didn't want to let her go, even though I could see how hard it was for her, and getting harder every day, and night.

I was young and scared and just wanted my Mom. Gran said that made all the sense in the world, and I shouldn't feel bad about not wanting to let her go.

This was what I thought of when Professor Barbour taught us about the Examen. That a person could feel a deep love in the middle of a deep sadness, or deep sorrow even as they felt so blessed to have this person in their lives.

Whether I focused on the 'negative' feeling of grief at my mom's death, or the 'positive' of feeling grateful and so adoring of her, there was love somehow, simmering at the centre.

I still miss Mom, of course.

(Note to self- maybe write something about the paper angels I made for Mom and Gran, to hang over our tree, as a way to signify their presence.)

I think of Mom and Gran every single day and often wonder what they'd think or say about something. I get why people latch on to all this spirit and ghost stuff.

This fall I went to a psychic fair. Stacey got me there with the promise it was about holistic wellness, whatever that means.

At the first booth on the left after we paid our admission the vendor was reading people's auras so he could match them with their soul stones. Right.

There was some nice amethyst, and something called labradorite I'd never seen before. The man at the booth wanted to know if "anything spoke to me".

I held back from saying I was looking for an infinity stone, like the ones Thanos used to destroy half the universe in that Avengers movie. He seemed so earnest, with his three little ponytails each a different colour, and I knew Stacey wasn't into Marvel movies, and wouldn't get it.

It turned out Stacey had driven us the 90 miles to this community centre so I could "get a reading" from her favourite psychic.

My twenty minutes with "Mr. Qarlz" (pronounced Charles) cost seventy-seven dollars and was pleasant enough. I can see how people are sucked in by his deal, which seems to be a lot about making the client feel special.

He said, "Are you aware you descend from a long line of seers?"

I said that was news to me.

Mr. Qarlz also had messages to relay. My Mom is very proud of me, and still walks with me, and my Gran wanted me to know that even though my Dad has been through a rough patch, he'll be okay, because he is being healed by love and light, which didn't sound like Gran, at all.

While we shared a vegan charcuterie board and a tasting flight of energy teas, Stacey swore up and down...

Zeke was back at the window, barking and making wet nose marks on the window.

Hope set her laptop on an end table, wrapped the quilt around her shoulders, and went over to stand behind the dog, who was still worryingly close to the Christmas tree. He might knock it over, with the way he was throwing his head back and forth, looking from the window to her and back again.

Shee rubbed the special spot between Zeke's ears, which were both pointed straight up.

"Zeke, buddy! What's your deal?"

She followed his gaze out the bay window and towards the church, and for the third night in a row, Hope saw strange lights flicking around inside the sanctuary.

"Okay, Zeke. Let's go."

Hope pulled her Gran's quilt tighter around her, stepped into a pair of her dad's boots and headed out the front door.

Cars passed by in both directions as they stood on the sidewalk in front of the parsonage. Hope figured some of the traffic was due to the big visitation at the funeral home, just two blocks south on Sharpe Street.

Hope did a little startled jump at the whoop of a siren, and the quilt almost slipped to the ground. By the time the emergency bar on the cruiser lit up, she'd remembered the police detachment was just across the street.

As the car with the flashing lights took off down the road at speed, she looked over at the sanctuary windows.

Once again Hope saw yellow-white light bouncing around inside the church.

Her father said most of the windows were original, and had suggested the beveled panes might do odd things with refraction and reflection, because of the bubbles and impurities in the old glass.

Was that a factor in what she kept seeing? Or was there something else happening here?

What would Mr. Qarlz think?

The previous summer Hope had attended a screening of a documentary made by a woman from her father's former church. Her father was in the movie, which was called The Ghost of Saint Mungo's and The Book of Answers.

Hope thought the title needed tweaking.

She'd been surprised by the opening scene, in which her father admitted he'd seen the ghost of a long-dead friend, who'd been the caretaker at Saint Mungo's back in the day. He said he'd kept his experience under wraps, even when quizzed by those who'd heard the rumours, and came to the church hunting for the ghost.

Hope had always thought he was the cautious, down-to-earth parent, who balanced out her mother's mystical inclinations. He tended to be the calm voice of reason.

The night before her father had vetoed going over to the church to investigate the reappearance of the weird lights. It wasn't hard to see his point, after what they'd walked into on Tuesday night.

Hope didn't think her father would be thrilled if she and Zeke checked out the church. Even less so if she said they were doing a little ghost hunting of their own.

He was already having a day as it was, what with being run off the road and totalling the Range Rover.

Hope was about freezing, standing on the street. She led Zeke back into the house, grabbed him a treat to lick out of her palm, then sat in her recliner to dial Detective Sergeant Barbara Palmieri.

"You stay put," the detective said. "I'm just across the street, writing reports. I'll do a walk through and let you know how I make out."

Fifteen minutes later, Hope still had her Gran's quilt wrapped around her when she answered the knock on the front door.

Barbara said, "I didn't see or hear anything in the church, and there was nothing on the camera we've got pointed at the front door."

"Thanks for checking it out, anyway."

"Now worries. It's why we gave you our numbers. You doing okay?"

"I'm good. Just tired, and a little freaked out by all that's been happening. The thing with my Dad today, just brought up a lot of old feelings."

Chapter 15

Later Thursday Evening (9 days to Christmas)

Penny Oltmann-Potter pushed open the door to the old Victorian dining room, which served as Jesse King's office, and the funeral home's arrangements room.

"I'm so very sorry to keep you all waiting."

She shrugged and half-spun, with what Tom deemed exaggerated effort, displaying her desire to escape the confines of her over-sized parka and get down to business.

Jesse was out of his chair and behind Penny in a flash. Tom felt bad that he wasn't up to moving that fast, but Jesse was ten years younger and hadn't rolled a car the day before.

"Let me get that for you."

Penny flounced her shoulders. The drab olive parka fell to the floor before Jesse could grab it.

He bent to retrieve the garment, then hung it on the coat tree near the door, which was already weighed down with outerwear.

"I'll note the arrival of our church treasurer, a half hour late."

Liza Testardo's withering tone interrupted Tom's thoughts.

Tom looked across the oak table to Liza. Her pen was poised over her secretary's minute book, but her dark eyes were aimed at Penny.

Jesse returned to his seat at the head of the antique dining table. He straightened and tightened his tie.

He said, "Penny did tell us she'd be delayed, and we were able to make good use of the time."

Penny claimed the far end of the table, opposite Jesse. She opened her grey Coach leather bag and placed a thin pile of printed pages where a dinner plate would have gone.

Liza said, "Shall I read back the minutes to catch her up?"

Jesse said, "We can save that for another time."

While waiting for Penny, the executive had reviewed the plans for the Sunday School Christmas Party, scheduled for the weekend. They agreed the younger families needed a lift, in light of Sylvie's death, and were grateful it would be held off-site, considering the grim discovery in the church.

Shelley Tinsel-Smith had offered to host it at Tinsel Acres, her family's Christmas Tree farm.

The executive considered a request for the baptism of a newborn, whose family did not live in the community, and hoped to "have the baby done" on Christmas Eve.

Shelley said, "If you can text me the child's full name, and those of the parents, I'll make sure we have a welcoming gift, with a nice card."

Jesse said, "That's a lovely gesture."

Liza said, "We've never done that before."

The balance of the time before Penny arrived was exhausted debating whether the welcoming gift would set a worrisome precedent.

Tom chose not to engage. Neither did he mention the latest email from the Donaldson's, the baptism family. The Honourable Robert Sharpe would not only stand as godfather, but he also planned to speak at the service.

Tom felt he'd done well to divert the baptism to Sunday morning. He'd have to tackle the issue of the speech from the Member when he met with the couple. He didn't want to think how Liza would react to Sharpe angling for the spotlight on that day.

Liza said, "Reverend Tom, what do you say? Should I go over the minutes so Penny can get caught up?"

Tom said, "I think we're good, Liza."

Jesse said, "Let's carry on. Penny, tonight's meeting was called at your request."

Penny rose to her full height, which just over five feet. She was in her mid-forties, with shoulder length brown hair. She'd worn a stylish blazer and pant set in a shade the salesperson might have called azure, but in contrast to her bright yellow blouse, Tom saw as Walmart Blue. She stood out boldly against the room's subdued floral wallpaper.

Tom wondered if this was her version of a power suit.

Penny said, "Poor Gloria shone such a bright light in our church, and now it's been snuffed out."

"Oh please," Liza said, "Just a few days ago you were angling to take over her big solo on Christmas Eve."

Liza was an alto. Gloria had been a soprano. Penny took her solos, on the rare occasions Gloria was out of town.

The Sharpe Street leadership, as with most churches Tom had served, was drawn largely from the choir.

"We had our creative differences, but I've always just wanted what's best for the choir, actually for the whole congregation. Which is why I've been beating the pavement to raise money."

Jesse, who was a baritone, but sang tenor in the choir, said, "That's something we'll need to..."

Liza cut him off.

"You've been telling people Gloria lost all the church's money, and only you can save us from ruin!"

Penny said, "I shared with a few people, in confidence, that Gloria ignored my best professional advice..."

"Professional advice? From you? The credit union manager nobody wants to work for?" Liza said.

Penny gripped the edge of the table with one hand. She exhaled a loud breath before speaking.

"There were a few occasions when the transfers from the Sharpe Trust were delayed. It led me to think it was time to ask the trust to transfer the money directly to the church account, as they once did. I of course had to speak to Gloria, and it was awkward. I worried that... well I wondered if she was becoming forgetful..."

Liza said, "Gloria was as fit as I am..."

Penny said, "Perhaps physically, but..."

Liza said, "You have a nerve, you do! Gloria was... well, she was sharp! Sharp as anybody here. She could have run the family business, except she had the misfortune to be born a woman, before her time. She would have done a much better job of it than her brother, who was always more interested in being top dog, than doing any actual work..."

Marco cleared his throat.

Liza shook her head at her husband.

She said, "Gloria was more on top of things than you know, and you need to be careful."

Marco's deep voice rumbled, "Liza."

He sings bass in the church choir.

"Don't you Liza me, Marco Testardo. I won't sit here and let this... let her... she can't talk about Gloria that way."

Jesse cleared his throat and looked at Tom. His eyes spoke volumes about the rising volume of the exchange.

Tom gave the slightest shrug, then said, "Liza. Penny. Emotions are high, and it's been a very tough week. Let's all try to be kind."

Having counseled others to be charitable, Tom regretted his mean-spirited judgment of Penny's clothing. He offered what he hoped was an encouraging nod.

Jesse said, "We'll have to talk about your impromptu fund raising, but it might be best to first get a picture of our finances."

Penny said, "Well, if it wasn't for my hard work these last two days, it'd be much worse. We can now cover most of the December expenses, including payroll..."

Shelley said, "Excuse me, but what about the Manger Market? What did that bring in?"

"After paying for advertising, table and chair rental, and the linens for the Jingle All the Way Cafe, the Christmas Bazaar cost us about $3200."

Shelley said, "Which explains why the fund-raising line is a negative number."

Penny said, "It's historically been more of a social event for the more senior women. It was one of Gloria's pet projects, and she'd usually make a special donation to cover the cost."

Shelley said, "I couldn't attend. It's our busy time at the farm, but I remember the ladies talking about their holiday crafts."

"Total sales from the craft tables were just under $72."

Penny failed to suppress a grin as she said, "The demand for Christmas-themed toilet paper covers has declined."

Tom said, "This was only my second year, but it seems people attend mainly for the lunch."

"It's always a big draw," Jesse said. "They haven't raised the prices... well, ever. Where else can you get soup, sandwich, beverage and dessert for $1.50?"

Penny lifted some stapled pages from the pile in front of her.

She said, "I've brought copies of my report... Shelley, can I trouble you to pass these around?"

Shelley smiled as if she'd love nothing more and rose to help.

Penny said, "As I began to say, we're now able to meet payroll, and cover utilities. Our assessment to the national church will come due in February, but we can hold them off for a while. As you can see, there've been no repairs to contend with...".

Marco's deep voice rumbled.

"Liza said some guys she didn't recognize looked at the boiler yesterday. I didn't know they were coming. They leave an invoice?"

Penny said, "I haven't seen one. And Brian over at Sun Parlour Heating and Cooling asked how everything's been working since they did the fall checkup. He also gave me a generous cheque for the church."

Marco huffed a laugh.

"Least he can do, with all the business we've given him."

Jesse held up the printed pages.

He said, "This looks better than I'd expected, after your phone call. But..."

Jesse paused, looked to Tom, and raised his eyebrows.

Tom said, "As grateful as we all are to finish the year in the black, we need an overall strategy for moving forward. One that's a team effort, not one person out there on their own."

Shelley said, "What about the Christmas Eve offering? At my church in Newmarket it was the biggest of the year."

Liza said, "We've never taken an offering at that service!"

Penny turned to stare at the church secretary. Tom saw the colour rise in her face.

She said, "That's one of a few changes I'm suggesting!"

Liza said, "Did you not just hear Reverend Tom tell you to back off?"

Tom said, "That's not exactly..."

Liza said, "Gloria's not even laid to rest, and you're already..."

Jesse said," Can we just..."

Penny shoved her remaining papers in her briefcase and stepped towards the door.

Jesse said, "Penny..."

She said, "I was expecting a little more..."

"A little more what?" Liza said. "Gratitude? Is that why you're here? You're as bad as Robert Sharpe out there in the visitation room, sucking up for fame and fortune!"

Penny said, "You have my report. I think I'd better be going."

She slung the brief-case strap over her shoulder, then opened the door with one hand as she grabbed for her coat with the other. She pulled the big parka off the heavily laden coat tree, which toppled with a muffled thump as she made her exit.

Chapter 16

Mid Friday morning (8 days to Christmas)

"Tom, have you done it that way before," Shelley Tinsel-Smith said, "have the burial before the service?"

Tom could see her breath in the cold December air. They were walking the two blocks from the funeral home to the church.

He nodded.

"A few times. Albert wanted the service to be a chance for people to say their goodbyes. But he also needed a moment for himself."

Tom didn't add that he and Jesse King had stood with Albert for a silent moment at the grave before Tom offered a prayer for the unborn child Sylvie had been carrying. Albert wasn't ready for that to be common knowledge.

Tom's neck and shoulders were stiff from the Range Rover rollover, which reminded him to be careful. He scanned the street in both directions.

"Let's cross here, there's a break in the traffic. Looks like a lot of cars headed to the church."

Shelley said, "Was it Albert's idea to have the service at the chapel, and the reception in the church hall?"

"He felt we needed to have Gloria's funeral in the sanctuary, before anyone else's. I kind of agree with him. I also think hosting the lunch gives the congregation a way to show their support."

"I think you're right. The people I called were all eager to help. We'll probably have a lot of food left over."

Tom had heard the rattle and scrape as the town's snowplow truck passed by the funeral home as he offered the closing blessing. They walked on gritty sand and heard the crunch of salt crystals underfoot as they crossed the road.

"I don't know how I'll feel being there on Sunday morning," Shelley said. "It will be strange to stand in the choir loft and see her empty space in the first row."

Just as they stepped up to the sidewalk in front of the church, Tom felt a bold brush of air as a vehicle rushed past on the road behind them. How had he missed seeing it coming?

He turned and caught a glimpse of the tail end of a black Cadillac Escalade, pulling away from them, and accelerating hard. He couldn't make out if it had a license plate.

"It's been a lot of mayhem and loss for a small town in one week."

"And at this time of year," Shelley said. "I liked what you said about Mary and Joseph being homeless when the baby was born."

"Let's go around to the side door," Tom said. "I don't want to walk in through the sanctuary."

They rounded the corner of Sharpe and Grenville and joined the line of those waiting to enter the church hall.

"I've never thought about Christmas that way," Shelley said. "Growing up at Tinsel Acres, we always focused on the joy of the season."

"There's nothing wrong with that," Tom said. "But working with families who've suffered losses at this time of year, I needed to learn how to help them hold on to Christmas."

"I don't know that I could do your job."

"A wise person taught me it wasn't my job to explain the terrible things, but to remind people we aren't alone in our mess. The image of the special baby born in the midst of peril does that. And shows us we're here to help each other."

"I heard that in Jesse's song. I'd never heard him do a solo that wasn't Elvis."

Tom said, "He really feels for Albert, and having him sing was better than me reading the lyrics and talking about them."

"I like the line about the humblest of people catching a glimpse of their worth."

"It's Bruce Cockburn. My favourite is where it talks about a future shining in a baby's eye," Tom said.

Shelley said, "Grab a table. I'll duck into the kitchen and get us coffee. There's something else I want to talk about."

The church hall was warmed by the crowd, thrummed with conversation, and smelled of good coffee and homemade egg salad.

The congregational life committee had set up all the round tables and chairs the space could safely hold, and most seats were occupied.

Long tables close to one wall were laden with trays of sandwiches, baskets of buns, and plates of cheese, cold cuts, home-canned pickles, cut fruit and vegetables. There were other tables set up near the coffee station, for desserts.

Members of the committee moved from table to table with carafes of coffee and tea and encouraged people to refill their plates.

Shelley approached with their coffees on a tray, which was also loaded with sandwiches cut into quarters.

Tom pointed to a corner near the stage, where the committee had set up kid-size tables and chairs, and put out paper and crayons.

"That," Tom said, "was a great idea."

Sylvie had been a classroom aide at Sun Parlour Primary School. Most of her class, their teacher, and the vice principal came to the service.

Shelley said, "I've been at way too many functions where parents feel like they have to keep the kids quiet. I'd much rather make them feel welcome. I took a peek on the way to the kitchen. Some of the kids are drawing pictures to give to Albert."

"That's really good," Tom said. I'm excited to see what you've got in mind for tomorrow."

Shelley said, "Steve's been like a big kid all week, trying out the crafts and games. I made him leave the piñata alone."

Tom enjoyed the spark of delight in Shelley's eyes when she mentioned her husband.

He thought about Annika, who'd be starting a day of travel when he was at Tinsel Acres for the party.

He said, "I can't actually tell if you're kidding about the piñata, but I appreciate all you're doing. Suddenly you're right in it with back-to-back events."

Shelley said, "Everybody's pitching in. With all the sadness, it's been good to have things to do that feel like they matter."

Tom pulled out his phone to check the time. Jesse would be waiting outside in about fifteen minutes to drive him to his next appointment. After that he'd be picking up the other Range Rover Paul kept at the Quiet Centre.

He said, "I stopped by this morning during set up, and told the committee they were doing great, but please thank them for me. I can't stay for the whole lunch. I have to meet that couple about the baptism."

"Then I won't keep you long. Please, have a sandwich," Shelley said. "I wanted to say that after the meeting last night I talked more with Liza and Jesse."

Tom wouldn't have blamed her if after the previous night's meeting, she'd want off the executive.

Shelley said, "Penny's comment about the payments from the Sharpe Trust set off an alarm bell for me."

Tom picked out a triangle of tuna salad on whole wheat. He could smell the mayonnaise, which was a good thing.

He said, "The whole trust set up is kind of weird. Nothing like it in any church I've heard of."

"It wouldn't happen in the church I grew up in. They were strong on tithing, and historically, did not put a lot of store in banks."

Tom said, "So what set off your alarm?"

"Penny talked about asking the trust to make an annual disbursement, rather than monthly installments, presumably to avoid the situation we currently face. I wondered why it hadn't been done before now."

"It does seems like busy work for Gloria, to be passing on the funds each month."

"I asked Liza for the terms of the original trust. Are you familiar with them?"

"I know about the open-door policy. It's hard to miss the plaque at the front entrance, with the Revelations quote: 'I have set before thee an open door, and no man can shut it.' "

Shelley said, "That was the first condition George Sharpe set. Unhindered access to the sanctuary. The second was like it. All aspects of church life must be open to all."

"George was Gloria's grandfather," Tom said. "Local lore says he was a fisherman who made his fortune as a rumrunner, and some uppity church elders gave him the stink-eye. They got over it when he paid to rebuild the church after a fire."

Shelley laughed at that.

She said, "The last two terms were more technical. The trust continues as long as there is a Sharpe on the church board and is to be managed by that descendant of George Sharpe, or their designate."

Tom sipped his coffee while he considered. Could killing Gloria be a way to dissolve the trust? Where would all that money go? He wondered if Michael and his team would see that as a motive for murder.

He said, "It sounds like Gloria could have the money go straight into the church account on any schedule she chose."

"Did you know that Jesse's boss, Mrs. Bower used to be the church treasurer?"

Tom swallowed the last bit of sandwich as he shook his head.

He said, "That'd be before my time."

"Jesse called her while we were talking. She said the trust money used to come in once a year, after the annual budget was set. That way the amount could be adjusted for projected needs. There was also a contingency fund, built up over time from surpluses, that was available if needed."

"For unexpected issues," Tom said. "Like our current pickle."

Shelley's eyes brightened with humour.

"You should try a pickle, they're very good. We get them from Lakeside in Harrow."

Tom said, "I know about Lakeside pickles. There's a local legend that says a Russian premier tried them on a visit to the Agricultural Research Station, and had a case sent back to Moscow."

Shelley laughed.

"That's great. I hadn't heard that one. I'll get back to the contingency question, but first I should tell you what Liza found in the minutes. This was from before she was the secretary. About a year after Penny took over, the executive discussed Gloria's announcement that the trust payments would now arrive monthly."

"I'm not sure what to make of that," Tom said. "But tell me about the contingency fund."

"That's the thing. Liza let me take home the minute books, and financial statements going back a ways. I could not find any reference to the contingency fund after the payment schedule changed."

Tom swallowed down the last of his coffee, and said, "Uh huh."

"I chatted with Mrs. Bower at the funeral home this morning. Gloria told her that if the church ever ran into problems, she'd take care of it, but she'd returned the surplus funds to the trust to be invested at a better return than the church could get."

Tom said, "I wonder why Penny didn't mention any of this. It sounds like it happened on her watch."

"Speaking of watches, I'm guessing you need to get going. We can talk more about this another time. Should I pack up those sandwiches to go, along with some of those famous pickles?"

"No, thanks. The thing with the baptism couple is over lunch at Smuggler's Point."

Chapter 17

Lunchtime, Friday (8 days to Christmas)

Tom scanned the dining room of the Smugglers Point Winery. Most tables were occupied. A team of servers, uniformly dressed in black, were kept busy bringing out food and topping up wine glasses. The murmur of multiple conversations was masked by a jazzy instrumental version of Winter Wonderland.

He felt out of place in his black suit and clerical collar but thought it might help the Donaldsons spot him.

A tall, middle-aged man approached. He sported an emerald-green jacket over a white dress shirt open at the neck. He had well-styled copper brown hair, a deeply tanned complexion, and a realtor's smile, which put Tom on guard.

The tight lines around the man's cold blue eyes reminded Tom of his father, at that moment he'd drained the last damn can of beer in the house.

"You're either the minister, or the headwaiter. You dress like a server, except for the doohickey in your collar."

He punctuated his observation with a hard-edged laugh.

"I'm Troy, and that's Haley. We're over here. Can we call you Jesse? Reverend King feels too formal."

The woman across the table wore a creamy white jacket over an aquamarine blouse that matched her eyes. Her short blonde hair was cut in the same pixie style of the wig Tom's wife wore when the chemo made her hair fall out.

Tom wondered what was triggering such painful memories.

Haley said, "Jesse, we're so excited to meet you. We've heard great things about your work at Sharpe Street."

Troy gestured with his glass and said, "Sit. What can we get you?"

Tom sat.

Troy drained his glass, then lowered himself to sit beside Tom.

Haley flashed a bright smile and wobbled her empty glass.

"Another bottle of the same please, Sonja. And whatever Reverend King would like."

"I'm... fine with water, thanks."

Troy said, "That's hardly the holiday spirit Jesse..."

"Actually, Troy, I'm Tom Book. Jesse is our board chair."

Haley said, "Are you sure you won't join us in a drink... Tom? We each did tasting flights before you arrived. I'd recommend the Smugglers Point Chardonnay."

Tom turned to the server, who seemed to be waiting for him. He read her name tag and said, "Sarah, I'd love a coffee, but there's no hurry. We'll likely need time to look at the menu."

"I'll get that coffee. But... they've already ordered for you. I came over to say we're ready to bring everything out."

"That's great Sonja! "Haley turned her smile Tom's way and said, "We thought it would save time."

Tom said, "I'm sure whatever you bring will be fine."

Troy said, "We've enjoyed everything they've poured for us, and the decor is great."

The walls were panelled with wide planks of reclaimed barnwood, upon which hung numerous wine barrel heads engraved with laser-cut images of old-time Lake Erie fishing boats and cargo vessels.

Antique captain's wheels wired to serve as chandeliers, suspended on heavy black chain, added to the nautical air.

Smuggler's Point juts out towards the American side of Lake Erie. Some of the area's most respected families made their fortunes during Prohibition.

Another server brought coffee and a small tray of fixings for Tom and refreshed the Donaldson's glasses.

Troy said, "We know it's been a challenging time, with the death of Robert's sister."

Tom said, "Gloria's death has been a shock."

Haley said, "We've been assured by Robert that it won't interfere with our plans. His aide penciled us in for the service, and Robert's already drafting his remarks."

Troy said, "Today's about firming up that we're good to get the baby done on Christmas Eve."

He emptied his glass in one long swallow, and said, "Sure you won't sample the Chardonnay? It's really quite good, for a local wine."

"No, but thank you."

Haley said, "So, we're all set then, for Christmas Eve? Robert will pop in for the first part of the service, make his remarks, allow time for a few photos, then we'd all be out of your way, and you can carry on with the mass or whatever."

Sarah and another server brought large platters of food. They were all having the panko breaded Lake Erie Perch, with slaw and fries.

Tom reached for his fork, then paused in case the Donaldsons wanted him to bless the food.

Troy said, "Do you guys do the fish on Friday thing? I wasn't sure, but it's the house specialty, so dig in."

Haley said, "Yes, please, eat. We don't want to keep you any longer than necessary... I mean, you must have somewhere else to be."

Tom cut into the fish. The breading was light, and crisp. He applied a squeeze of lemon, and the tartar sauce, then tasted his first bite, while thinking about how to have this conversation.

"The church board met last night and were happy to approve your request to have Miriam baptized."

Haley frowned, and said, "We were off to such a good start."

Troy said, "Hale? What's the matter, honey?"

"Tom's about to show us his but."

Tom said, "I... oh, I got you. Yes, there is more to talk about."

Troy lifted his empty wine glass, then waved it above his head.

He said, "We're going to need another bottle."

Haley said, "We thought everything was arranged by Robert's office."

"The board was not comfortable with a baptism on Christmas Eve. They offered this coming Sunday morning as a less hectic alternative."

Troy said, "Is there any wiggle room?"

"If Sunday doesn't work, they'd be open to another date."

"Are they aware," Haley said with a rising voice, "that Robert Sharpe, our very good friend, will be the godfather?"

Tom sipped his water.

"It would be unusual to include the godparent's name when bringing a request for baptism."

Troy said, "So they don't know who they've said no to..."

"They've said yes to welcoming your child..."

Haley said, "But only on their terms! That seems..."

"Most congregations require at least one parent to be an active member, who lives in the area. They are being kind, and trying to balance your wishes, with the needs of others, at a busy time."

"So, no wiggle room," Troy said.

Sarah appeared with another bottle of the Chardonnay and refilled the Donaldsons' glasses.

Haley said, "We'd originally planned to get her done at the Catholic Church."

Tom tried the slaw. It had a strong vinegar bite, which he thought suited this conversation.

"The nannies are very religious," Haley said. "The baptism is very important to them."

Troy said, "Sifra was our surrogate mother, and her sister Púa has also been with us for years."

Haley said, “If it weren’t for them, we wouldn’t have all the joys of parenting. They care for the baby and run the household, and we’re at the office more than ever.”

Troy said, ‘Their priest in London said we’d have to take in-person classes...”

“Which could take months,” Haley said.

Troy said, “When Robert heard the priest gave us a hard time, he assured us you would be more accommodating.”

“His family has a long association with the congregation. I’ve never met him.”

Troy said, “He moves in pretty high circles.”

Haley said, “We feel so privileged he’d take the time, with all the important things he’s involved with.”

“Privileged may be exactly the right word. Can I ask about his connection to your family?”

Haley said, “Troy and Robert were at university together...”

“We’re fraternity brothers. Beta Rho Omicron forever! Right now, we’re helping restructure his family business.”

“Are you a lawyer?”

“Haley’s the lawyer. I’m more of a big picture guy. I see what needs doing, and get it done.”

“I can see you being good at that.”

Troy smiled. He had something in his teeth.

“I usually find a way. Like when we had trouble getting permanent residency for the girls... the nannies. All it took was one call to Robert.”

Haley said, “We’re so excited he’ll be Miriam’s godfather.”

A loud voice boomed behind Tom.

“It sounds like I picked a good moment to make my entrance!”

The Member bent to kiss Haley, then elbowed across Tom’s plate to share a robust handshake with Troy.

Troy said, “We were just getting down to it.”

Robert Sharpe claimed a seat at the table.

Tom wiped the corners of his mouth, re-folded the napkin, and placed it near his plate.

Haley said, "Let's get you a glass. Or just take Tom's. Would you like some food?"

"Thanks no, Haley. I don't expect this will take long."

The Member turned his full attention to Tom.

"My aide called the church this morning, to confirm the Christmas Eve booking."

"Booking?"

"John was shocked to learn the baptism was rescheduled without consulting my office."

"I'm a little surprised Mrs. Testardo talked to him about it."

"Liza's worked for my family for many years."

Haley said, "Tom just said the board won't allow Miriam's baptism on Christmas Eve."

Troy said, "They counter-offered with a slot this Sunday morning."

"That's not quite how I'd put it. We aren't actually in negotiation."

Haley said, "In our world, everything is negotiable."

Troy said, "It's the art of the deal."

Robert gestured with both hands as if calming a crowd.

"My aide had the impression you didn't tell the board I'd be speaking at the service."

"That's true."

There was a pause, that Tom suspected was meant to rattle him.

Above the restaurant noise, Dean Martin sang about a marshmallow world in the winter.

"When were you planning on telling me?"

Up close, Sharpe's eyes were a reptilian shade of green, which was picked up in the muted pattern of his silk tie. His face was tanned a light bronze, not easy to maintain in December.

"I assumed the Donaldsons would share as much of our conversation as they deemed appropriate."

Tom felt his own face getting warm, as if he was the one under a tanning lamp.

Robert said, "Were you planning to reach out to me at all?"

"Mr. Sharpe, I've called your office twice this week, with regards to your sister's death. Your assistant assured me you'd be in touch, if you deemed it necessary."

This yielded another longish break. Dean Martin sang that the sun is red like a pumpkin head, which seemed an odd image for a song about winter. And weren't most pumpkins orange?

"As you can see, it has become necessary," Sharpe said. "As Haley said, everything is negotiable. There is always give and take."

Tom said, "I wouldn't go against the board's decision."

Sharpe flashed his teeth in a quick smile.

"We'll give you that. You'll be able to tell the board you upheld their decision about Christmas Eve. In return, you will agree to the following..."

Robert looked over at Troy, who gave his fraternity brother a thumbs-up.

"On Sunday morning, I will stand with my good friends as their daughter is baptized. I will shake Troy's hand and offer Haley a hug. I will refrain from kissing the baby, because that's a little too on the nose. Then I'll stand behind the pulpit my grandfather paid for. I will speak, humbly and profoundly, about the blessed event in which I have been honoured to take part."

Tom said, "Is that all?"

"I'll hand you an envelope and explain that my personal gift is intended to tide the congregation over while the question of ongoing financial support is being... re-examined. You will thank me and carry on with your service."

Tom said, "Haley... Troy... does this arrangement suit you both?"

Troy smiled his almost smile, and said, "We're good, Tom."

Haley raised an empty wine glass.

"See you on Sunday, Tom. On your way out, can you grab Sonja and send her over here? I'm parched."

Tom rose from his chair.

"Mr. Sharpe, I'm sorry for your loss."

He nodded to the Donaldsons and said, "Thank you for lunch."

Chapter 18

Friday Afternoon (8 days to Christmas)

"I brushed away the dry golden brown pine needles with my bare hands," Tom said. "Then I hollowed out a cavity like a bowl to receive my Mom's ashes, as I poured them out, at the base of an ancient white pine."

Tom was in the midst of telling Paul Bennett about a dream he'd had after his late-night phone call with Annika.

They were up in the Aerie; a glassed-in observatory Paul built atop an old brick grain silo at the end of the Quiet Centre property that overlooks Lake Erie.

As he'd walked away from the winery, and across the road that separated it from the Quiet Centre property, he'd noticed a matching pair of shiny black Cadillac Escalades idling.

He noted the plate numbers on his phone, and jotted down a reminder to look into some things he'd heard over lunch.

Tom felt more at ease as he came closer to the retreat centre.

He didn't relish a life in which everything was part of some negotiated deal.

The winter breeze had felt cleansing to Tom as he ascended the metal staircase that wound around the silo.

He willed himself to let the unpleasantness of the time in the restaurant fall away, like the snow he knocked off his overshoes before Paul opened the glass door at the top of the stairs.

They sat in comfortable chairs, that were arranged for conversation but angled outward for the view of the calm grey water and the pale blue sky.

It was a good place to for Tom to talk about his dream.

"Her ashes poured out smoothly, like a ribbon of smoke. I noticed shiny glints, and then the flow became pale, as if it was being blanched by the afternoon sun. The ashy powder turned pure white as it streamed into the hollow. This made me think of bones, then calcium, and finally, milk."

Paul smiled.

"As in mother's milk?"

Paul was in his late eighties. He was mostly bald, with fringes of short white hair that began above each ear and met around the back of his neck. His broad, bare forehead added to a gentle openness of expression, and there was a sparkle of delight in his clear blue eyes.

"Mother's milk? Yeah, maybe," Tom said.

He smiled back at Paul, and went on.

"Then I was pouring milk into the bowl, which soaked down through the old pine needles, and into the soil. I imagined it reaching the tendrils of roots and being drawn up into the tree."

Tom appreciated that Paul listened with his whole self. It invited him to focus on the dream.

Paul said, "Were there other sensations? Any smells around you?"

"The sun was warm on my back. There was a mild breeze. The forest smelled old, like soil just turned over."

Paul was thin and sinewy, in the way of old men who still chop wood and dig post holes. He dressed the part, with his pressed denim work shirt, faded jeans and beat-up work boots.

When Paul hosted retreats at the Quiet Centre or ventured off the property, he wore a roughhewn brown cassock tied at the waist with a cotton rope. It was part of the monastic rule he'd adopted when he took vows as an associate of a small order.

Paul said, "Do you remember other details? Sounds?"

Tom closed his eyes.

"The soft call of Canada jays. The whistling of a sparrow. The deep chuckle of a raven, like she'd just heard a good joke."

"Interesting. What happened after that?"

"I stepped away from the base of the tree and looked for the raven. I thought she might be perched in the higher branches of that old white pine."

"Did you see her?"

"No. But in the brief time I was searching, the milk had all been soaked up, and the bark of that tree, as far up as I could see, gave off an amber glow."

"And how did you feel, as you stood there?"

"Like I understood, in my bones, what the raven had been laughing about."

"That's lovely," Paul said. "As you told me about this dream, what came to mind for you?"

"Hope and I flew up to Thunder Bay a few months after Mom's funeral. I'd called ahead to ask permission to spread her ashes on the land of the First Nation where she had her first teaching job. It was what she'd asked us to do. The box was in my lap for the whole flight, and then Hope held it for the three-hour drive north."

"The woman at the band office knew why we'd come and walked us out to where the old school and teacher's house had been. She suggested we go a little deeper in the bush, to a spot where a small stream joined a larger one."

Paul said, "That would be considered a special place."

"She knew my mother's name. She said Mom taught her, and that she'd been one of the good ones."

"What does your dream say to you?"

"Mom's back where she wanted to be. In a way, she's home."

Paul said, "The dream-maker inside of us gathers bits of material from our lives to tell a story we need to hear. Like ravens in the waking world, who pick up shiny things to bring back to their nests."

"I've heard you say that before, without the bird part."

"In many cultures, the raven is considered a messenger from one world to another. There are also creation stories where they are the bringers of the first flame. Fire often represents life, or change, or more properly, transformation."

"It always seems to come back to that."

Paul smiled with his whole face.

"What happened when you poured out your mother's ashes at the place she wanted to be? Another way to ask is, what happened when she found her way home?"

"Things changed. The ashes became milk, which fed the tree, and became part of it. Then there was that amber light from within the tree, and the laughing raven."

"If this raven was in your waking life, what shiny bits might she pick up?"

"Hope and I found the corpse of a woman about the age my mom would be, if she hadn't died. She was under a fake pine tree, in a pool of her own blood. Her nephew told me she poured her life into that church."

Paul nodded.

"Yes."

"And Gloria held the purse strings for a congregation that wants me to stay on permanently."

"It's almost like you're being invited to set down roots."

Tom said, "It's all connected with what happens next with Annika... who has amber eyes."

"And with whom you had an important conversation before you had this dream."

"I asked if she'd like to come back early and be with Hope and I for Christmas."

"How did that go?"

"She's flying in tomorrow evening. I'll pick her up at the Detroit airport."

"How do you feel about that?"

"Anxious. Happy. Frightened. Excited to see her. Worried it's a big mistake. And yes, I know... that's all normal, even healthy."

Paul said, "The grieving soul may fear to love again. It's not just loving a person that bears inherent risk. New life... daring to love a place, a new role... investing in anything means accepting the possibility of loss."

"Thank you, Paul."

"If you have time, we can go down to the main house for tea. I'm interested to hear more about your misadventure with the black Cadillac before I give you the keys to the other Range Rover."

Chapter 19

Early Saturday Morning (7 days to Christmas)

Hope hit the brakes hard.

"Shit! Sorry!"

Tom's phone flew out of his hands.

Panic surged through him. He was back in that moment two days before when his Range Rover slid out of control, spun 180 degrees, then rolled over.

"Hold on, Dad!"

His chest, still bruised from the crash, was pressed with painful force against the shoulder belt.

It hurt to breathe.

He'd felt the soreness at the gym that morning, and realized he'd be tender for a while.

Hope said, "Okay, we're good."

She let off the brake and the SUV's tires crunched over snow-crusted gravel. They were stopped, safe on the shoulder of the county road.

"What the..." Tom began. The pressure on his chest subsided. He turned his head to peer over his shoulder.

Hope said, "We're good Dad. There's nothing, nobody coming up behind us."

Looking out the passenger window, Tom saw remnants of the previous nights' dusting of snow lingering in rutted lines across a farmer's field, and in the shadows of the windbreak trees.

Just a few car lengths ahead of them, brake lights glowed red on a salt-stained blue Tesla as it skidded to halt at an angle, just behind a caramel-coloured Fiat 500.

Tom said, "What happened?"

"Sorry," Hope said. "That idiot in the blue car whizzed past, then pulled in front of us. He didn't seem to notice the little brown car until he was right up on their ass... I mean tail."

"You did great," Tom said.

He looked out and saw they were well over on the shoulder of the road.

"I need a second. I'm still a little sore from the other day."

"Sure. I'm going to the back to check on Zeke... Hey! Zeke, buddy..."

Somewhere on the floor Tom's phone played the Batman ringtone.

Tom grunted as he released the shoulder belt, then groaned as he bent to feel for his phone. His fingers found it as Hope opened the driver's side door, which let in a rush of cold air.

Tom answered his phone. "Hey, Michael. That was fast."

"You okay, partner? We show you as stopping suddenly on 77, north of Leamington. I can have someone there in... under six minutes."

Over the wind rushing in through the back hatch, Tom heard Hope say, "Sorry about that Zeke."

Tom said, "Thanks, but we're good. Hope was driving. Someone passed when they shouldn't have, and then had to stop short. Hope handled it well."

"How are the other drivers?"

"Must be okay... both vehicles are back underway."

The back hatch closed with a thunk.

"And you? You could still be feeling it from Thursday."

"Yeah, but I'm good, just shook up... Hope's getting back in. I'll put you on speaker."

Seconds later the driver's side door was open, with another cold blast.

"Zeke's good," Hope said.

She pulled her door shut, buckled back in, and pointed to the road.

Tom nodded. He spoke into his cell.

"My phone's not synced to this car, so you'll hear some noise. Hope's getting us back on the road."

"Good morning, Hope," Michael said. "You alright?"

"We're good. Zeke's fine. Dad's sore, but that's from the other day. I'm guessing that's why you're tracking us."

Tom said, "Hope's up to speed. She knows I'm trying to help sort things out."

The normal deep resonance of Michael's voice was flattened by the cell phone speaker.

"Barbara gave him the puck to keep in his pocket. She stuck another on the new Range Rover you came home with yesterday."

Tom said, "We're headed to a church function. Hope will keep her eyes and ears open."

"Does that mean you're okay with your dad helping us out this time?"

Hope said, "I think he's more up for it than he was back in Oakville. And I get it. I saw what someone did to that poor woman."

"I'm pretty sure I don't need to say this," Michael said, "but..."

"Dad told me. It's like the first rule of Fight Club. Or being a pastor's kid."

Michael laughed.

"Okay."

"Excuse me," Tom said. "That was the 4th concession," Tom said. "Our turn will be a right on to the 8th."

They were headed to Tinsel Acres for the Sunday School Christmas Party.

Hope said, "I have it on the nav screen. We're good, Dad."

The phone produced a clipped version of Michael's chortling.

"Sounds like you've got it Hope. After Barbara checked the church building last night, she went back over the video from the camera we have pointed at the church, as well as the parking lot camera."

Hope said, "Did she see anything helpful?"

"We only started recording the feed from the parking lot camera Wednesday morning. We see some regular users, and we've run all the plates. It's mostly neighbours using the lot overnight."

"We're interested in an older model brown Plymouth Voyager that arrives, and leaves a few minutes later, around the time you saw light moving around inside the church."

Tom said, "Can you see who's gets out of the van?"

"They wear dark loose clothing, ball caps pulled down, and Covid masks. Barbara ran software that looks at body shape, how they walk, and other factors. It seems to be two women. They walk slowly, which may indicate illness, or age."

Hope said, "Did you look up their license plate?"

"The minivan is registered to a numbered company."

Hope said, "What does that mean?"

"A business has a legal identity. Some owners gives them a name. Lots of companies just use their business numbers. But the van looks too old and beat up, for anything legit, and that tells us something."

Tom said, "What do you think it means?"

"Local cops tell us they see a lot of unlicensed taxis and delivery vehicles that service the greenhouses. There's a whole infrastructure, some of it underground, set up to meet the worker's needs."

Hope said, "What kind of needs?"

"Same as anywhere," Michael said. "Rides to town and back. Familiar food delivered when you're too tired to cook. Alcohol. Sex workers. Drugs, although we think it's mostly soft, recreational use. The work is tough for hard-core users to sustain and doesn't pay all that well."

Tom said, "Most make minimum wage. They work hard, and send money home. A lot of them live in bunkhouses like that one we're passing right now."

Essex County is wide and flat. Even the massive greenhouses looked small against the vast grey winter sky.

Michael said, "You've picked up quite a bit about the greenhouse workers."

"The church has partnered with the Migrant Workers Support Group on a few things."

Hope slowed the SUV to accommodate a transport pulling out from a driveway.

"Dad," Hope asked, "Didn't you say Gloria's family business is into greenhouses, and logistics?"

Michael said, "You're good at this, Hope. We were already looking at possible ties between their company and the darker side of the industry."

Hope said, "Darker than the underground economy you mentioned?"

"We estimate somewhere between ten and twenty percent of the workforce is undocumented. They're used as floaters, brought in for extra shifts to deal with time-sensitive harvests, orders that need to get out fast. There are also a few unlicensed cannabis operations. That end of things is handled by some very nasty people."

Hope said, "You mean organized crime."

Michael said, "That's what the media calls it."

Tom said, "Speaking of nasty people. I'd suggest having Lawrence and Barbara look at a couple from London. Troy and Haley Donaldson. She's a lawyer. He's some kind of fixer, who's also a fraternity brother to Robert Sharpe. They're tied into Sharpe's efforts to restructure the family business."

Michael said, "Anything specific?"

"Troy bragged that Sharpe helped him jump the queue on permits for their nannies, who are from the Philippines. It spoke to their willingness to work outside the rules."

"Not a good look," Michael said, "for a guy who wants to run the Treasury Board. I'll get Barbara to do some digging, and Lawrence can start building profiles."

Tom said, "Thanks. I'll keep you posted if we pick up anything else."

Hope said, "We're almost at the farm."

Michael said, "Okay. Hope, go see what you can see. Tom, when you get a chance, ask Barbara to show you the footage she found from our camera on the church, from Thursday night, when Hope saw the lights again. We want to see if you recognize someone."

Chapter 20

Mid Sat Morning (7 days to Christmas)

An elfin red-headed child wearing a pointy green paper hat peered up at Tom, giggled, and said, “What’s he doing?”

Tom Book stood in the midst of a merry troop of elves. They sat on carpet squares that were either holly berry red or ivy green. He waved his right arm as if hitting an unseen nail with an invisible hammer.

For a moment, the Sunday School children were quiet, and the only sounds were the crackling of the fire in the woodstove, and the faint lilt of Christmas music coming from an old floor-model radio.

“...all is calm, all is bright.”

Then another elf, whose long brown hair emerged unevenly from under her slightly crumpled hat said, “Yeah, what’s Reverend Tom doing?”

Most of the kids’ hats had survived the brief journey from the craft tables over to the story circle. They were green construction paper cones with bright yellow pompoms on the point, and a red paper band around the bottom, with spikes like a crown. Also, liberal amounts of gold glitter, of which there was now a scattered trail.

Tom imagined the hardwood plank floors would have an extra sparkle for the rest of the season.

The Tinsel Acres reception centre was where customers came to pay, and warm up after their search for their perfect tree. Shelley Tinsel-Smith had offered it as a space for the Sunday School party.

Tom continued his strange arm waving, as little voices offered opinions.

"He looks like's he's hanging from a rope."

"That's funny."

"He looks like a monkey."

Much high-pitched elven laughter ensued, fuelled by the iced sugar-cookie stars and Christmas trees the kids had picked up on the way to story-time.

Tom and the elves were surrounded by a circle of folding chairs, set up for adults, and kids who might feel too grown-up to sit on the floor.

The story circle and the craft tables were at opposite ends of the room. In between, a Sunday School grandma had been stationed to keep little ones at a safe distance from the woodstove that provided warmth and added the smell of seasoned wood burning to the aromas of hot chocolate and spiced, mulled cider.

Strings of old-fashioned Christmas lights with the big bulbs in solid colours, each with their own pressed tin reflector, were wrapped around the rafters above the craft area and the story circle.

Ten-year-old Sadie Bower was the only Sunday School student who'd opted for a grown-up chair. From her seat on the edge of the elven gathering she spoke with somber authority.

"He's not being a monkey."

It was Sadie's grandmother on woodstove duty. Andrea Bower, who was also Jesse King's boss at the funeral home, brought Sadie and her sister to church anytime it didn't conflict with their hockey.

Sadie scratched her head, pushed some strands of curly brown hair behind her ear, and said in a serious tone, "I think he's only doing it to get you to look."

Tom waved his right hand towards the older girl.

"You're right, Sadie. But do you know why?"

She smiled. "You wanted our attention. Maybe to get everyone to be quiet."

Sadie was missing a front tooth. Tom couldn't remember when his daughter's teeth finished coming in, but thought she'd been a bit older. He hoped the gap in Sadie's smile wasn't due to a hockey injury.

Tom said, "My mother started as a teacher in a one-room school smaller than this building. It was way up north, in a little village totally surrounded by Christmas trees. It was a long time ago."

The red-headed elf shot his hand up for a question. Had the mention of school activated his kindergarten programming?

"Was it the olden days?"

"Yes, Declan, it was. Way before I was born. When she wanted everyone to stop talking, and look at her, she'd ring a big bell on a handle. I have it at home but forgot to bring it."

Declan said, "So you just pretended."

Tom said, "For some reason the pretend bell often works better than a real one."

Sadie said, "Because we wondered what the heck you were doing."

Tom said, "Exactly. You saw something you didn't understand, which made you wonder. To me, that sounds like the beginning of a story. Can I tell you one?"

Declan said, "Is it a Christmas story?"

"Yes," Tom said. "It's about the time Mary talked with an angel."

Sadie said, "Like the one on top of that tree?"

She pointed to the Christmas tree in the corner near the door. The angel on top was crafted from a tin funnel and had chicken wire for the halo and wings. It fit right in with the Grandpa's Workshop theme in which the space had been decorated.

Tom liked the faux fireplace built with stacked red metal toolboxes. The mantle was hung with heavy wool work socks, embroidered with the names of members of the Tinsel family.

"That's the thing Sadie. The Bible doesn't describe Mary's angel. The story just says they talked. We don't even know if she actually saw it, or if she just heard it, or maybe..."

"Maybe she was having a dream?"

"Could be," Tom said. "Some of my dreams feel really important. Sometimes they tell me something I need to know."

Sadie said, "So what did this angel tell Mary?"

"The angel told her not to be afraid, that they'd come to bring her some Good News."

"Why was she afraid?"

"According to the story, Mary was just a few years older than you, Sadie."

"Like maybe Savannah's age? She didn't come today. She said this was just for little kids."

"How old is Savannah?"

"Fourteen. She acts like she's all that because she goes to the high school."

"Mary was about Savannah's age when she got the news about the baby."

"That's pretty young. Who was going to help her with it?"

"Good question. Mary might have wondered that too."

"What about Joseph? Wasn't he Mary's husband?"

"This was before they were married. Mary's family had promised her to Joseph, and when she was old enough, they would get married."

"Savannah says she has no time for boyfriends or girlfriends. Says she's too busy."

Tom said, "I'm guessing your parents are good with that."

"But what about Mary? Did she want to marry Joseph? Did she even want to have a baby? Did he want to have a baby?"

"All good questions, and we don't know for sure. We think Joseph was kind to her, but it seems like the baby was a surprise."

"So, what if Joseph found out, and was like, I'm outta here?"

Tom said, "The angel told Mary not to be afraid, that this was good news, and part of God's plan. This was going to be a special baby."

"Well, duh! Aren't all babies special?"

Tom said, "Sadie, I should get you to help me with my stories at church. Yes, I think all babies are special."

"Savannah's friend Daphne from hockey's a year older than her, and she's only in grade ten, but she's having a baby. Savannah says her parents are all mad about it."

Tom said, "That happens. It could have been like that for Mary too."

"So how can this be good news?"

"I think what Mary heard from the angel was God would help her, and that God loved her and the new baby, and the child would grow up to tell lots of people about God."

"But why did it have to be so messy and complicated?"

"That's another good question, and I don't have the answer. But what I think is that when life gets complicated, and it gets hard to see good in the world, it's important to know we aren't alone."

As Tom heard himself, he wondered how old Bobby Sharpe was, when his mother died, and his Aunt Gloria stepped in to raise him. He thought he should give Bobby a call before the visitation for Gloria on Sunday afternoon.

Chapter 21

Later Saturday Morning (7 days to Christmas)

Tom lay on his side in the soft snow at the base of the tree. The cold soaked through his jeans into his left hip.

He leaned into his left hand for balance as he wielded the hand saw with his right. Each push and pull on the saw sparked a sharp twinge in his shoulder.

Hope said, "You okay Dad?"

"Uh, maybe you should do this. I'm still pretty sore from the other day."

Hope reached for the saw, then gave her father a hand up.

Tom brushed the snow off his pants as Hope took his place under the low limbs of the tree.

She said, "It's like where we put Gran's ashes. I love the smell."

Tom said, "I didn't know we were putting up a second tree."

"What did you think would happen when you sent Zeke and I out here?"

At the sound of his name, the German shepherd raised his big head. His lead was tied to the handle of the Radio Flyer wagon Hope borrowed for their walk through the rows of Christmas trees.

"It's probably good to support the farm, since Shelley and Steve hosted the party."

Tom held the tree steady as Hope made quick work of sawing through the trunk.

They maneuvered the six-foot white pine to lay flat across the little red wagon's wooden rails.

Tom took charge of Zeke's lead. He yawned and raised himself off his haunches.

Hope pulled the wagon along the track of boot prints in the snow that would take them back to the sales barn. The wagon's over-sized tires rolled easily over the snow, but not without a squeaky protest.

"It'll be perfect in the living room. We can get Annika to help us decorate."

"You don't think that's a little too... happy family?"

"More than asking her to cut short her trip to Europe?"

Tom looked up at the grey sky and decided to switch to a safer topic.

"Did you pick up anything to point us towards a murderer?"

Some of the adults who dropped their children off for the Sunday School party took the opportunity to walk amongst the Christmas trees. Tom had suggested to Hope that Zeke might also appreciate a chance to stretch his legs.

"This one lady said you ruined Christmas when you said Matthew and Luke tell different stories about Jesus' birth."

"I heard pretty much the same thing at the Bible study. Gloria didn't like that either."

Hope paused at the end of their row of trees. When she spoke again it was at a lower volume, and in a more serious tone.

"Someone remembered Gloria saying there'd be a real tree in the sanctuary over her dead body."

"Sad thing is it'll happen now because of her dead body," Tom said. "Steve's going to haul a big one in this afternoon. Kelly Halligan, Lori Gregoire and some of the other firefighters will help set it up."

"Did they think of maybe getting the Sunday School to help decorate?"

"Not a chance. That'll be handled by the Manger Market ladies, who want it done just so. That's part of the compromise Jesse worked out. He wants the tree in place for his big concert tonight."

"The ladies and their Manger Market. I heard about that, too."

"You picked up a lot."

"It was actually amazing. People walked around, looking at the pretty trees, oblivious to how far their voices carry. Except for this one time, when these two ladies stopped cold when they heard the squeaky wheel on this wagon."

"What about the Manger Market?"

Tom could see his breath as he spoke.

"One lady worried what will happen now that Gloria's gone. She'd heard the treasurer was against it."

"That's Penny. At the executive meeting she said without Gloria chipping in, the event lost money."

He'd told Hope to wear a heavier coat. He wished he had taken his own advice.

"Penny's name came up in the last conversation I overheard. Someone wondered if Penny would finally get to sing O Holy Night on Christmas Eve. The other person said Gloria got the solos because she wrote the endowment cheques. She called her G Sharp and laughed a mean laugh."

"I've heard that before. G Sharp because she didn't always hit the notes."

"Really, Dad, some of them act like they're the cool kids in high school."

Hope pulled the wagon towards the back of the reception centre.

The Tinsel Acres reception centre was a one-story metal building with garage doors on either end, which on another farm would likely serve as a shop. The back end, where Hope and Tom were headed, was where Steve and Shelley helped customers get their trees ready to take home.

Steve Tinsel-Smith stood next to a boxy blue metal platform. It was about a foot high and had a heavy orange power cord running from it to an outlet box mounted on the pole for a yard light.

Tom thought Steve looked snug and warm in his rust-brown insulated coveralls, and pine green Tinsel Acres toque.

Steve said, "That's a nice tree. Let's give it a shake."

With practiced efficiency, he lifted the tree off the wagon and stood it up straight, with the trunk on the blue metal device.

He tapped a foot switch with the toe of his boot, causing the metal box to vibrate. There was raucous mechanical percussion that postponed conversation.

Long pine needles, cones, and a sifting of dust fell from the limbs, joining layers of detritus from other trees, that had settled around the edges of the shaker.

Steve toe-tapped the foot switch again, resulting in a moment of stillness.

He said, "The white pine is called the tree of peace. We learned about it a grower's association meeting."

Hope said, "Why do they call it that?"

"We had an elder in from Six Nations, near Brantford. He said the Haudenosaunee have stories about a man who came to end the conflict amongst their nations. He gathered the leaders together under the shelter of a white pine, which became a symbol of lasting peace."

Steve lifted the tree from the shaker and pushed the cut end into a wide hoop mounted at one end of a long metal rail, which was supported by metal sawhorses.

He pulled a cable from a winch at the other end of the rail and hooked it on the trunk. He toe-tapped another foot switch. The cable was tugged taut, then pulled the tree through the hoop, which compressed the limbs as they passed through. As the much-narrower tree emerged from the hoop, it was wrapped snugly with white netting.

Steve sliced through the netting at the crown end with a jack-knife, freeing the tree from the machine. He lowered the wrapped tree to the snowy ground, folded the knife, and tucked it in his pocket.

"The elder told us sometimes warriors would pull a young white pine out of the ground, place their weapons in the cavity, then replant the tree."

Tom said, "I like that."

Steve said, "Me too. I figure we could all do with more peace in our lives."

Steve helped Hope load the newly wrapped tree back on the Radio Flyer wagon with the squeaky wheel.

He said, "I'll give you a hand tying that on your roof."

Tom held Zeke's lead, and Hope pulled the wagon.

Steve led them around the reception centre and back to the parking lot, a large sheltered area defined by big barns on either side.

Annika's SUV was one of about a dozen vehicles parked in an area that could easily hold a few dozen more.

Steve pointed to the older barn on the right.

"That's where we store the big equipment, and fix what breaks."

Directly opposite stood a new barn. It was several storeys high and looked big enough for indoor basketball.

Hope said, 'What's that one for?"

Steve said, "Someday it will replace the old one."

Hope said, "Looks like a great place for a party."

Chapter 22

Saturday Evening (7 days to Christmas)

"Partner!" Michael's voice boomed through all 19 speakers of the Range Rover's high-end sound system.

Tom said, "You know that song Elvis does, or did, where he sang 'out there in the dark, there's a beckoning candle'?

The lights of Windsor, and Detroit beyond it, were visible as Tom drove northwest.

Michael said, "If I can dream. Last song on the '68 comeback special."

"How, and why do you know that?"

"Mom was a big fan. We watched that DVD over and over. What got you thinking... oh, it was Blue Christmas tonight."

Tom was in a steady stream of vehicles on Highway 3, which cut a flat, and mostly straight diagonal across the county from Leamington up towards the Ambassador Bridge to Michigan.

"Jesse dedicated the song to those who've been a candle in the night for someone who was lost. His dad completed suicide when Jesse was in high school, and he remembers the person who was there for him...

Tom felt his throat tighten.

"You were there for me, Michael, when my Mom died."

Tom slowed for a red light.

"Right back at you, partner. My Mom liked you, even though you only got to meet her that once, before..."

Tom checked the time, and the nav map on the in-dash display. He was on track to be early to the Detroit airport, unless things were slow at the bridge.

"I wish I'd had a chance to get to know her."

"You made an impression on her. That's why she told me I needed to look out for you."

"So not because we're friends or anything."

"A crusty old copper and a soft-hearted pastor? How could that happen?"

"Before this thing with Gloria, we hadn't talked for a while. I'm sorry about that, and don't want it to be it takes a murder..."

In the rear-view mirror, Tom caught sight of a vehicle with a big glaring light bar, coming up fast, then stopping hard, and up close behind him. It was a tricked-out Jeep Wrangler in classic Tonka yellow. Windsor had a big Chrysler plant where they built mini-vans, and a lot of the workers seemed to use their employee discount to buy big toy trucks. At least it wasn't a black Escalade.

"We're good, Tom. How was the concert?

The light changed, and Tom accelerated. The Tonka truck came up around him, passed, and left Tom far behind.

"There was one little glitch, and another, bigger annoyance, but I'm glad I went."

"What was the glitch?"

"Jesse did the intro I told you about. With that candle song he does the thing where you pass the flame from person to person. Everybody picked up a candle in a clear plastic holder as they came in the church."

Michael said, "Just like Christmas Eve."

"Yeah, same deal. Everybody's all ready, holding up their little candles, and Jesse goes for the taper thing."

"Taper thing?"

"The long wooden handle with the adjustable wick on the end, that also has the brass part that looks like a dinner bell, to put out candles. We had one at Saint Mungo's."

"Gotcha."

"I saw him do this last year. He lights the taper from the tall pillar candle at the front of the sanctuary, then uses it to light the little candles for a few people in the front pews, and they pass the flame on, as the lights are dimmed."

"You okay with him stealing your whole Silent Night deal, less than a week before Christmas Eve?"

"He's being doing this for years, and a lot of his audience wouldn't otherwise go to church, so this is a big moment for them."

Tom passed through the intersection with Walker Road. To his left was a monument store, with sample tombstones on outdoor display, which struck him as an effective reminder to drive with caution. To his right was a discount cannabis shop.

"You said there was a glitch?"

"He reached for the taper thing, and I could see he wasn't finding it. That was weird because there's a certain place for everything in this church, and Jesse knows all the places."

"So, what happened? Guessing you held back from jumping up to help him look."

"That would have broken the spell. I thought of it, because we were on the near edge of awkward, but he looked at me, and I could tell he had it covered."

"So what did he do?"

"He borrowed one of the small candles everyone else had. He went to someone he knows smokes, and in his best Elvis voice he said, 'Hey buddy, you want to help me take care of business?'

The guy obliged, and Jesse did the, "Thank you... thank you very much."

That got a laugh, and he moved on, got the moment back."

Highway 3 transitioned into Huron Church Road, the five mile-long approach to the Windsor-Detroit bridge. Three lanes in each direction.

Tom had allowed time in case it was jammed up with big trucks, even on a Saturday night.

"So that was the glitch. What was the other thing? The annoyance?"

Tom was happy to join the steady flow towards the bridge.

"So, after Jesse rescued the candle-lighting, and all the lights are dimmed, he sang the song to end the show. The lights came up, and because a lot of this crowd comes every year, they know there's no encore. They're being sent out into the world to be candles."

"I headed down the centre aisle, on my way to the exit. Then there was this rude thunking on a microphone, and it wasn't Jesse, because Elvis had already left the building."

"I looked to the front of the church, and saw our treasurer banging on the pulpit mike, and yelling, 'Hold up everyone!'"

"She's pretty short, so she was mostly hidden behind the pulpit, but her voice cut right through the murmuring and footsteps of the departing crowd."

"I have an emergency announcement."

"Like a lost kid," Michael said. "Or a fire?"

"She said the church was broke and needed their help to survive to host the concert next year. She'd be in the narthex waiting to take their donations."

"So you didn't know about this?"

"Not a chance. We wouldn't have let her, if she'd asked. Not the time or place. Most people were there because they'd suffered a loss, and find the holidays really hard. As my Mom would say, they didn't need to borrow our troubles."

"They have enough of their own. My mother said that too. So what'd you do?"

"Nothing. I had to leave. I'm on my way to the airport to pick up Annika."

"Traffic's moving pretty good, once you get clear of the border. It's good you kept moving. Not much you could do there."

"I really didn't have the heart to try. It seemed so important to Penny, even if it's misguided."

"You're allowed to not work all the time."

"And what are you up to tonight?"

"Yeah. But you've got something, someone good to focus on, after all that's happened this week."

"Absolutely."

"How are you feeling about seeing her?"

"Honestly, I'm a little nervous. Feels like a really big step, asking her to cut her trip short to be with us... with me."

"It's probably a good sign you have some butterflies. But Tom, she's a grown-up woman, who can say yes or no, and what did she say?"

"That if I hadn't asked, she was going to bring it up."

"So go get her, partner."

Chapter 23

Late Saturday Evening (7 days to Christmas)

Hope thought it had to be something biological that had caught Zeke's attention. Annika told her he'd been trained with blood, bones, and human remains.

The sable coated German shepherd had his snout close to the hardwood surface of the centre aisle of the sanctuary, at a spot very close to where Hope and her father had found the pool of blood flowing from under the fallen Christmas tree.

That blood was long gone, Hope thought. After the crime scene techs had done their work, trauma cleaners had been brought in. They wiped away all signs of what had happened, using chemicals that left the sanctuary smelling like a dentist's office.

How could Zeke sniff out anything?

Hope shone the beam of her dad's big flashlight across the area the dog was sniffing, and then further up the aisle. The bright light reflected off a trail of what appeared to be droplets of clear fluid.

Hope shivered, despite the warmth of her father's heavy barn coat, which she'd pulled off a hook on the way out the side door. She grabbed it because one pocket held a stash of K-9 treats.

"What is it Zeke? What do you smell?"

Hope remembered more of what Annika said about Zeke's training.

"Zeke's a qualified cadaver dog. We've searched for, and found people we could help, and some we couldn't."

Zeke's nose hovered over that one spot on the hardwood floor, and his whole body vibrated, like his muscles were getting him ready to pounce.

It struck Hope the big dog was waiting for direction.

"Bones, Zeke."

To her ear it came out more like a question than a command, but it seemed to satisfy the search dog, who turned his face up to her, let out a sharp bark, and tugged on his leash.

She unclipped him, and he sniffed his way up the centre aisle, past the front pews on the left side of the church, then over to the outside wall.

A balcony ran all along that wall, and jutted out above him, casting Zeke deep in shadow.

Hope ran through the list of what her Gran had called could'ves and should'ves.

She could have called her father when she saw strange lights in the church, for the third night in a row, but he was on his way to pick up Annika at the Detroit airport.

She should have turned on all the lights when Zeke led her into the sanctuary, but she hadn't wanted to attract a lot of attention if it turned out to be nothing.

She could have called the police. The Sun Parlour detachment was across the street, and Detective Barbara had been great about it the previous night.

Hope hadn't wanted to be the girl who cried wolf, again. Instead, she was in the dark with a dog as big as a wolf, looking for only Zeke knew what.

"Zeke, I hope you'll stay between me, and whatever it is you're tracking."

Annika said Zeke was very protective if you were part of his pack.

Hope also had the flashlight Michael Powers gave her father last Christmas.

It's a couple feet long, made of machined aluminum, and feels like a billy club, which may be the point. The leather strap loops around your hand, so you won't lose it if you have to swing hard at something. Michael said it's heavy enough to shatter a car window, if you hit it just right. The weight comes from all the batteries.

Hope followed Zeke with the high-powered beam of the flashlight, and it lit up the space under the balcony. The wall was finished in oak panelling, which glowed golden in the intense light.

Zeke nosed his way along the wall, halting at a spot about halfway between the front and back of the sanctuary.

Hope stepped closer and swept the light up and down that section of the oak-panelled wall. It seemed that Zeke had stopped in front of a well-camouflaged door. There was no handle, so she pressed her palm against it.

The panel gave a little inwards, as if on a spring latch, then popped outward a few inches.

Zeke pushed his snout into the newly opened gap between the wall and the door panel. He really wanted to go in there.

Hope stepped around Zeke and shone the bright light into the gap and pushed the door open with her free hand.

Zeke stepped into the gap, then turned his head back towards Hope, with a look she read as "What now?"

"Steady, Zeke," she said, hoping it was the right command. Then she tried, "Heel, boy!"

At that command, Zeke seemed to relax, which Hope thought was a good thing.

The bright beam lit up a long storage area, in the space under the balcony. Hope wondered if her Dad knew it existed. She saw an old wooden filing cabinet, a few boxes that over-flowed with yellowed paper, a length of thick hose that might be for a 1950's vacuum cleaner, and what could have been an old sleeping bag, pushed back into a corner.

The light also revealed two figures, standing near the outside wall. One woman looked very pregnant, the other quite concerned. The pregnant woman was at least a foot shorter than the woman with her, and appeared very thin, except for the baby belly.

She was leaning forward with both hands on the wall for support, and she was sobbing.

Hope saw wetness spreading on the woman's pants bottom and down the inside of her legs. It appeared her water had broken, and contractions had started.

The other woman rubbed her back, and spoke softly, "Estarás bien, Marta."

Hope didn't want Zeke's presence to complicate things.

"Good boy Zeke, stand down."

Zeke looked like he expected a reward.

Hope used a chunk of dried meat from the pocket of her father's barn coat to lead the German shepherd to a spot just outside the storage area.

"Sit, Zeke."

Hope gave him his treat, then rubbed between his ears and said, "Good boy, Zeke. Stay."

She stepped back into the hidden room and pulled the chain on the hanging bulb she'd noticed.

"Um, hi? I'm Hope. My dad is Tom Book, the minister. I want to help. We should call 911."

The pregnant woman gasped, "No! No policia!"

Hope learned the pregnant woman was named Marta, and her friend was Estrella. They'd both come to Canada as temporary workers from Mexico, and there were issues with their documents.

Marta seemed to understand much of what Hope said but only spoke in Spanish. Estrella spoke English, which was a relief to Hope, who only had what her Latinx friends at school mocked as Taco Bell Spanish.

Hope assured them the police wouldn't be involved. She used a line she'd picked up while volunteering at the free clinic in Atlanta.

"It's not a crime to need help."

With their permission, she called for an ambulance.

Her next call was to Paul Bennett, a friend of her father who lived fifteen minutes away, at a retreat house he called The Quiet Centre.

Hope left Zeke at the parsonage, so she could drive Paul's car, a very cool mini-Cooper, in British racing green, to the hospital.

Paul sat in the back with Estrella, who hugged a beat-up looking backpack to her chest for the whole ride. She was upset she couldn't ride in the ambulance with Marta.

Paul was dressed in a brown monk's robe, tied with a length of cord.

He was mostly bald, and Hope had heard someone say he looked like Captain Picard on Star Trek. She thought he was more like the older Obi-Wan Kenobi.

While Hope drove, Paul taught a meditation technique. He encouraged Estrella to imagine a calm inner sea, to help her continue to be a soothing presence for Marta when they met her at the hospital.

Paul had his clergy credentials, so they were able to help Estrella find the waiting room outside the birthing suite.

The charge nurse said Marta would likely be in labour for quite some time, but that everything looked good. She invited Estrella to go in with Marta.

Paul drove Hope back to the parsonage, so she could tend to Zeke, and check in with her father, who was on his way back from the airport with Annika.

Paul said he was headed back to the hospital and would let Hope know how things went. He promised to text her, which sounded odd coming from a Jedi Knight.

Hope settled into her favourite chair in the parlour, and wrapped herself up in a quilt. She'd turned on the gas fireplace, and the lights on the Christmas tree.

Zeke was soon snoozing at her feet.

She tried to visualize herself floating on her calm inner sea, but a storm of thoughts and questions churned the waters.

Was there a connection between Marta and Estrella and the strange lights she'd been seeing?

Who were they hiding from?

Were they involved somehow in the death of Gloria Sharpe?

Chapter 24

Later Saturday Evening (7 days to Christmas)

Tom thumbed the steering wheel control for the radio. WNIC supported its claim to being Detroit's Christmas station by playing the Bing Crosby and David Bowie mash-up of Peace on Earth and Little Drummer Boy.

"Hope likes this station. I normally keep it on CBC."

Annika yawned. She brushed an errant strand of her blonde hair away from her face, and said, "It's fine."

"When did your day start?"

"We left Nijmegen at ten a.m. to get me on the three p.m. flight to Detroit."

Tom said, "So that was what, four a.m. my time? What time did you have to get up?"

"I guess two a.m. But I napped a little on the plane."

They'd shared an awkward hug and a tentative kiss when she emerged from baggage claim at the Detroit airport. Things had shifted between them.

All lanes of the freeway were running fast and full. Tom stuck to the slower lane but still felt the push to keep pace.

A rumbling diesel pickup zipped by, then veered sharp into the lane ahead of them, tall chrome stacks pumping up a cloud of oily black exhaust. Tom checked behind them, then let off the gas to widen the gap.

"We need space to breathe and the exit should be coming up soon. Can you help me watch for it?"

"Of course," Annika said. "Hope told me about last time."

Two weeks earlier, after dropping Annika at the airport, Tom missed the signs for the bridge to Canada. He'd ended up stuck in the tunnel to downtown Windsor at rush hour.

On the radio, Santa promised driveway delivery of a gift-wrapped Ho Ho Hyundai, with a big red bow shinier than Rudolph's nose. The elves would even bring it on Christmas morning. No money down, and no payments 'til the fourth of July.

Annika shook her head and said, "I must be tired. Is that really a thing?"

Santa's promises were followed by Chris Rea's blues-worn voice singing Driving Home for Christmas. Tom reached to switch it off.

"No," Annika said. "You can leave it on. I like this one. Reminds me of Dad."

"I thought he was more a classical music kind of guy."

"He was," Annika said, "but he had a soft spot for sappy Christmas songs."

Tom said, "I just thought, it's about going home for Christmas..."

"Look, there's the big maple leaf sign for Canada." Annika smiled. "That's the way home."

"Got it, thanks."

Tom braked for the off-ramp, then slowed the Range Rover further for the big S-curve to the toll plaza for the Ambassador Bridge. He picked a line and pulled up behind a brown Honda Accord.

Tom said, "I'm glad you're here, but I'm still worried it was a big ask, to have you cut your trip short."

"To be honest, it felt weird over there. I hadn't seen the cousins since Dad took me the summer after high school."

Tom risked a smile. "That long ago?"

"Uh huh. They seemed glad to have me, but... it still felt like a lot of effort, for them, and for me. I didn't like being a guest in someone else's space at Christmas..."

Tom let off the brake to move up towards the toll booth. There was now just the Accord ahead of them.

"And yet..."

"I know. But this is different. I've stayed at Paul's before, and he's always so good about it. And the property is great for Zeke."

Tom lowered his window to pay the bridge toll. The wintry breeze carried an acrid whiff of exhaust. He powered up the window and they rolled on.

Annika said, "The cold air felt good for a second. Revived me."

"Maybe you should stay with us at the parsonage, at least for tonight. Hope would love it, and I..."

"Your church people don't know me. This is not a great time to be the strange woman sleeping over at the minister's house."

They motored past a line of transport trucks in the lane beside them as they came onto the bridge. The radio offered "Baby It's Cold Outside". Tom turned it off.

He said, "It's a big house, and it's not 1950. They might not even notice, with all the cops coming and going."

"That's pretty naive, Tom. It's a small town. There'd be talk."

"We could sneak you out in the morning. Nobody needs to know."

"Somebody would see, and it would get out."

"Probably, but I'm not sure I'd care. And besides, I'm not sure how long I'll be there."

Annika said, "What do you mean?"

"Jesse gave me a letter from the church board. They want to call off their search for a new minister and offer me the call."

"And?"

Tom said, "I figure I have to either accept, or say no, and get ready to move again."

"What do you want to do?"

"When I left Oakville, I wasn't sure I'd ever want to work in a church again. The chaplain job in Windsor was good. I worked one-on-one with people and didn't have to worry about keeping the hospital going. They have managers for that."

"You are definitely not a manager."

"And I don't want to be one. For me the best part of the job is what Paul calls the care and feeding of souls. The worst is the care and feeding of the institution. Some at Saint Mungo's were so focused on protecting the image of the church, it got people killed. That was an extreme reminder of what I don't want to do."

Annika said, "So can you be the pastor, and not the manager?"

"That's what I've been asking myself, since Jesse gave me the letter."

"You've mentioned him before."

"He's the board chair. He also runs the local funeral home. He's a good guy. I admire his commitment to his community, and to his work. He's the good kind of funeral director, in it for the right reasons."

Annika smiled. "You seem to make friends with the funeral directors wherever you go. Is he a good manager?"

"I think he likely is. This next little while will be a challenge."

"Because of the death in the sanctuary?"

Tom said, "Most of this church's money has come from a trust fund controlled by the woman who was killed. There are questions about the solvency of that fund. The treasurer's been telling people the church is broke."

"I didn't think churches were supposed to have a lot of money," Annika said. "Dad used to say a hungry wolf is bound to hunt."

"That literally sounds predatory."

"He was talking about some of our neighbours, who gave their kids everything. Dad believed everyone needs to learn the value of work. He also thought it was good for people to have to learn to work together."

Tom said, "Not for the first time, I wish I'd got to meet your father."

Annika smiled. "To be honest, I'm not sure what he'd make of you. He wanted me to find a good farmer."

"Is it too late for that?"

She reached for his hand.

"I think it is, Tom. My life is already too... complicated for another involvement."

They rode in silence towards the middle of the bridge.

"If you thought Jesse could handle the business side, would you want to stay with this church?"

"The congregation does some great things. I care about the people, and it's a good little town. But... there's more to consider. Where's Hope going to be? She's dropped a few hints she doesn't want to stay at Emory. And there's you..."

"And there's me."

Tom saw Annika's struggle to keep her eyes open and stay in the conversation, and it softened something in his chest.

Traffic in the middle lane slowed.

"Before the big trucks roll up beside us and block the view, look to your right. Those big lights shining upriver show where they're building the new bridge. It's supposed to really change things around here."

Annika said, "Speaking of change. I've been meaning to tell you... before I left, I got a written offer from the Pieter's. They're ready to buy me out."

"You talked before about selling most of the land but keeping the house."

"I'm ready to let them have the whole thing."

"And then what?"

"When I was over there with the cousins, I realized home is less about where I am, and more about... well, who I'm with."

Brake lights shone from the back of vehicles as they neared the multiple lines for Canadian customs. Tom slowed to roll in behind a shiny white Tucson with Michigan plates. It had a big red bow on its roof and Santa's face on the rear door.

Tom said, "Annika, I don't want to stop what you're saying, but look... is that a Ho Ho Hyundai?"

Annika laughed. "You're an idiot, Tom Book. I'm trying to say I want to be with you."

Tom lifted his foot from the brake, and they moved up for their turn at the customs booth. As he rolled his window down to hand over their passports, he felt his phone buzz in his pocket.

He said, "I..."

The Range Rover's dashboard screen lit up with a text from Hope.

"Come straight home, asap. If I'm not here when you get back, call me. Don't worry, Zeke and I are okay."

Chapter 25

Late Saturday Evening (7 days to Christmas)

Tom pulled a blanket down from its shelf and closed the hall closet door with care. He paused to look in the parlour, before stepping through the doorway.

The gas flames of the fireplace cast a soft light and radiated needed warmth.

Heat rose in the room, gently buffeting the memorial origami angels hanging above the Christmas tree.

The tree itself was lit by a starfield of tiny white lights.

Tom looked over at Hope, nested in her favourite of the two leather recliners he'd brought from Oakville. Everything up to her neck was snug under her grandmother's comforter, the one decorated with a waterfowl family painted in Norval Morisseau's Woodland style.

He tread into the room softly, sock feet on the age-worn area rug that came with the parsonage.

He bent over Annika, who was slumped into a cushion tucked between her and the sloped arm of the camelback sofa. Her eyes opened as he arranged the blanket on her.

She said, "Thanks... I still don't like this couch."

The couch also came with the house.

He said, "Is she awake?"

From within her nest, Hope said, "My body's tired, but my head is buzzing. I'm not sleeping anytime soon."

Tom said, "I called Lawrence, and told him about you and Zeke finding Marta and Estrella in the boiler room."

He leaned down to scratch between Zeke's ears. The German shepherd lay on a thread-worn oriental rug, his bulk pressed up against Annika's legs.

Tom said, "You did good tonight, Zeke."

Zeke licked a chew snack out of Tom's palm.

Tom said, "Lawrence will send Barbara over to the hospital."

He set his cell phone on a narrow oak side table and settled into the empty recliner beside Hope.

She said, "What will happen? Will Barbara arrest them?"

"Lawrence said she'll treat them as potential witnesses. The Leamington detachment has a Spanish-speaking officer on tonight, so she'll translate, and help keep an eye out."

Hope said, "They were so scared."

"I also called Paul," Tom said. "He'll stay at the hospital as long as they want him."

Annika covered her mouth for a yawn and looked at her watch.

"It's pretty late, and Paul's what, eighty? Where does he get the energy?"

Tom said, "Paul goes to bed a couple hours after sundown, unless there's something on at the retreat centre, or he's watching the night sky. He was probably asleep when Hope called him."

"He sure didn't sound like it," Hope said. "He was bright and cheery, and ready for action... unlike some people I know when they first wake up."

Tom said, "Paul claims he needs less rest with each passing decade. Maybe when I get to his age, I'll be a morning person."

Annika said, "That's something to look forward to."

There was silence until Zeke opened his mouth for a wide yawn and re-arranged himself at Annika's feet.

"Even Zeke's tired," Tom said. "It's been a long day for all of us. Especially you, Annika."

Annika raised her chin a fraction and opened her eyes a bit wider. "I'm okay for a while. It sounds like Hope needs to talk, let the little guys say their piece."

Hope's face showed her confusion.

"Uh..."

Tom said, "The monkeys in your head. All the thoughts, questions, worries."

Hope said, "You two have your own language. I'll have to decide if I like that or not."

Tom smiled, turning his head to take in both Hope and Annika. "Should I ask Lawrence to send us a translator?"

Hope shifted under her quilt, as if about to stand, then settled back into the recliner.

"You probably think I shouldn't have gone over to the church. But I wasn't alone, I had Zeke with me."

Zeke stirred, angling his head in Hope's direction.

"But it's good we went. Marta and Estrella needed help. They knew your name, Dad. It helped when I said Reverend Book was my father."

Tom said, "They came to an event we did with the Migrant Workers Support Group. Someone, it may have been Gloria Sharpe, heard Estrella singing, and invited them to church."

Hope said, "I was thinking they could be the women Michael mentioned from the parking lot videos."

Annika said, "Sounds like I've got some catching up to do."

Tom said, "After we discovered Gloria's body, Barbara tapped into the church's back door camera and started recording. It also picks up the lot where you parked your car. Looking back at the times Hope saw lights in the sanctuary, she found a brown minivan in the lot on Wednesday night. The video shows two women getting out of the van."

Annika said, "I saw a brown minivan back there when Zeke and I went out for our little walk. That reminds me to ask about the Christmas tree strapped on top of my car."

Tom said, "My guess is Barbara's already seen the minivan. The tree is from Tinsel Acres. We were thinking it would be fun for the three of us to decorate together."

Annika turned her head towards the tree by the window.

"Any idea where you'd put a second tree?"

Tom said, "We hadn't actually got that far in our thinking. There's been a lot going on."

"After Tuesday night," Hope said, "they aimed a camera at the church from the OPP station across the street. They have a video they want Dad to look at, of someone else going in the front door on Thursday night."

Annika said, "So just one person, not the two women on the video from Wednesday. But if it was Marta and Estrella in the church Wednesday night, why?"

"Exactly," Hope said, "And why did they come back tonight?"

Annika said, "Part of my nurse training was on a maternity ward. Water breaking doesn't always mean labour has started, but I agree, for someone that far along, she must have had a really strong motivation to be out anywhere."

"I wonder," Tom said, "if they were in the building on Tuesday night, when Gloria was killed."

Annika said, "Could one of them have..."

Hope said, "They looked so scared when Zeke and I found them. And it was even worse when I mentioned calling 911."

Tom said, "Something I learned from Lawrence Kitchen, during the mess at Saint Mungo's, is that fear does not always indicate guilt."

"It is hard to believe," Hope said, "... that either of them could do something so vicious."

Annika said, "On the other hand, if one of them was protecting the other..."

"Yes," Tom said. "But from who, or what? It's hard to see Gloria as any kind of threat to them."

"But if they saw what happened to her..."

Tom said, "That's a reason to be frightened, but not a reason to keep coming back to the church."

Annika said, "There must be a lot more to all of this."

Hope said, "This is the stuff, the monkey voices in my head. I thought I was doing a good thing. But what if I read them all wrong, and helped the people who killed that poor lady?"

She squeezed fist-fulls of her grandmother's quilt.

"That would mean I put Reverend Paul at risk. He sat in the back of his little car with Estrella, trying to calm her down. What if there's something wrong with her? She might have hurt that nice old guy."

Tom said, "I don't know anyone better at reading people than Paul Bennett. If he thought Estrella was a danger, he might have got in the car with her, but he would not have let you come along."

"Are you sure?"

"I'd trust Paul with my life. He has good instincts."

Annika said, "Hope, even if Marta and Estrella are mixed up in something bad, you helped protect that unborn baby, who deserves a chance. I'm proud of you for that."

Chapter 26

Early Sunday Morning (6 days to Christmas)

Tom fastened buttons on his heavy barn coat while stepping into his Timberland boots.

He'd got the coffee going and a breakfast casserole out of the fridge and into the oven before rousing Zeke.

During the night, the big dog had made his way downstairs from Annika's guest room to the dog mattress near the back door.

The sable-coated German shepherd seemed sound asleep, but his ears perked up when Tom shook the clip-on lead and said, "Walk, Zeke?"

Tom felt the buzz of a text alert in his trouser pocket. He thought he knew who'd be texting at 6:45 am.

He pulled out his phone as Zeke pulled him out the back door.

At Zeke's urging, they headed left towards a small park they could access from the lane running behind this block of Sharpe Street.

The security lights for the parsonage and the church had come on as they walked out, illuminating his route down the back lane. They'd stay on for at least half an hour, giving plenty of time for both Zeke and Tom to do what was needed.

He checked his coat pockets for gloves, compostable bag, and flashlight, just in case he needed to hunt for Zeke's morning deposit.

As Tom had expected, the text was an update from Paul Bennett.

Paul had spent most of the night with Marta and Estrella, then gone back to the Quiet Centre for a restorative nap and an invigorating shower. He'd soon return to the hospital.

Judging by the lights he could see from the laneTom noticed very few of his neighbours were up and going this early on Sunday morning, .

The frigid morning air and overnight dusting of snow did not put a chill on Zeke's enthusiasm. The big dog strained at the leash with each step until Tom summoned his stern tone.

"Zeke, heel!"

Zeke only needed to be told once but would test Tom until he heard the word. They made good progress down the back lane.

Paul reported he'd had the brown minivan moved to the Quiet Centre, which Tom thought confirmed it was the vehicle Michael had described from the parking video.

Estrella had been resting when Paul left the hospital, and Marta wasn't yet in active labour. The nurses were monitoring and expected things to pick up in a few hours.

Horace, the beagle who lived two back yards from the park entrance offered his loud, unfavourable opinion on Zeke's presence in the back lane.

"Easy, Zeke." Tom said. "The little guy's safe behind his fence."

Paul wished Tom all the best with the Sunday morning service, including the baptism and speech from the godfather.

As they reached the park entrance, Tom felt a slight increase in tension on the lead.

"Zeke."

The big dog slowed his pace a fraction and turned his head back towards Tom. When Zeke opened his mouth that way, Tom often took it for a smile.

"Good boy. But I'm still not letting you off the leash."

At the close of his text Paul declared that he'd be offering sanctuary to Estrella, Marta and their child, when the time came for them to leave the hospital.

Tom knew what that meant.

Whatever they were caught up in, Paul had judged they weren't the culprits, and he'd put considerable effort into protecting them from further harm.

Chapter 27

Sunday Morning Breakfast (6 days to Christmas)

"Dad, what took you? We've got an online meeting with Barbara and Michael in less than five minutes."

"Good morning, dear daughter. And how did you sleep?"

"Never mind being fake cheerful, Barbara says something big is about to happen."

Hope pointed down the hall.

"We're set up in the dining room."

Tom shed his boots and hung up the barn coat.

Hope said, "Zeke, come with me. We'll get you something to eat."

Tom headed down the hall. The aroma of spicy Italian sausage, sharp cheddar cheese, onions, potatoes, and cooked egg stoked his appetite.

Annika said, "Hey, Tom. Can you grab these plates? Hope has us on a schedule."

He stepped through to the kitchen, thinking of leaning in for a quick good morning kiss.

Annika held the steaming breakfast casserole in front of her in oven-mitted hands.

"Uh... okay. I'll just wash the dog off my hands. Then I'll bring the plates. How about cutlery?"

Annika went into the hallway, aimed at the dining room.

"Already on the table, and the coffee's poured. Hope's been in high gear since Barbara called. I think she's impressed with the detective sergeant."

Tom followed her to the dining room, where he saw that Annika and Hope had been busy.

Boxes he'd left on the table were now stacked in front of the massive sideboard and hutch.

The heavy velvet drapes had been tied back to let in the early morning light, such as it was. Tom didn't want to think of the dust that would have been released.

The chandelier above the table, and all the wall sconces burned bright.

Hope sat in the second of three chairs on one side of the heavy oak dining table, which was built to seat eight.

Annika set the casserole dish and serving spoon on a hot pad and sat on Hope's right.

"How's this?" Hope said. "Can you see me okay?"

Barbara's voice came from Hope's MacBook, which was raised up on a short stack of bible commentaries.

"That's great, Hope. Hey Annika! Long time. Michael's about to come on. You okay if I talk and eat at the same time?"

Tom was glad to see his old books put to good use.

Hope said, "We'll be eating, too. As soon as Dad gets here with the plates."

"Right behind you, Hope," Tom said, "Morning, Barbara. What's going on? Looks like you're still at the hospital."

Tom set the plates out, and sat beside Hope, who was focused on the laptop.

The screen showed Barbara with a breakfast wrap in one hand, coffee in the other, and what looked like a nurse's union bulletin board behind her.

"I'm in the break room, right across the hall from Marta. Things are beginning to happen for her and the baby. But that's not why we wanted to check in."

Annika said, "You look good in scrubs, but Tweety and Sylvester?"

"The night shift scrounged them up. It was either these or Care Bears."

Barbara's image halved in size, to make room for Michael Powers, who seemed to be joining the meeting from a seat on a plane. There was a strong hum in the background.

"Hi Hope, Annika, Barbara. Hey partner! Sorry to interrupt your morning. Just wanted you to have a heads up."

Tom said, "No worries, Michael. Okay if we eat while you talk?"

Tom nodded to Hope, who served squares of the casserole onto their plates.

Michael said, "This shouldn't take long. Annika, I feel like I don't really need to say this... but I've asked Tom and Hope to keep these conversations confidential. I know you get that from your search and rescue work with law enforcement."

"Absolutely, Michael. And I appreciate being kept in the loop."

"Okay, thanks. First off, Hope, that was good work last night. It was crucial to get Marta and Estrella to a safe place... and not just because of the baby."

"Thanks Michael. I couldn't have done it without Paul's help."

"We also owe him a thank you. He stayed with the women, and from what Barbara's said, helped them get very good legal representation."

"Michael," Hope said, "are they in trouble?"

"Not with us. They've had a really rough go, that you'll hear more about, I promise. For now... Barbara, can you fill them in?"

"Tom, Michael's authorized me to send you the video of my interview with Estrella, to watch when we're done here. For now, I'll touch on the highlights."

Barbara set her breakfast wrap down on the table in the nurses break room.

"Turns out Estrella Guerrero is an investigative journalist. She's been tracking the movement of undocumented workers from her home state in Mexico, to operations in New York, Ohio and here in our area."

Hope said, "Michael gave us some background on that."

Barbara said, "Ms. Guerrero got on driving for a woman who owns a few piratas... unlicensed taxis. It gave her the perfect cover to come and go where the workers live."

"That's very brave," Hope said. "And maybe explains why you're there undercover."

"At this point it's about keeping them safe. We have a uniformed officer downstairs but want to avoid a visible police presence on the obstetrics ward. No reason to spook the other patients."

Tom said, "So you've had a long night."

Barbara said, "But absolutely worth it."

Michael said, "Our analysts have also been at it all night with audio, video and photo files from Estrella's cloud storage. By four a.m. they'd found enough to corroborate information gathered from less credible sources. By 5:30 this morning we had warrants in hand for a multi-agency raid on a greenhouse complex outside of Leamington."

Barbara said, "Lawrence just texted, Superintendent. He's at the County detachment on Manning Road, suiting up with the tactical guys. RCMP and Border Services are also on hand. The incident commander says they're good to go as soon as they confirm with EMS."

Michael nodded.

"That's good. The pilot tells me we're about to land in Leamington. I need to pack away this laptop. I'll catch up with you all later."

Michael's square disappeared from Hope's laptop screen. Barbara's grew to fill the space.

Hope said, "I wanted to ask Michael why they have to wait on EMS."

Barbara said, "It's standard to have a medic on hand, but there's more going on. We got a fast go ahead for today's operation because Estrella documented horrific conditions inside that compound. We're very worried about what we'll find."

Chapter 28

Sunday Mid-Morning (6 days to Christmas)

Tom cleared the breakfast dishes and Annika refreshed their coffees while Hope opened the video Barbara sent of her interview with Estrella.

Barbara had said, "I did not actually have to ask a lot of questions. It was clear Estrella had given a lot of thought to her statement. I bet she's a great reporter."

Hope's MacBook was still perched on a pedestal of Tom's old books, on the dining room table. Estrella's image was frozen on the screen, with a time-stamp indicating 2:37 that morning.

Estrella looked directly at the camera. Her thick black hair was pulled back in a ponytail. Wire-framed glasses drew attention to intense dark brown eyes.

It appeared Barbara had borrowed the same staff room she'd used for the breakfast Zoom meeting. The bulletin board behind Estrella bore a poster for the Obstetrics staff holiday party, and a notice about union elections.

On the table in front Estrella there was a turquoise hospital water pitcher, a paper cup, and a legal pad.

Tom and Annika took their seats on either side of Hope. She started the video.

"I am Estrella Maria Guadalupe Guerrero. I've been advised of my legal rights and have an attorney present. I make this statement voluntarily."

"I entered Canada last January, on a temporary work visa, which has long expired."

Barbara's voice could be heard from off-camera.

"We aren't concerned about your immigration status, or Marta's."

Estrella flashed a warm smile.

"Thank you for that, Detective Sergeant."

"It's no secret people from my country who work in your agriculture sector face many difficulties. Less well known is that some who come here are never heard from again."

"When my cousin Ricardo became one of *los desaparecidos*, my Tia Isabel was devastated. I wanted to find a way to help."

"During the COVID pandemic, my country threatened to cut off the supply of workers, prompting your government to address concerns for their safety."

"I hoped to draw similar attention to the plight of the disappeared. I left my newspaper job and applied to come here."

"I was well treated at my greenhouse job, and heard about other good companies, but there were stories about less scrupulous employers. To dig deeper, I left my job and got on driving a taxi pirata."

"There are many such ghost cabs shuttling people between the bunkhouses and town and making deliveries."

"In my taxi I could go anywhere, and I was invisible."

Annika looked at Tom.

"She's really something."

On-screen, Estrella said, "This was how I met Marta. I soon contrived to be the regular driver bringing meals to that greenhouse."

Tom saw a hint of a tear behind her glasses.

"We come from different villages, but are from the same place, if you can understand my meaning. Marta has my heart. I vowed to stand by her, and to protect the little one.

"Marta paid a large fee to an agency that promised good jobs. They took Marta's papers and smuggled her here in the back of a trailer with fourteen other women."

"They were all raped in that trailer, but only Marta became pregnant."

Estrella rose from her chair and leaned toward the camera. She rubbed the table with the flat of one hand. Her other hand was a fist wrapped around a pen.

"These women work long hours cultivating cannabis and packaging it for shipment. Their handlers do not allow them to cook for themselves and do not provide enough food. Most of the others lost weight, even as Marta's belly grew."

"The time came when Marta could no longer hide her condition."

"She knew she had to flee, to protect her unborn child, but feared for the safety of her friends. Marta worried they would be punished if she escaped."

Estrella returned to her chair, shifting it closer to the table. She poured water and drank from the glass.

"Only after she was raped again did she allow me to help her get away."

"It was one of the bosses, who arrived in a big black SUV, driven by bodyguards who carry themselves like policia."

"This man enjoyed degrading Marta. When he was done, he pulled bills from his wallet, wiped himself, and tossed them at her."

"Marta stored his filthy money and other items in the bag from that day's sandwich. She wrote the date and time on the outside and signed it. A friend signed as her witness."

"It became my mission to preserve this evidence, and to learn about this man. His name is Troy Donaldson."

At the dining room table, Tom turned to Annika.

"I knew I didn't like that guy."

Barbara's voice came through the television.

"When the time is right, we will ask Marta to do a photo line-up. Our lab is analyzing the evidence you passed on to us."

Estrella nodded.

"Marta escaped, but without her papers."

An unfamiliar voice could be heard.

"Ms. Guerrero, if I may ask, why did you not approach our Leamington consulate?"

"Mr. Donaldson's men were hunting Marta. We'd heard comings and goings at your consulate are closely watched."

"That is... most concerning."

"I kept driving the taxi pirata. We saved for a car, to get us to the consulate in Toronto. Marta could not fly without papers, and we could not risk the train or bus stations."

Barbara said, "Estrella, can you tell us how you came to know Gloria Sharpe?"

"Yes, of course."

"We lived out of the taxi. Some nights we parked behind the church and slept there."

"One evening there was a meal for migrant workers. The food smelled like home, so we took the chance."

"People were good to us at the church. Marta and I attended worship when we felt safe."

"Miss Gloria heard me sing and invited me to join the choir."

"One Sunday someone broke into the taxi. They didn't find anything. I had my backpack with me. We believed it was Donaldson's hired cops."

"Miss Gloria saw our fear, and we told her our story. She showed us where we could sleep. A hidden closet, under the balcony. She said the front door would always be open, and as long as she lived, the church would be a sanctuary. It is very sad to think of this now."

Estrella drank from the water glass.

"As the baby's time approached, Marta found it harder to get comfortable. We often went to the closet so she could rest."

"This is where we were on Tuesday evening."

"Marta was deep in sleep. I must have drifted off as well, because I was awakened by Miss Gloria singing."

"I rolled off our air mattress and pushed the closet door open a crack, so I could peer into the sanctuary."

"The only light was from the single bulb in the brass lamp on top of the piano."

"Miss Gloria stood near the piano, with her spine straight, and her hands cupped one in the other over her diaphragm."

"She was practicing O, Holy Night. We call it 'Oh Noche Santa'."

Estrella cleared her throat.

"The lamp glowed behind Miss Gloria, and it lit up her hair like a silvery halo."

"Miss Gloria stopped singing when she saw me walking up the side aisle."

"We repeated a conversation we'd had before. She wanted me to sing on Christmas Eve or join her in a duet, because her voice was not as strong as it once was."

"I was reluctant. I didn't know who might be at that service, or who might take notice of us."

"I also knew there were... others who felt entitled to sing the solo. Strong feelings had been expressed at rehearsals."

Hope paused the video.

"Mom always said no when she was asked to join the choir. She couldn't stand the politics."

Annika nodded.

"It was the same at my Dads' church. Part of why I quit going, after he died."

Hope hit play.

"Miss Gloria's phone rang, and she had to take the call."

"I checked on Marta, who needed help to get up. I knew when she stood, she would soon need the bathroom."

"We waited a moment before leaving the closet but still heard the end of Miss Gloria's side of the conversation. There was tension in her voice."

"She said, 'If you think it can't wait, and can't be settled on the phone, then come to the church. I'm here now, but I'm expecting someone else in an hour.'"

"Miss Gloria dropped her phone into her big purse and snapped it shut."

Tom said, "I'm going to text Barbara to see if they know who called Gloria that night."

On the screen, Estrella said, "I told Marta that Miss Gloria had people coming to see her, and we had to leave."

"Miss Gloria seemed to understand, and said, 'I'm sorry, but I don't trust either of them farther than I could throw them.' "

"I said we understood, and we'd be on our way after Marta used the bathroom."

Tom's phone buzzed.

Barbara's reply read "Gloria received calls from Liza Testardo, her brother Robert, her nephew Bobby, and from a landline at the Sunny Shores Credit Union."

Tom returned his attention to the video.

"As we walked, Marta whispered to me in Spanish. She said to tell Miss Gloria I would sing with her on Christmas Eve.

"I wasn't about to argue. Especially not when I needed to get Marta to the bathroom."

"I told Miss Gloria I would join her in the song."

"The last time we saw her alive, Miss Gloria was smiling. Her face glowed, lit by that single lamp."

Barbara said, "What happened next?"

"We finished in the bathroom, and used the rear exit to the parking lot. I warmed up the minivan, to clear the frosty windows."

"Marta wanted chilaquiles, so we went to see a woman who makes meals for the greenhouse workers. She loves Marta and was happy to make her breakfast at 8:30 at night."

Barbara said, "Were you back to the church that night?"

"Yes. We drove around the building first. We only saw Miss Gloria's car behind the church."

"I parked and we went in through the front door. It was very dark in the sanctuary."

"I called out to Miss Gloria, but she did not answer."

"There was a strong, and very wrong smell, that upset Marta's stomach. I walked ahead, shining my phone light to guide us up the centre aisle."

"We did not get far."

"The big Christmas tree had been knocked down. Branches were jammed up against the sides of the pews. The narrow part of the tree was closest to us. Under it, I saw much blood on the wood floor."

"I told Marta to sit in a pew, close her eyes, and rest her swollen feet."

"I heard movement outside the church. Then the outdoor security lights shone bright through the big windows. In their glare I saw broken ornaments and coloured shards of glass on the floor. And much more dark red blood."

"I ran to Marta and guided her between the pews to the side aisle under the balcony."

"I told Marta to keep her eyes on the door to the church hall and to look at nothing else. She should not have any more horror in her life."

"I told myself there was nothing we could do for Miss Gloria, if it really was her under the tree. I had to get Marta away from the church, before the authorities arrived, and found two undocumented brown women and a dead body."

"Please remember, Marta was brought to Canada by brutes who ignored the law. We were hiding from other men who look and act like police officers but work for the man who savagely raped Marta."

"This is why we did not stay."

"We went out the rear exit. I helped Marta into the minivan."

"As we drove away, I saw lights come on inside the sanctuary."

Chapter 29

Later Sunday Morning (6 days to Christmas)

Standing in front of the chancel stage, Tom turned his back to the congregation. His lapel microphone picked up his voice.

"I'm going to talk to them now. But I'll try to be quiet, the baby is sleeping."

That got a little chuckle from the big crowd.

Tom was grateful and amazed so many people had come to church. It had been a hectic weekend, in a busy season, and people had a right to be tired. They'd had Sylvie's funeral on Friday, and both the Sunday School party and Jesse's Elvis event on Saturday.

The core of volunteers who kept things going wouldn't have time to rest anytime soon, with the visitation for Gloria Sharpe that afternoon at Aird and Bower, and her funeral and a lunch to follow, both at the church on Monday.

Tom nodded to Shelley Tinsel-Smith, who had just led the Donaldsons up to the chancel stage to stand next to the baptismal font.

Seeing Shelley reminded Tom the final planning meeting for the Christmas morning breakfast had been set for Tuesday, choir practice for Thursday, and then it was Christmas Eve on Saturday.

Shelley moved to the podium.

"It is my pleasure to introduce Haley and Troy Donaldson, who have brought their daughter to be baptized."

Haley Donaldson wore a shimmering calf-length silk dress; in the same aquamarine she'd worn for lunch at Smuggler's Cove.

Troy was in a smoke grey suit, with a tie and pocket square the same shade as his wife's dress. Beside him stood Robert Sharpe, the Member of Parliament for Sun Parlour. His suit matched Troy's and came across as more best man than godfather.

Miriam's baptismal gown was a miniature of her mother's. She was snug, with eyes closed, in the arms of one of the nannies.

It was either Sifra or Pua. The Donaldsons had not offered introductions.

The nanny looked very small standing between the child's parents, in a white long sleeve dress that made Tom think of an old-fashioned nurse's uniform.

The magnificent twenty-five-foot white pine brought in for the Blue Christmas concert rose behind the baptismal party. The long-needled green boughs were strung with tiny white lights and adorned with hundreds of red velvet bows.

Tom breathed in the tree's sweet, resinous scent, and it brought him back to the present moment.

He'd been operating on autopilot and his mind had wandered as he asked the Donaldsons formal questions about raising their child in the faith.

Had they noticed he hadn't listened to their answers?

The accusations made against Troy were unproven, but Tom believed Marta and Estrella.

The raid on the greenhouse complex would be launched in just a few minutes.

Tom knew he needed to set aside his feelings about the father and give his attention to blessing and baptizing the child. She deserved his full presence.

Tom doubted Troy and Haley had noticed his wandering thoughts. They were looking past him and posing for the high-resolution video camera wielded by John Freund, personal assistant to Robert Sharpe.

At the start of the first hymn, The Member's aide had popped up from his seat in the front row.

Leaning in a little too close, Freund raised his hands to show Tom the camera, rigged with an over-sized light ring. With an unctuous stage-whisper he'd said, "I'm sure you won't mind if I capture the special moment for The Member."

Tom pointed stage left.

"You are welcome to stand there."

It was time for Tom to pose the formal questions to Robert Sharpe as the godparent.

Could Tom focus?

Would Sharpe stick to the script?

"Will you give your prayerful support to this family as they continue in the life of faith?"

The Member said, "I will, God being my helper."

Tom breathed in the white pine smell. It also didn't matter how he felt about the couple's choice of godfather for their child.

"Do you promise to pray for Miriam, and by your life and words, share your faith with her?"

Robert Sharpe looked up from the page Tom had provided. When their eyes met, Tom felt a chill.

Sharpe said, "I do, by the grace of God."

Tom turned away from Sharpe to face the congregation and raised his arms to invite them to stand.

"The front door of this church is always open. We welcome all who wish to join us. Troy and Haley have brought Miriam here for the sacrament of baptism. Will you promise to support her, and their whole family in their journeys of faith?"

The near capacity crowd said in unison, "We make that promise, relying on God's help, and God's grace."

In the chorus of responses, Tom was sure he recognized a few of the higher-pitched elven voices he'd heard at the barn party. He felt a catch in his throat. He paused for a deep breath, taking in more of the nurturing forest freshness.

He was filled with the memory of his own baptism. He'd been four, and his brother John Paul a newborn. He'd felt his mother's soft fingers around his small hand as the minister spoke his name and put water on his forehead.

Tom looked out at the Sharpe Street congregation. He felt grateful for their willingness to welcome little Miriam. He nodded his thanks and gestured for them to sit.

He turned again to the family lined up beside the baptismal font, which in another setting could be taken for a marble birdbath.

A brass plaque on the base declared George Sharpe, the Member's grandfather had ordered it all the way from Vermont, as part of his restoration of the church, after the big fire in 1923. Tom wondered if The Member would mention that in his post-baptismal remarks.

Tom moved to stand in front of the nanny, his arms ready to take Miriam.

He muted the microphone clipped to his lapel, and said, "I'm sorry, I don't know your name."

In a soft voice she said, "It's Sifra."

"Mine's Tom. May I hold her?"

Sifra lifted Miriam toward him. She had a reverent look on her face.

Tom reactivated his microphone before taking the baby in his arms.

His chest was still sore from the shoulder belt the other day. He hoped they didn't see the twinge as he took the weight of the baby in his arms.

Miriam wriggled, to make herself comfortable against Tom's chest. He was pretty sure she'd also just passed gas, or something more substantial. He remembered that vaguely fluid sound.

He couldn't look Troy in the eye, so he focused on Haley.

"What is your child's full name?"

Troy opened his mouth, but Haley beat him to it.

"Her name is Miriam Antoinette Donaldson. Antoinette was my mother's name."

It was the most heartfelt thing Tom ever heard her say.

Tom said, "Miriam Antoinette Donaldson, I baptize you in the name of..."

He was interrupted by a discordance of electronic bells. Text alerts, which Tom's lapel mike picked up, so everyone in the church heard them. Many sneaked furtive peaks at their own phones.

Troy reached into his inside jacket pocket.

The Member already had his phone out.

Haley stared down at the diaper bag at Sifra's feet.

Tom caught a glimpse of John Freund lowering the video camera, switching off the ring light, and reaching for his phone, which by then was ringing for an incoming call.

Robert Sharpe held a phone in front of Troy's face.

Troy's eyes went wide, then quickly narrowed.

Troy said, "Hales..."

Haley Donaldson was attempting something like a curtsy in her long dress, so she could dip a hand into the diaper bag. It wasn't going well.

"Never mind that," Troy said. "Read the text on my phone."

Troy's phone began to ring, followed by the one in the diaper bag.

Troy said, "Uh, we gotta go."

Tom, who still held Miriam, said, "Is everything okay?"

Robert Sharpe said, "Something has arisen that requires our immediate attention. We..."

Abandoning her effort to reach the diaper bag, Haley Donaldson straightened her back, and said, "Can you just do your thing with the water?"

Tom did his thing with the water and passed Miriam back to Sifra, whose eyes shone with tears.

He reached out to shake hands with Troy and Haley, but they were already stepping past him to head down the centre aisle.

Sharpe and his aide were right behind them, which Tom took to mean he wouldn't be making his speech.

Chapter 30

Mid-Afternoon Sunday (6 days to Christmas)

"Reverend Tom! I hear your daughter's in town. She looking for a job?"

Catherine stood at the Wagon Wheel Diner's cash register. She was dwarfed by the big decorated blue spruce tree set up where patrons couldn't help seeing it as they paid their check.

The tree's fresh scent of spruce won out over lingering aromas of French fries, grilled onions and coffee.

Catherine was smiling, but Tom had seen her glare hard at regulars who failed to pick a gift tag from the tree. Each bore handwritten details of a gift for a child in need.

"Hope's only home for the holidays," Tom said. "She's still in school down south."

Catherine's glossy black hair, pulled up into a bun, seemed both impossible, and unquestionable on a person in her eighties, and added a good three inches to her height.

A red gingham apron hung loose over her thin frame, but the frilled short sleeves of her white blouse revealed wiry upper arm muscle that flexed as she picked up a large, insulated coffee carafe.

"Bobby just got here, poor guy..."

Catherine gestured with the carafe towards the back of the diner, and lowered her voice.

"Hey, I saw you with the fancy out-of-town cops. They figure out who killed his aunt?"

Tom said, "They're working on it."

"Lot of people had the wrong idea about Gloria."

"I wish I'd had the chance to really get to know her."

"She didn't make it easy," Catherine said. "But she had heart. Every year she'd come in two, three days before Christmas..."

Catherine nodded at the blue spruce.

"She'd scoop up any tags left, didn't matter how many, and she made sure those kids got their gifts."

Catherine led Tom to Bobby Sharpe, who straightened up from a slump when he saw them coming.

"Hey, Rev... I mean Tom."

The saddle brown vinyl upholstery wheezed out a sigh as Tom slid his knees under the orange Formica table.

Catherine set the carafe midway between their thick white mugs.

She looked at Bobby with gentle eyes.

"Sweetie, we were just talking about your Aunt Gloria. Coffee, and anything else is on me. We've got some nice roast pork, comes with mashed potatoes, home-made apple sauce, green beans and a salad."

Three booths down the line a tall young woman with streaks of Christmas red and green in her blonde hair was wiping down tables.

She called out, "Don't forget dessert. Still lots of the peach cobbler taking up space in the walk-in."

"Thanks Catherine," Bobby said. "We just needed to get away from the funeral home for a while. I'm not real hungry. Unless... Tom... unless you want a bite?"

"I'm good, thanks. My daughter's doing a stir-fry. We'll eat together after the second half of the visitation."

Bobby withdrew into himself for a moment. In the background Perry Como sang "There's no place like home for the holidays."

Tom wondered if Bobby had anyone left he considered family.

Bobby said, "Place looks the same, Catherine, and so do you."

She flashed Bobby a smile. "I hope you bluff better than that when you're in a big game, Mr. Fancy-Pants TV Poker Player."

Bobby said to Tom, "I've come here since I was a kid, and nothing ever changes."

Bobby pointed toward a light fixture, an actual wagon wheel, that had been made over into a rustic chandelier.

"I love this old ranch stuff," Bobby said, "I always thought she should put up some steer horns, so the old fellers could hang their hats."

"Look around, Bobby," Catherine said. "Think these guys ever take off their ball caps?"

There were only a few other customers in the diner. Older men nursing their last coffees of the afternoon. Catherine had it right. None of them had doffed their hats.

"I'll leave you two to talk. That coffee's fresh, and the creamers in that bowl are still cold. You need anything else, you let me know."

She touched Bobby's shoulder as she turned to leave. "You look good all dressed up. Better than those tracksuits you wear on the TV. I know it's for the visitation, but that colour is good on you. And I like that tie."

Bobby said, "Thanks Catherine."

Both men were in funeral black. Tom's suit showed signs of frequent use, as did the black shirt with the clerical collar.

Bobby's suit looked new. His shirt was a rich burgundy, and he'd added a gold silk tie imprinted with a poker hand. One card turned down, and the other four face up for viewing.

Bobby hefted the carafe, holding it as a question over Tom's mug.

"Sure," Tom said, "Might as well. I'll be up a while tonight working on Gloria's service."

Bobby said, "You don't need to stay for the whole thing. I don't even want to be there. Robert works the people in line like he's campaigning. When Marco Testardo offered his condolences, Robert went on about how his government is tough on crime. Marco just stared at him."

Bobby called his father Robert. Tom had never switched to calling his own father Frank, but he understood the sentiment.

He said, "I stayed because I thought you could use the support."

"I appreciate that," Bobby said.

Tom said, "And Catherine's right, that's a great tie for you."

Bobby said, "Thanks, Bobby said, straightening the gold tie.

"Are those special cards? Two black aces and two black eights?"

Bobby said, "In poker we call it the dead man's hand."

Tom said, "So why'd you wear it today?"

Bobby said, "It goes good with the shirt, and I figured Robert would hate it. And I was right. He sicced his skeevy assistant on me, to say it wasn't appropriate attire."

Tom said, "And you're still wearing it. Good for you, Bobby. Be yourself."

Bobby said, "I appreciate that Rev... I mean, Tom. And thank you for this, the coffee."

"I'm glad to talk, Bobby."

Bobby said, "I appreciate you meeting me the other day, and writing down all that stuff about my aunt, but you might not need to do that part.'

Tom said, "I want to make sure you get to give thanks for her life."

Bobby said, "Thing is, Robert wants me to meet him tomorrow, before the funeral. Maybe he'll let me say my piece. Probably want to preview it first, so I don't embarrass him and whatnot."

Tom remembered the classic from Peanuts. Lucy says she won't pull the football away, if Charlie Brown will try, just one more time, to kick it.

He said, "Bobby, I hope... I hope you're right."

In the silence that followed, Bobby lifted the carafe, topped up his cup, and offered more to Tom.

Tom shook his head.

"I'm good, Bobby, thanks."

Bobby said, "I wanted to ask... whaddya think about dreams?"

Tom said, "Do you mean like actual nighttime dreams?"

"I had this dream last night," Bobby said. "It felt like I've been having it for a while."

Tom said, "I have a friend who says sometimes we get the same sort of dream over and over, until we get the message."

Bobby said, "Like the dream wants to tell us something?"

Tom sipped his coffee, then said, "My friend says dreams come from inside of us, and we probably already know what they are trying to say."

Bobby nodded.

"So, in this dream I'm in an old timey casino."

Tom said, "Is this a place you recognize?"

"Only from old movies, like Ocean's Eleven. Frank Sinatra, not George Clooney. The way Vegas used to be."

Tom said, "What happens?"

"I'm sitting on a chrome bar stool with a red leather seat, in front of a huge gold-plated slot machine. It's all blinky with light bulbs around the edges, like a showgirl's makeup table."

Tom said, "What are you doing?"

Bobby said, "I'm feeding the machine. It's a nickel slot, and I have a paper bag full of coins. It's like one of the brown bags Aunt Gloria used to pack my school lunches."

Tom said, "That's interesting."

"I ate the same lunch every day. Peanut butter and cheese on whole wheat, cut in quarters, wrapped in wax paper. An apple, and two Oreos. And she always put in a little note. Like... you got this Bobby, love Auntie G."

"So anyway, I hold the bag in one hand, and grab nickels with the other. I do the same thing, over and over. I pull out a nickel, feed the slot, and reach up to pull the handle."

Tom said, "You mean like a one-armed bandit?"

Bobby nodded.

"Only the handle, is a little too long. It has a black ball on the end, size of a softball, and I have to half stand up off the stool and stretch to reach for it. The ball is slippery, and my fingers barely get a grip. When I get leverage, and pull down, the gears inside the machine get whirring and this same weird thing keeps happening."

Tom said, "What weird thing happens?"

Bobby said, "Those old machines, they had wheels that spun, and you'd see pictures roll by. The King, the Queen, the Ace, and something special for the big jackpot. There'd be three wheels all spinning, until they ran out of juice. If all the wheels stopped on the same picture, you were winner, winner, chicken dinner. On this machine, if they all lined up Lucky Seven, that'd be jackpot."

Tom said, "Did you win?"

Bobby said, "No cigar. Each time I'd drop a nickel, reach hard and pull the arm. The wheels would spin, and one, two, three, they line up on the red seven, and then poof, there's another wheel, and it winds down to stop, and instead of a jack or queen or joker, I see the words 'try again' on the new wheel. So I drop another nickel, get all the wheels spinning again."

Tom said, "Then?"

Bobby said, "I get sevens across all the windows, and then poof, there's another wheel spinning, until it rolls to a stop with try again. So I grab another coin, slam it in, pull the arm, and go again. It keeps on like this, and each time there's another window."

Tom said, "And you keep going?"

Bobby said, "Hell... I mean... heck yeah. Know that if I stop, some other chump will win big with the next pull. I'm too invested, and it's just about to happen..."

Tom said, "So what do you do?"

Bobby said, "I play and play. My arm gets sore from all the pulling. The lights around the edges of the machine are going out, one by one. And behind me, I can hear that the casino is emptying out. The staff want to go home, but that makes no sense. Vegas goes 24/7. Even in my dream."

Tom said, "What would happen if you just stopped?"

Bobby said, "I know that if I stop, even to rub my sore arm, or if I get off that stool to stretch, they'll toss me out on my ass. They'll reset the machine, and all my trying will have been for nothing."

Tom said, "So what happens?"

Bobby said, "I play until there are no more nickels. I fish around in the bottom of the bag. I find an apple core and crumpled wax paper. I toss those behind me, reach in again, and pull out a note from my Aunt Gloria."

Tom said, "Can you see what the note says?"

"I want to read it, but then the last light goes out, and I feel big meaty hands on my shoulders, pulling me off the stool."

Tom said, "And then?"

"Then I wake up. Weird hunh?"

Chapter 31

Late Sunday Afternoon (6 days to Christmas)

Detective Sergeant Barbara Palmieri, who'd just reminded Hope she should call her Barbara, rinsed a very impressive knife under a warm stream from the kitchen faucet.

She wiped down the shimmering seven-inch blade with a special cloth and then dried the beechwood handle and placed the knife in its cherry-wood case. She closed the lid, which was carved with Japanese kanji.

Barbara turned to Hope and raised her hands in front of her chest in prayer position, like she'd just finished yoga and was going to say Namaste'.

She closed her eyes and inhaled deeply.

Exhaling, she opened her eyes and in a solemn tone said, "How you do anything is how you do everything."

Hope's father had mentioned Barbara was into martial arts, and she was wearing a vintage Bruce Lee t-shirt over her jeans. Maybe this was some kind of ritual.

Barbara had shown Hope how to chop with the Santoku, a traditional Japanese kitchen knife, while they were prepping stir fry ingredients.

Hope said, "Is that like some Zen thing?"

Barbara sat on one of the breakfast nook stools.

"I'm just messing with you."

Hope and Annika had been laughing their way through photo albums when Barbara texted. She was looking for a time to show Hope and Tom some surveillance video and give them an update on the raid.

Annika said, "She and Lawrence must get tired of restaurants. We should invite them for supper. Michael too, if he's around."

Lawrence and Michael weren't available, but Barbara was keen and asked what she could bring, besides her own knife.

In the kitchen, Hope said, "It's a good saying. Seriously, is it some special teaching?"

Barbara grinned.

"It might be, but I got it from the Orphan X books. They're thrillers about this guy who helps people with nowhere else to turn."

Hope poured canola oil into a frying pan, waited for the sputter, then dropped in marinated chicken pieces.

"Lately most of my reading's been for school."

The kitchen soon smelled of sesame and ginger.

Barbara said, "What are you working towards?"

Hope poked at the chicken with a wooden spoon.

"I'd been thinking nurse practitioner, or physician."

"I note the past tense."

"Yeah. I've been volunteering at a community clinic in Atlanta. I love helping the patients, most of them, but..."

"But?"

"I feel out of sync with the staff. A lot of them are good people, just..."

"Not your people?"

Hope pushed the meat towards the edges of the pan to make a space for the sliced red onion, which was soon sizzling, and adding to the cloud of good smells.

"Did you know, before you went into policing, that you'd fit?"

"I had a pretty good idea," Barbara said. "My dad retired after thirty plus years on the job. Mom was a police dispatcher, then joined the wellness team. We've always had cops around the house."

Next to go in the pan were thin cut green beans and cubes of red pepper, which Hope thought added seasonal colour.

"How'd your parents feel about your choice?"

"They're supportive, and they worry. Dad thought I was too small to be safe on the job."

"Can you hand me that measuring cup?"

Hope stirred in sliced mushrooms, minced garlic, and her own sauce, which included honey for a touch of a glaze.

"Did he get over that?

"No. We began my judo training the day I told him I was serious about being a cop."

Hope scattered chopped cashews over the top, checked the rice, then called her father and Annika to the kitchen to fill their plates.

She hadn't peeked in the parlour but thought they might've fallen asleep leaning into one another on the ratty old couch.

Not long after Barbara arrived, Hope's father had come in the back door looking, as Hope's Gran used to say, like something the cat wouldn't bother dragging in.

Annika was also low energy. Hope assumed she was recovering from her travels, and the drama of the previous night.

Had they given up on Annika staying at the Quiet Centre? Hope wouldn't ask while they had company.

Hope led the way to the dining room. Barbara was behind her, then her Dad and Annika, who looked a little ruffled. Maybe they'd dozed in front of the parlour fireplace.

Hope said, "The original plan was to eat while we watched the Christmas Vacation movie. We've upped our game because we have a guest."

Barbara said, "I get to see the dining room in person."

Hope set her plate down, then lifted the stack of books she'd used that morning to prop up her laptop. She turned to her father.

Tom relieved Hope of the books, adding them to a pile on the sideboard.

"Guess I need to find better place for these."

Rather than any of the things she was thinking, Hope adjusted the dimmer for the chandelier over the table.

Tom and Annika sat together, with their backs to the sideboard.

Barbara sat facing Tom, and Hope took a seat across from Annika.

Hope was closest to the entryway in case she needed a trip to the kitchen, or to reach over and scratch Zeke's ears, as he'd parked himself in the hall.

Barbara said, "So Tom, how's your day been? Do you have it in you to say grace before we eat?"

Tom offered a quick prayer. Then he sighed.

"Worship was eventful. I spent coffee hour side-stepping questions about why the Donaldsons and The Member ran out like the church was about to explode."

Annika smiled at Tom.

"How about no church or crime talk during supper?"

Annika filled the vacuum with a story about her Dutch cousins taking her to three Christmas markets in one day, and insisting she try the bratwurst at each.

Hope was pleased to see the food was well received. The rule about no crime talk held until she asked Barbara, "if you're here, who's with Marta and Estrella?"

Barbara looked at Annika, who shrugged.

"There's a uniformed officer in a cruiser outside the hospital. Superintendent Powers is also there. That's why he couldn't join us."

Hope said, "Is he undercover, like you were?"

Hope saw that her father's smile reached all the way to his weary eyes.

"I'm picturing Michael, the ex-linebacker, in Hello Kitty scrubs."

"He opted for a white coat, with a stethoscope around his neck," Barbara said. "The staff know who he is, so he won't be delivering babies."

Hope said, "Does that mean they're still in trouble?"

"Michael spoke to the crown attorney about designating them witnesses to human trafficking, so we can look out for them."

Tom set his fork down. He looked a little more weary.

"Human trafficking? So Estrella's statement was accurate."

Barbara said, "Estrella's intel led to the rescue of twelve women. We seized a box of passports, driver's licenses and other documents. All the paper is for Mexican citizens, so we've reached out to their embassy, and their consulate in Leamington. It's a mess."

Dad said, "Words like 'rescue' and 'held' paint a grim picture."

Barbara said, "We are very concerned. As Estrella mentioned, Marta was one of fifteen women smuggled into the country in a transport trailer, all from rural villages in Mexico. We don't know yet how many of the women we rescued were part of that group and can't account for the ones we didn't find."

Hope said, "I'm just so glad they got them out."

Barbara said, "We are too. The men we arrested during the raid are well-known to us."

Annika said, "That's cop talk for they have criminal history."

Barbara said, "We have five Canadians and two Americans in custody. All with ties to criminal organizations. None seem inclined to talk. Michael said they were smug, like they think they have a get out of jail free card."

Tom said, "Was anyone hurt in the raid?"

"Nothing serious," Barb said. "Estrella's information was excellent, which made for a well-executed plan. Two officers were fired upon. One of the TRU guys took a round to his vest and will have a purple welt to show for it. The other was Lawrence, and he's okay."

Tom, Annika, and Hope all spoke at once.

"What?"

"Someone shot at him through the glass of one of the old greenhouses. The round missed, but a glass shard grazed his left arm."

Annika, went into nurse mode.

"I hope his tetanus shot was up to date. Did it hit a blood vessel?"

"No, thankfully. Our medic shot him up with antibiotics and a painkiller, cleaned and packed the wound, and put his arm in a sling. They checked him over at the hospital. His only complaint is the sling makes it hard to type."

Hope said, "I hope he's resting."

Barbara said, "Yeah. He said to thank you for inviting him."

Tom said, "I'll give him a call."

Barbara said, "I think he'd like that."

Hope said, "So what time was the raid?"

Barbara said, "They were at the staging area by 9:00 am, and on site by 10:00 am. It was all done but the mopping up by noon. But we'll have people working the scene for quite a while. We won't be called off like we were with the church."

Tom said. "Are there connections to what we talked about on Wednesday? Because some phones went off in church this morning."

"Some of the men we're holding have ties to the Kazinski family. The greenhouse complex and the land are owned by a company connected to your new friends, the Donaldsons, and to Robert Sharpe. There were also farm trucks and a transport trailer registered to Sharpe Logistics."

Tom smiled.

"I shouldn't be happy, but I really don't like those people."

Hope said, "How about I get dessert going? Maybe Barbara can use the TV in the parlour to show you that video."

Tom said, "If it's what I think I'm smelling, I'd say that's a great idea. I think we can all use a bit of a lift."

Hope portioned out bowls of her mother's brownie pudding. It's like a chocolate cake served warm out of the oven that creates its own gooey sauce.

Tom found the French vanilla ice cream while Hope took beverage orders and got tea and coffee going.

Barbara set up the TV while Annika took Zeke outside.

Minutes later the group reconvened in the parlour, dessert bowls in hand, their eyes on the flat screen TV over the fireplace.

Hope and her father were on the couch.

Annika and Barbara sat side by side in the leather recliners.

Zeke planted himself at Barbara's feet.

"This won't take long, and then I want to eat before the ice cream melts," Barbara said. "This is from Thursday night, about 7:20 p.m."

She ran the video from her laptop, which had a yellow and black bat signal decal on the top panel.

They watched a person on the screen cross the street from in front of the OPP detachment to approach the main door of the church. Their back was to the camera, and they wore a dark, loose-fitting winter coat that disguised both age and gender.

Barbara said, “My analysis app estimates this person is five feet tall, give or take two inches. There are no other identifiers.”

She fast forwarded a few minutes to when the same figure could be seen leaving the church, walking with a strange gait not evident earlier. A hood kept their face in shadow.

Hope said, “It’s like they are trying to stand extra tall.”

Her father said, “I can’t say I recognize them.”

A moment of quiet ended when the Batman theme rang out from down the hall.

Barbara said, “Does the caped crusader call here often?”

Tom handed his dessert bowl to Hope.

“My phone’s in my coat, at the back door. That’ll be Michael, calling from the hospital.”

Chapter 32

Sunday Evening (6 days to Christmas)

Tom said, "Is it okay if I put you on speaker? Barbara's here with Annika, Hope and me."

He walked the hallway towards the parlour, where they all waited to hear the news from the hospital.

An image of the hooded figure leaving the church on Thursday night remained frozen on the screen above the mantle.

"Sure, partner." Michael Powers said. "That'll save me another call."

Barbara looked up from her laptop.

Tom pointed at the television.

She nodded to Tom, then said, "Hey boss, what's going on?"

"Just calling to report the baby's arrived, and everyone's healthy and safe."

Tom reclaimed his seat on the couch.

Hope bounced up on her feet and walked three paces to the Christmas tree.

Zeke looked up for a moment, then nudged in a little closer to Barbara's legs.

Hope said, "That's such good news."

"Reverend Paul is in with the happy family right now."

Hope stood by the tree, looking up at the paper angels she made for her Mom and her Gran.

Barbara shut down the video feed to the screen over the mantle and closed the laptop cover.

The big screen reverted to the previous feed. Christmas Vacation was on pause.

Barbara said, “I showed Tom the video from Thursday night. No bells rung. Anything else… going on around there?”

“Ortiz says it’s a normal weekend in Leamington,” Michael said. “Lots of customers for Emergency, but nothing for us to worry about.”

“That’s good,” Barbara said. “Heard from Lawrence?”

“He’s at the motel, pecking away one-handed on reports. When my relief gets here, I’ll stop by and tell him to knock off.”

“So, am I your relief? I can be there in twenty.”

“No, Detective Sergeant, I want us all bright-eyed tomorrow.”

“Who’s spelling you off?”

Michael said, “One of the local crime guys volunteered.”

Barbara smiled.

“That mean we’re no longer the enemy?”

“The raid this morning was a big win. We gained some cred.”

Hope walked to the couch, knelt close to Zeke, and wrapped her arms around his neck.

She whispered, “You’re such a good dog. That baby’s okay, because of you.”

Annika leaned towards Tom’s phone.

“This glimpse into the world of policing is fascinating,” Annika said, “but can I ask something?’

Michael said, “Of course.”

“Boy or girl?”

Michael’s laugh rumbled through Tom’s phone.

“I should’ve opened with that. She’s a beautiful little girl. Alegria Maria Guadalupe Benito-Guerrero.”

Annika said, “I like it. And that’s a lot of name for a little one.”

“Estrella says Alegria means Joy.”

Hope said, "I love it."

"They're also naming her for Saint Maria of Guadalupe," Michael said. "Because where they come from, she represents strength and resistance to oppression."

Tom said, "Considering what they've been through..."

Annika interrupted.

"And?"

"Oh, gotcha," Michael said, "Alegria weighs in at just over seven pounds, or about 3.2 kilograms. She measured 19.4 inches or a little over 49 centimetres in length. I'm told this all bodes well for the little one."

Annika was using her phone to consult a neonatal nursing site. She nodded.

"Yes, those are good numbers."

I'm also to tell Hope they're both grateful you convinced them to go to the hospital, and they'd love to see you, and have you meet the baby.

Hope looked at Tom, who nodded.

She said, "Tell them we'll come by tomorrow."

"Will do. Night all!'

Annika said, "Well that's exciting."

Tom said, "We were overdue for some good news."

Hope said, "But now I'm too wired to sleep. Want to watch the rest of the movie?"

There were no objections, so Tom hit the remote, and the dark screen lit up.

Chevy Chase stood near a Christmas tree. He wore a white Chicago Blackhawks jersey with the name Griswold on the back and was hugging Beverly D'Angelo.

Hope turned to Barbara and said, "Don't you think they look like my Dad and Annika?"

Chapter 33

Late Sunday Evening (6 days to Christmas)

Hope's Journal

It didn't last long, but when I was in grade eight, I kept a diary. Stay with me, this really does relate to what I want to write about.

I was into this show about a girl detective. The Secret and Dangerous Adventures of Sadie Alexandra D'Amico. Each episode opened with her sitting on the floor in her bedroom closet, jeans and leggings hanging down around her, with her computer on a beanbag lapdesk, typing away. I always wanted one of those lapdesks.

They'd show Sadie's screen, and you could hear clicks on her keyboard. That kid typed fast and words appeared as she said them in the voice-over.

"Dear Diary; It feels like it's been a while since my last entry. I have so much to tell you. The Secret and Dangerous Adventure of the Unprincipled Principal ended with Ms. Timmons getting escorted off the school property, and charges being laid. But let's go back to the beginning..."

Sadie and her little band of buddies tackled injustice where they saw it, always had each other's backs, and looked cool while they did it. Or at least as cool as you can when you're 14, and in a show shot in the Toronto suburbs, on a Canadian network's budget. Like a cross between Degrassi Street and The Littlest Hobo.

I loved Sadie, and her crime-fighting friends, Georgia and Kennedy. They brought down a different suburban evildoer each week. They faced perils, but almost always got their homework done, and nobody ever died.

Mom was in the midst of her own dangerous adventure with the tumour on her brain. This was the first time. Dad was focused on her, and I figured he needed me to handle my own stuff.

I could have used some friends to help me fight evil.

This all came back in a heartbeat when I sat down to type tonight, and my first thought was, "It feels like it's been a while since my last entry".

While we made supper Barbara and I talked about the importance of finding your people. The ones you connect with because you have similar mission and purpose. She says she found that in policing, and especially on Michael's team.

I get why Dad is drawn to working with them.

Dad's always been a kind of a loner. He grew up having to protect his little brother from their father. Then he took on a lot when Gran finally got them away from him.

Dad learned from a young age to watch and listen carefully, and to kind of stay on the edge of things, in case he needed a quick exit. He still has that in him, and it can make it hard for him to fully invest.

I've only met his father a couple of times. It's hard to make space for him in my heart, knowing how he cruel was to Gran, and Dad and his brother JP, and seeing the scars it left.

But it seems like good came out of that horrible situation. It formed my Dad to be a compassionate watcher and listener. He sees into situations and into people. Picks up on stuff others don't notice. That's been his strength as a person, and a pastor, and apparently makes him a good whatever he is on Michael's team. Consultant?

This time, I'm also kind of on the team, and like I said, I get why Dad likes it.

My project for Professor Barbour is about how joy can find a way even when life is hard.

Dad talks about how devastating it can be for families when someone dies close to Christmas, and they lose the capacity to celebrate the holiday.

I wonder how it is for Bobby Sharpe. His Aunt Gloria was killed in her own church and left in a pool of her own blood under a Christmas tree. How will he find joy?

Marta, from what Estrella said in her statement, has been through so much. When I found them hiding in the church I saw the hurt and fear in them both.

Estrella was there for Marta, and from what she told us, vowed to be there for the baby, even before she was born.

And now she's here, and they named her Alegria. Which means Joy!

I am excited to meet the little one. A child conceived in the midst of people being trafficked, and terrorized.

It's definitely got a Christmas feeling to it. Not so much the North American consumer Christmas, but more like the original story. Two people out on a cold night, looking for shelter, and a baby born in a rough place where animals are kept.

We respond to the vulnerability and the basic neediness of a baby, and it brings out good things in us as humans. We want to be more loving, more compassionate.

The impulse to be kind puts us on the same team, or maybe it reminds us we were actually always on the same team.

Dad asked Jesse to sing a Bruce Cockburn Christmas song at the funeral for Sylvie, the woman who died in the snowmobile accident.

It's the song Dad used in the Christmas Eve service the winter Mom was in her first fight with brain cancer.

I've been listening to it again.

In the chorus, Bruce sings about redemption entering our reality like a stone on the surface of a still river. His poetry makes me see ripples going outward like when you toss even the smallest pebble into a body of water.

In the song it's not a stone, that creates this concentric, expanding effect, it's a sound. The cry of a tiny babe.

I don't know what Cockburn means by redemption.

One summer we drove out to New Brunswick to visit where my Dad was sent when he first became a minister. We went through New England on the way back.

A lot of little towns had signs for Redemption Centres. I wondered if they were some kind of church I'd never heard of, because they also had a lot of those.

Mom laughed and said people brought bottles and cans to redemption centres to be recycled. They got paid the deposit charged when the beer or soda was bought in the first place.

In one little town I saw this old guy with a long ZZ Top beard and a leather biker's vest open the side door of a rusty old van. He pulled out two big clear plastic garbage bags full of cans, and I could see there were a lot more bags in the van.

Mom saw the question in my eyes. Did that guy drink all that beer?

She said, "Could be he works at a bar, and they save up the empties."

Dad said, "I think there are also people who gather what others toss on the side of the road."

My idea of redemption is that things that maybe were going to be thrown away, still have intrinsic value, and can be of use again, given a chance.

Dad asked me to help with the service that Christmas Eve when I was in grade eight, and Mom was so sick, from the treatments to fight the tumours. She couldn't go to church, so Gran stayed home with her.

My part was near the beginning of the service. Dad had just welcomed everyone, and we sang "In the bleak mid-winter", which is his favourite hymn. Then the lights were dimmed.

I stood at the reader's lectern, at the front of the dark sanctuary, and recited the first few lines from John's Gospel.

"In the beginning was the Word, and the Word was with God, and the Word was God. He was with God in the beginning. Through him all things were made; without him nothing was made that has been made. In him was life, and that life was the light of all humanity. The light shines in the darkness, and the darkness has not overcome it."

Then Dad lit the big pillar candle at the front of the church. For a moment, that little flame was the only visible light.

The sanctuary lights were brought up slowly as we listened to a recording of Bruce Cockburn singing Cry of a Tiny Babe.

Chapter 34

Early Monday Morning (5 days to Christmas)

Tom emerged from deep sleep, like a diver coming up for air.

Zeke was barking and Hope was calling out.

Her voice grew louder.

"Dad!"

He was no longer in a dream. Hope was outside his door.

Tom pushed back the heavy duvet. Dropping bare feet to the hardwood floor he felt a stream of cold air.

A chill breeze pushed out the room-darkening drapes, allowing flashes of faint light to hit the floor.

He turned on the bedside table lamp, but that was too bright, too soon.

He rubbed his light-dazed eyes and saw sharp edges, shiny glints on the floor below the bottom edge of the drapes.

Fully awake now, a memory surfaced that he'd felt the house rock, and heard the raucous sound of glass shattering, followed by something louder than thunder.

An explosion. Close and powerful enough to shake the walls of the parsonage.

"Hope! Annika!"

"Dad!"

"You okay?"

He opened his bedroom door.

"Yeah, we're good... but what's happening?"

Annika and Hope stood together in the hallway.

The sight of Annika's calming hand on his daughter's shoulder mended something in Tom.

He knew they'd find a way through whatever was happening.

Zeke bounded up the stairs, a large furry missile propelled by concern for his humans.

Annika said, "Good boy, Zeke! We're all okay."

Tom said, "Let's see what's going on, then maybe change out of our pyjamas."

They were met by new sounds as they descended the stairs.

Horace, the whiny beagle from down the street sounded a mournful complaint.

Car horns sounded, and the panicked whooping of house alarms.

There were also sirens of different tones, telling them someone who knew more than they did had already called 911.

Reaching the main floor, they heard voices. People outside on the street.

As they moved towards the front door, Hope in the lead, with Zeke by her side, Tom peeked his head in the doorway to his left.

Since he'd remembered hearing the breaking of glass, Tom wanted to check the parlour.

The paper angels still hung from the ceiling but spun madly from their threads as cold air rushed in through the broken panes of the front window.

The Christmas tree had toppled over, sending ornaments to scatter on the hardwood floor.

A few older glass ornaments had hit the floor hard enough to smash and leave impact trails of bright coloured shards.

Tom dropped to his hands and knees, to look for the presents he and Annika and Hope had placed under the tree. Six gifts, one for each of them, from each of them. He hoped they were unharmed.

"Dad," Hope said, "You need to get out here, and take a look at the church."

Chapter 35

Monday Morning (5 days to Christmas)

Lawrence Kitchen was on the landing outside the front door of the parsonage.

"Annika, we'd be grateful for your help, but we can't guarantee your safety."

His cheeks were flush and he had a thin line of dried blood under his chin, near the spot you might feel for a pulse. Had Lawrence cut himself shaving, or was it from greenhouse raid?

Tom shivered at the thought.

Annika, who stood with Tom in the open doorway, tightened her one-armed hug around his middle.

Lawrence had just explained there'd been an explosion in the church, most likely the boiler. They had reason to believe someone could still be in the building, but the fire crew had yet to find them.

His OPP bomber jacket was open, and the left sleeve hung limp, because his arm was under the jacket, hanging against his tactical vest in a sling.

She said, "Lawrence, it's cold. Maybe you should come in."

Lawrence shuffled his feet but made no move to accept the invitation.

"Sorry, that's the other reason I came over. We're evacuating everyone in a three-block radius."

Zeke pushed his big head between Tom and Annika's legs.

Hope also joined them, leaning into Tom's right side.

She said, "So whatever happened at the church, it's not over."

Lawrence said, "We've got the gas and power to the church shut off, but we can't take any chances."

Tom said, "So you're clearing the neighbourhood, but also hoping Annika and Zeke will stick around to help search the building?"

Hope said, "And telling her it might be dangerous."

Lawrence nodded.

"It's technically an active crime scene. Barbara would go in with her and Zeke, and somebody from the fire department."

Annika pulled a key ring from her pocket and handed it to Lawrence.

"My gear bag is in my car, in the lot behind the church."

She pointed to sawhorse barricades already in place to block Sharpe and Grenville Streets, and the officers in military style fatigues who stood by them.

"It looks like they've got things locked down. Tell whoever you send it's the Santa Fe with a Christmas tree strapped on top."

Lawrence looked at Annika.

"Thank you for this."

Tom felt Annika's arm pull him a little closer in a side hug.

She said, "We should get going. I'll just grab a coat. Anything else Zeke and I need is in my gear bag."

Lawrence said, "Tom, you and Hope are welcome to come over to the detachment if you want to stay close. We're transporting everybody else to the arena."

Hope said, "Do we have time to grab some things?"

Tom said, "Based on what I see our neighbours doing, I'm guessing not."

Lawrence said, "Your Dad's right."

As Lawrence escorted them across Sharpe Street, Tom saw uniformed officers knocking on doors and leading households of people to waiting school buses.

Children plodded along in snow boots, some wearing winter jackets over pyjamas. Tom guessed that many of these families had been enjoying a lazy Christmas vacation morning.

Tom saw a man headed to a yellow bus balancing a baby in a car seat in one hand and a large diaper bag in the other. It got him wondering what supplies might be needed at the arena, if the evacuation lasted more than a few hours.

He thumbed out a quick text to Jesse King and Shelley Tinsel-Smith, summarizing what he was seeing.

There was thick grey dust in the air, that settled on the snow and made it look like cat litter, but no smoke.

If there'd been a fire at the church, it had already been dealt with.

Emergency flashers glared from two big fire trucks, an ambulance, and a half dozen police vehicles, including a large black panel truck marked OPP Emergency Response Team.

Tom waved at Lori Gregoire, one of the firefighters, who was pushing up the sliding door of a storage compartment on the rescue truck. She nodded back, then returned to her work.

There was a generator running nearby.

The cold air smelled of dust, diesel exhaust, and something like mouldy food.

Lawrence pointed the toe of his black tactical boot at sharp crystals glinting in the dirty snow.

"Watch your step as we go. I'll try to take us around where the explosion blew most of the shards of glass."

The blast blew out every pane of the sanctuary windows that Tom could see, and the front door of the church hung open at an angle, hanging on by the bottom hinge.

They veered right, and a few houses down the block before crossing the street. Tom realized Lawrence was making the detour for the sake of the pads of Zeke's feet.

Every house he could see had broken windows. Tom wondered about the extent of damage to the parsonage, and the homes of his neighbours.

Lawrence led them down to the basement of the detachment.

Barbara met them at the door of a conference room.

"They just put your bag in the women's locker room, second door to the right. You need a hand with Zeke?"

"No, we're good," Annika said. "This is what he lives for."

Tom saw what she meant. Zeke's big head was up, and his eyes were bright as he followed Annika down the hall.

Barbara was already geared up. She wore a ballistic helmet with a head-lamp, and a respirator mask hung ready to pull over her face. A coiled wire ran from her left ear to a radio mounted on her armoured vest, next to a body cam. Her duty shirt and tactical pants matched the desert brown uniforms of the officers who'd secured the perimeter around the church.

The holstered sidearm on Barbara's hip was a reminder the church was still considered a crime scene.

A long board table had been pushed against the wall opposite the door to the conference room. Above the table a very large wall-mounted flat screen showed a still image of the corner of Sharpe and Grenville Street, focused on the main entrance of the church. The timestamp in the bottom right corner showed 7:14 am, just before the blast.

It was the same camera angle as the video they'd watched the night before.

At the end of board table, a uniformed officer sat at a workstation. He had a keyboard, a flat box with a lot of switches, a smaller monitor, and a controller that reminded Tom of the joystick from his prehistoric Atari game console.

Lawrence stood to one side of the big flat screen, as if about to offer a lecture.

"While Annika and Zeke get ready, we can show you why we think there may still be someone in there. Ron, can you take us through it?"

Ron typed, then said, "At 7:15 we see a person approaching the church on foot."

Barbara stood with the thumbs of each gloved hand tucked in the arm holes of her tactical vest.

Ron said, "We see him climb the stairs, and enter through the main door. I'll fast forward to our next activity."

The timestamp read 7:31 a.m. A matched pair of shiny black Cadillac Escalades were pulling up in front of the church. Both vehicles parked illegally, facing against the flow of traffic.

Tom said, "They must realize they're in full view of the police station."

Ron said, "These guys do what they want. We got a good look at the plates. The front vehicle belongs to a private security firm out of Gatineau, does a lot of high-level corporate work. The second has parliamentary plates, registered to Robert Sharpe. We're about to see him get out."

The sun wasn't up yet, but the scene was well lit by the corner streetlamp. The second-row door on the driver's side of the Escalade opened from within, and the top of The Member's head appeared above the roof line.

He was visible from behind as he strode toward the church and climbed the stairs to the main entrance. He faced the camera for a moment as his head swiveled to scan up and down the street.

Lawrence said, "It's like he's hoping no one's looking."

Barbara said, "If you don't want to be noticed, maybe don't travel in a motorcade."

Ron said, "I'll advance this some more. Sharpe is inside for a little less than twenty minutes. He comes out in a hurry."

Ron hit some keys to show a close-up of The Member's face.

Robert Sharpe seemed to be shouting at his phone as he came down the steps. A thin man in a black topcoat hopped out of the second Escalade and scooted over to open The Member's door. He climbed in after his boss, and both SUVs sped away before the door was shut.

Ron said, "We don't see the first person exit the building. Less than three minutes after The Member is driven away, the explosion happens."

Barbara said, "We were still tapped into the church's camera at the back door. We'd have seen him if he'd gone out that way."

Lawrence said, "We hope he's not in the basement. Preliminary report is the boiler exploded."

Annika said, "From what the deputy chief just told me, there's going to be a lot of particulate in the air. Let's hope Zeke can sniff out a trace."

Tom had been so intent on the monitor, he hadn't noticed Annika and Zeke in the doorway.

Kelly Halligan, the deputy fire chief stood behind them. His bunker gear smelled of ash and dust.

Annika had changed into the khaki tactical pants and shirt from her Halton Search and Rescue gear. The cops had loaned her a body armour vest, a ballistic helmet with a headlamp, and a respirator mask that matched Barbara's.

Tom noticed Zeke was wearing thick grey dog booties, secured with black Velcro straps. His khaki search and rescue harness had a big orange patch that said LIVE FIND.

Tom met Annika's eyes. He felt his throat get tight and wondered if he could speak without choking up, and what he might say.

He took a breath, then pointed to Annika's desert brown belly pack.

"I hope you've got plenty of treats for Zeke."

The big dog's ears perked straight up, and his face angled towards Annika as if to say, "So are we doing this?"

Chapter 36

Monday Mid-Morning (5 days to Christmas)

Hope stood with her hands on her hips, leaning in towards the large screen in the basement conference room.

"It's like there's a snowstorm in the church entryway."

Tom was beside his daughter. They were waiting for the search party to move into the sanctuary.

Lawrence Kitchen sat next to a uniformed constable, who watched a smaller version of the feed at his workstation.

"There's still lots of particulate in the air, but it probably looks worse than it is, if it's getting on the lens of Barbara's bodycam," Lawrence said. "The Deputy Chief... Kelly, is watching the levels."

Hope said, "Is it safe for Zeke? They all have respirators."

Tom said, "Hopefully, they're in and out of there quick."

Lawrence said, "The respirators are protocol. Kelly was concerned about asbestos but hasn't detected any."

The big screen showed Deputy Chief Kelly Halligan from behind. His turnout coat was heavily dusted with the same grey ash that coated the floor, evidence of the time he and his squad had already spent at the scene.

Kelly said, "Annika, let's work the sanctuary, then maybe move on to the church hall."

He held up a bright yellow handheld device.

"It's not bad in here. The breeze through all the broken windows is helping."

Barbara's vest-mounted bodycam gave a view of her gloved hand moving outward and pointing down.

She said, "And the basement?"

Kelly said, "Lot of excavation before we can get down there. Incident commander said rule out the main level first. I agree with her."

Kelly nodded towards Zeke. The orange LIVE FIND patch on his khaki harness stood out bright in the gloom.

Kelly said, "Let's go."

They stepped towards the entrance. The swinging doors built to welcome worshipers had been blasted off their hinges.

Three headlamp beams cut lines of brightness into the dust-thick air of the sanctuary.

Annika knelt in the fine grey ash to unclip the lead from Zeke's tactical harness.

"Good boy, Zeke! We've got work to do."

Zeke's ears perked, and he stood a little taller.

Annika said, "Bones, Zeke!"

Zeke lowered his nose towards the dust, and padded through the doorway, to start his search. The protective boots on his paws added smooth ovals to the other footprints.

Barbara's camera showed Kelly and Annika following the big dog into the larger space.

Hope said, "It's really sad to see it like this."

It was as if a monstrous wave had barrelled through, twisting and smashing the first few rows of seating and scattering splintered wreckage over the remaining pews, and against the back and side walls of the sanctuary. The whole mess was coated with grey ash.

The brass pendant lights that used to hang down from the high ceiling had crashed to the floor, pulling their heavy chains down with them.

The twenty-five foot white spruce had been torn apart, and bare bits of tree limb, now dusted grey, could be seen in the rubble, which also included mangled vestiges of hymn books and pew bibles.

The white marble baptismal font had toppled off the chancel stage. The bowl had cracked and was separated from its base.

Zeke raised his snout to sniff the air, and picked his way around the wreckage, to take a few steps to the right. He was headed towards the north wall of the sanctuary.

Kelly pointed to work lights set on tripods along the north and south walls.

"The sun wasn't quite up when we did our first walk-through. Don't really need those now, with all the natural light coming in."

Hope said, "Lawrence, can we talk to Annika? I have an idea."

Lawrence turned to the constable beside him.

"Ron?"

Ron said, "Our audio feed is from Barbara's radio, which is locked on transmit. Best thing would be to call them."

Hope said, "Dad, do you have your phone, mine is..."

"Calling Annika now."

They watched Annika pull open a Velcroed pocket and retrieve her phone.

"Tom?"

Hope grabbed her father's cell phone.

"Annika there's like a hidden closet, about halfway along the north wall, close to that yellow tripod. It's where we found Marta and Estrella. I think Zeke's heading that way."

Hope's voice was picked up by the mike inside Annika's mask, and with a slight lag, came through the big television.

Annika pointed, and said, "Kelly, you get that?"

Kelly was already moving past Zeke, who continued to step with care around rubble, sniffing as he went.

The comms picked up Kelly's boots pounding across the floor.

"Barbara, give me a hand."

The on-screen image bounced as Barbara moved to join Kelly at the north wall.

Two sets of black-gloved hands lifted chunks of splintered wood, which lit up under the glare of head lamps until they were heaved out of the way.

Kelly said, "Hold up."

Zeke had advanced to a position near the tripod, and Annika moved to join him.

"Stand down, Zeke," she said. "Good boy."

Kelly switched off the work lights.

He said, "Too much heat off those spots."

The Deputy Fire Chief raised a device that looked like a cross between a water pistol and a video camera. A red dot appeared on the wall. He moved the dot up and down and back and forth in increments of a foot or so at a time.

"I'm seeing heat behind this wall, enough to be a person."

Kelly stuffed the thermal imaging camera into a pocket of his bunker coat. With gloved hands he pulled and twisted a splintered timber that had punctured the paneling.

Ron said, "Tell them the medic is standing by, and the ambulance is at the front door."

Hope said, "Annika, the medic's ready."

When Kelly wrestled the timber free of the wall, a section of paneling sprang free.

A flurry of grey dust swirled as Kelly aimed his headlamp at the opening.

"10-52," Kelly said, "Send the medic in now."

The comms picked up the heavy footfalls of the ERT medic and escort entering the sanctuary.

Barbara called out, "Over here!"

Barbara stepped closer, and her bodycam captured the sight of a prone man in an overcoat, shrouded in grey dust. He was curled up in the fetal position and did not appear to be breathing.

Chapter 37

Late Monday Morning (5 days to Christmas)

"... a joint task force involving the OPP's Tactical Response Unit, the RCMP, the Canadian Border Service Agency, five Canadians and two Americans are in custody. Items seized include a massive quantity of cannabis and other controlled substances, numerous weapons, unregistered firearms, ammunition, explosives, and large amounts of Canadian and American currency."

The commentator's deep voice rattled the speakers on Jesse King's office laptop, which sat at the head of the oak dining table that dominated the arrangements room.

As Tom entered, he saw the brass sconces glowing on all the walls of the former dining room, an indication power had been restored to the neighbourhood.

Jesse was seated on the left side of the long table. He reached out to pause the video, then gestured for Tom to take the seat beside him.

"C'mon in Tom. We appreciate you taking time to meet, considering how your day started."

Jesse was in his usual three-piece charcoal suit with the subtle grey pinstripe, and less understated purple silk tie and pocket square.

"Not just my day. The whole street's a mess. Good morning, Mrs. Bower, John."

Andrea Bower, owner of the funeral home, sat across from Jesse. Tom guessed she might have been headed to yoga, before the morning took a turn. The eighty-year-old looked trim and spry in raspberry leggings, a matching zippered jacket, and a headband that tamed the wiry grey curls above her forehead and ears.

John Freund sat beside Mrs. Bower, who'd taught him and Jesse at Sun Parlour District High School, back in the day.

She said, "How is Bobby Sharpe doing? We saw the respirator over his face as they put him in the ambulance."

"I hear he's recovering well. The doctor says forty-eight hours bed rest, lots of fluids, and he should be fine."

"I'm so relieved to hear that. We're just catching up with John and working out our response to the events of this weekend."

Tom took the chair beside Jesse.

He pointed to the screen.

"Anything on there about the church? I haven't seen any cameras around, yet."

John Freund said, "Not so far. We were watching the 11 a.m. update when you came in."

He wore a textured olive-green sweater over a blue oxford shirt, and jeans Tom guessed cost at least as much as his last suit. Even so, this was dressing down for Robert Sharpe's personal assistant. There was no product taming his ash brown hair, and he needed a shave.

Freund had a tooled leather folio on the table in front of him, which bore the logo of Sharpe Holdings. Next to the folio was a cell phone, and what looked like a page torn from a yellow legal pad.

Tom pointed to the laptop.

"What are they saying?"

The screen was frozen on an image of Michael Powers, in his dark blue OPP dress uniform. Tom guessed it was a press conference. The strip on the lower third of the screen read Joint Task Force Raids Sharpe Holdings.

Jesse pressed play. The loud commentary resumed.

"...charges are expected to be laid in relation to numerous offences, including but not limited to, unlicensed cultivation of cannabis, possession of controlled substances for the purpose of distribution, weapons charges and multiple counts of human trafficking."

On the video, Michael stood at a podium bearing the OPP crest. There were uniformed officers from several police services lined up behind him.

"This positive result comes after months of coordinated work by agencies in three countries, and multiple jurisdictions here in Canada. Excellent intelligence made it possible to execute a raid that..."

The audio switched back to the deep-voiced commentator. The image on the screen shifted to the glass front of an office building on a busy city street. The camera pulled in tight on the words "Sharpe Holdings", and the company logo, a capital S tightly imposed over a capital H, to create a stylized dollar sign.

"Onlookers at a nearby farm reported seeing multiple ambulances and a school bus being used to transport an unconfirmed number of workers away from the site. Public records indicate the property is a commercial greenhouse and packing facility owned by Sharpe Holdings. A tractor-trailer and several farm vehicles bearing the company logo are parked near the complex. The CEO of Sharpe Holdings, Sun Parlour Member of Parliament Robert Sharpe was unavailable for comment. Reporting from Leamington, this is Dale Molnar, CBC News."

"That's it," Jesse said.

Tom looked at Freund. He'd try to remember not to call him Johnny Friendly.

"I haven't seen your boss since he and the Donaldsons left the baptism service. I'm thinking this had something to do with their abrupt departure."

John Freund picked up the ragged-edged note and tore it in half, and then again into quarters. He then crumpled the fragments with a tight fist.

"Robert is... he's... he's been lying. To me, to the PM's office, to everyone."

He held his arm out over the folio, and opened his hand, allowing the pieces to fall on the Sharpe Holdings dollar sign logo tooled into the leather.

Mrs. Bower reached for his hand.

"John, take a breath, and start with what you told us earlier."

John said, "I asked him, what do we do? About the raid, about Bobby, about the church, about Gloria's funeral? He left his instructions on that page and then jumped in a car headed to the airport. Want to know what it says?"

"John," Tom said. "How can we help you?"

John freed his hand from Mrs. Bower's grasp. He raised both arms and laced his hands behind his head.

"He wrote three words. Deal with it. But I don't think I can."

Mrs. Bower said, "We'll start with the basics. And we'll take his written instructions, such as they are, as his authorization to make decisions as needed."

John nodded his head.

"Okay."

"The first thing is the service for Gloria, which was meant to happen today," Mrs. Bower said. "It obviously cannot happen without her surviving family. We will reschedule."

Tom said, "I'll be dropping in at the hospital later, but I won't get into this with Bobby unless he's up to it. My suggestion is we aim for a service on Thursday. That will hopefully give Bobby the recovery time he needs."

Jesse met Mrs. Bower's eyes, then said, "We're on the same page, Tom. Whatever Mr. Sharpe had to attend to, hopefully he can be back by then. John, what do you think?"

"I'm not aware of any government business. Parliament is on holiday recess until the first week of January. There's really nothing on his calendar that can't be rescheduled, but there also wasn't anything about a flight today."

Mrs. Bower nodded in the general direction of the church, and said, "Under the circumstances, our facilities are at your disposal. Jesse, do we have anything this week I don't know about?"

"Sylvie's service, and Gloria's were all we had, and there are no pending arrangements."

"Well, let's pencil the service for Gloria in for Thursday. That way we have something to work around, when our schedule starts to fill in."

Tom knew what she was getting at. Every year it seemed there were folks who held on, and then felt they could let go, once they'd lived to see Christmas.

Mrs. Bower turned to look at Tom.

"Jesse and I have been chatting about Christmas Eve. The congregation would be absolutely welcome here. It may not be the most festive setting, but..."

Tom said, "I appreciate that Mrs. Bower, and I will pass on your kind offer. I was going to wait until after this meeting to talk to Jesse, but Shelley and Steve have offered the big barn at Tinsel Acres."

Jesse said, "That's wonderful. We'll need to look at how we let people know, and make sure people have rides. Maybe we could run some buses from the church parking lot."

John said, "I keep hearing your church is bankrupt. How can you afford..."

"Jesse, that's a great idea," Mrs. Bower said. "Tom, let me run with that one. Stanley at County Buses is in my hot yoga class."

"Sorry John," Tom said, "We've got days to sort out Christmas Eve. Right now, we're here for you."

"It's okay. What I really want to ask about is that cop we saw in that news clip."

"Superintendent Powers?"

"Jesse says you know him, and that he's a good guy."

"I do, and he is."

"I need to talk to him."

Chapter 38

Tuesday Morning (4 days to Christmas)

Tom parked the Range Rover in a spot near the office entrance to the Sun Parlour fire station. He knew better than to block the three over-sized bay doors out front.

He felt the shock of the chill breeze as he stepped out of the SUV. His hair was damp from his quick shower at the gym, and the only hat in the vehicle was his new SPFD ball cap, which he felt self-conscious about wearing, especially at the station. He left it on the dash, as a way of signalling that his car belonged.

The sun was a mere suggestion over-ruled by grey clouds, and the outside air was just a vague hint above freezing, but Kelly Halligan had just washed the rescue truck.

Water dripped from the gleaming vehicle, a super-duty pickup with a large metal box fitted on an extended chassis, with rolling doors to allow access to side compartments.

Rivulets of water carved their way through the thin layer of packed snow on their way to the parking lot drain.

Tom said, “Hey Kelly. Got your text. What can I do for you?”

There were water spots on Kelly’s bright yellow bunker boots, and suds on the hi-vis strips above on his navy-blue duty pants.

"Two things, Tom. The first is the crew talked it over, and we have an idea about the Christmas morning breakfast. If it's okay, we want to try to do it in the church parking lot..."

Kelly laid out a plan involving open-sided tents, patio heaters, tables and chairs from the church hall, and a drive through lane for those who didn't want to eat outside.

Tom said, "That's... very generous, and it sounds like it could be a lot of fun. I'll talk to Jesse and see what he thinks."

Kelly said, "We have plans for him too. Tell him to call me. The other thing is the crew hopes you can join us at the Spitfires game tomorrow night. It's our way of saying thanks for coming on as chaplain. You're the first pastor in town we could all agree on."

Tom laughed. "Maybe because I'm the new guy, and they haven't got to know me yet."

The short-sleeved red polo, with the words Deputy Chief embroidered below the SPFD logo was stretched tight across Kelly's well-muscled frame and had somehow escaped getting splashed.

He handed Tom an envelope.

"I've got three tickets for you. You can bring your daughter, and your... friend.

"Thanks. I'll ask them... Kelly, aren't you freezing? I'm cold just looking at you."

Kelly rolled up the door on a side compartment of the rescue truck and removed a bright yellow tote.

"Mom says I always ran hot as a kid. She could never keep a jacket on me."

"I actually have no idea if Annika would like it. Hope might be interested. She started watching hockey while going to school in Atlanta."

Kelly clicked open the clasps and popped off the lid. The yellow bin was lined with black anti-shock padding.

'I just need to check some things in here," Kelly said. "Georgia seems a weird place to get into Canada's national sport."

Kelly lifted two hard-shell cases from the yellow bin and set them on the deck of the open compartment.

"That's what I said. She was very quick to say, 'Dad, our national sport is actually lacrosse.' She said 'Dad' in that way that reminded me how little I know about... well, everything."

Kelly opened a lunch box-sized case and lifted out a bright red instrument that resembled a hair dryer with a four-inch video screen welded to the handle. He powered it up and read the unit's display.

"Your daughter talks to you, which is good. Ben's barely speaking to me. He still blames me for the divorce, and he can't stand Penny."

Tom said, "I'm sorry."

Kelly turned off the non-hair dryer and set it back in its cut-out within the black case.

It seemed easier for Kelly to talk, if he didn't have to look at Tom.

"He said if Penny's going to be around, he and his girlfriend will spend Christmas with his mother. I won't be seeing them, because I don't go to Jan's house."

"Does Penny know how Ben feels about her?"

"I tell her how much it bothers me, and she just says Ben's a grown-up, and no longer my responsibility. It's like she doesn't care. At least not the way I do."

Kelly closed the small black case and set it back in the yellow tote.

"This sounds like it's about more than whether Ben likes Penny."

Kelly said, "Yeah, I guess it is. She's focused on different things."

"Like what?"

"Like when I asked her to move in. We're together half the time anyway."

Kelly made a half turn to meet Tom's eyes.

"Should I be telling this to a minister?"

"It's all good, Kelly. What'd she say?"

"That I was putting the cart before the horse."

"Uh-huh. What did that mean for her?"

"She was happy to sell her place and sock the money away in her personal account. But now she wants me to put her name on my house, and on all my banking. She wants to manage my money but keep hers separate. When I asked why, she said she can't commit to someone who doesn't trust her."

"Sounds like trust is a big issue for her."

"It is for me too. She doesn't even let me drive her car. She only gave me a keyfob so I can move it, if I need to get my truck out of the driveway."

"How long have you been... seeing each other?"

"Not even a year. I waited until the divorce was final. I didn't want to rush into anything. And now..."

Kelly opened a smaller black case and lifted out a device that reminded Tom of his old Nintendo Game Boy, except it was bright yellow.

Tom said, "I've seen that one before."

"It's a multi-gas meter," Kelly said. "We use it to see if the air is safe to breathe. It can also tell us if anything like natural gas, or particulate in the air, is approaching explosive levels. It sees dangers we can't see."

Tom said, "That came in handy on Sunday."

Kelly said, "I wish there was one of these for relationships. The way things went with Jan, I had no warning. And with Penny, I just don't know. Sometimes I think she's not like other people."

"How?"

"The other night when I said I was relieved we got called away, and I didn't have to see who was under the tree, she gave me this icy look, and said, 'it comes with the job, Kelly. Grow a pair.' "

Kelly's words reminded Tom how the cold was seeping into him. He was ready to get back in the car, or maybe go in the fire station, but feared that if he made a move, Kelly would shut down.

"Is it different for Penny because she doesn't have the history you have with the people here?"

"Maybe, but you're not from here either, no offense. But I heard you at Sylvie's funeral. You care about people."

"Thanks, Kelly. Sylvie's was a hard one."

Kelly nodded. "I think they all are."

He waved a hand at the rescue truck, and the fire station behind it.

"It's why we do this. Human life..."

Kelly returned the yellow device to its case, which he placed in the larger tote.

The way he rubbed his hands together made Tom wonder if Kelly was finally feeling the cold.

"I told Penny about the explosion at the church, and she didn't even ask if anyone was hurt. When I said Bobby could have died, you know what she said?"

Tom waited while Kelly hefted the yellow tote back into the side compartment. He pulled hard with both hands, and the compartment door came down with a loud clang.

"Sorry, it sticks sometimes... When I told her about Bobby, Penny wondered if he was in Gloria's will, and who'd inherit if he'd been killed."

Chapter 39

Tuesday Mid-morning (4 days to Christmas)

The morning sky was heavy with dark, low hanging clouds that made Tom wonder just how snowy Christmas might be.

He said, "Will you get home for the holidays?"

"That's not really how this job with Michael works," Lawrence said. "We go where we're needed and stay until we're not."

Lawrence was driving the unmarked sedan he shared with Barbara, a Ford Taurus in a shade of grey that matched the sky. They were headed to the Leamington hospital to interview Bobby Sharpe.

"What about your daughter?"

"Emily's part of why I said yes when Michael made the offer. She went to Melbourne for university and says she won't be back until she graduates."

"Australia's about as far away as there is. I'm sorry," Tom said.

"She wanted out from between her mother and me."

"Still."

"Yeah."

They rode in silence until they approached a retired police cruiser parked in a drift of snow beside a long driveway. A sign next to the car welcomed visitors to the Canadian Transportation Museum and Heritage Village.

Lawrence turned his head towards the car. It was white, with the words Essex Police lettered in red across the side doors.

"I've heard mixed opinions about that old Crown Vic. Some enjoy the throwback to when the town of Essex still had its own force. Others don't appreciate the Tim Horton's cups displayed on the dashboard."

"Sounds like things have warmed up with the locals. Michael said the raid helped."

"I hate to say it, but so did this." He raised his left arm up out of the sling.

They traveled a few more miles before speaking again.

Tom said, "Being on the road, how do you have a life outside the job?"

"A lot of detachments have their own weight room. And Barbara's got me sparring."

"That's good, but it's all physical," Tom said. "What do you do... for the rest of you."

Lawrence slowed for a turn.

"I'm writing a book."

Tom nodded.

"That fits. You pay attention, and don't settle for the obvious. You look at the who, to understand the why."

Lawrence said, "That's a good line."

Tom said, "What kind of book?"

There was a smile in Lawrence's eyes.

"What do you think?"

"I hope it's a mystery," Tom said. "I remember our talks about Holmes and Watson."

"It's based on my if onlys."

Tom said, "As in if only I'd thought of that sooner?"

Lawrence said, "Times when if I'd taken a breath, and the wider view, I might've noticed something earlier. So, I thought, how about a cop who knows to do that?"

"What will you call it?

"The Cases of The Reflective Detective."

"That works on more than one level. Your sleuth looks outward, and ponders the details of the crime, but maybe also looks inward, and notices the effect working the case has on them. I had a supervisor once who said we should consider our gut feelings as information."

"That's good. Maybe I'll use that one too."

Lawrence pulled the Taurus into the hospital parking lot. They sat in the unmarked for a moment, to allow the plow truck to pass.

The front blade pushed a thin scrape of snow, and a spinning disk over the trailer hitch scattered tiny blue salt crystals.

Lawrence locked the Taurus, and they walked through the plow truck's diesel fumes towards a marked SUV in the police-only slot outside the emergency entrance.

The officer at the wheel lowered her window and waved them over.

"Hey Lawrence. Reverend Book! How are you?"

"Better now, Manuela." He raised his left arm up out of the sling. "It took a few days before I could move without complaining."

"Anybody listen?"

"Not with the level of sympathy I deserve."

"You going up to see the baby?"

Tom said, "I hope to meet her later. We're here to talk with..."

Tom looked to Lawrence. He wasn't sure how much he should say in the parking lot.

Manuela said, "Our poker player? He's a character. But not as interesting as la niñita. She reminds me of my own, fifteen years before the sass and snark."

The automatic doors slid back as they approached the main entrance. The security guard at reception gave Lawrence a nod of recognition.

Not for the first time, Tom appreciated the humour of the gift store sign, which read "Shopping Therapy".

An untouched box of disposable masks on a stool near the elevator brought Tom back to how things had been two years earlier.

When they were alone in the elevator, Lawrence said, "Thanks for sending Mr. Freund our way. He's had a lot to say."

"Anything you can use?"

"It's going to take some time to evaluate it all. He passed on a very detailed rundown of The Member's movements, for the days leading up to Gloria's death, and after. He also provided a long list of tasks Sharpe ordered that involved using his office and parliamentary resources for personal gain."

A bulletin board was mounted on one wall of the elevator. Next to a poster about an increase in the hourly parking rates was a reminder that physical or verbal abuse of hospital staff would not be tolerated.

Tom said, "He told us Sharpe had been lying to the Prime Minister's office. I wonder how many kinds of trouble he's in."

Lawrence said, "We know he's been keeping bad company. When you mentioned Sharpe was in town the day his sister died, Barbara tapped into her magical search engines. She found him on the passenger list for a private flight into Leamington. The jet's tail number identified it as a long-term lease to the Kazinski family. That same jet was waiting for Sharpe yesterday morning."

"Wow," Tom said. "I'm glad I called when John said his boss was heading to the airport."

"That was a good catch. We prevailed upon Mr. Sharpe to postpone his travel plans."

"He needs to be here for Gloria's funeral anyway."

Lawrence said, "We asked John about the name Kazinski. He showed us how often the name comes up in Sharpe's appointment diary. You'd already given us the piece about Sharpe and Troy Donaldson being fraternity brothers. It turns out Brad Kazinski is also a Beta Rho Omicron bro."

"Is that really the name of their fraternity? They're the BRO bros?"

Lawrence grinned.

"I'm surprised you didn't study Greek at seminary. Barbara tells me the Greek letter Rho looks like a capital P, which kind of ruins it."

"Why... how does she know things like that?"

"She'd tell you it's not what she knows, but that she knows how to look. You know she has a master's in library and information sciences? It's actually from Western, where the bros went."

"She's impressive. I think she's been a good influence on Hope."

"So, some good comes out of this mess," Lawrence said. "I'm glad about that."

"And I'm glad to hear John's been helpful," Tom said. "He didn't make the best first impression."

"I don't think he's been all that impressed with himself lately. He was all in with his role as Sharpe's right hand. I think it provided the identity and purpose he craved."

"Until it didn't," Tom said.

"The last straw for him was having to tell Bobby he couldn't speak at his aunt's funeral."

"Sharpe tried getting me to do it," Tom said. "But I don't work for him."

"John realized he'd been bending over backwards to please someone who really only cares about himself."

Tom said, "Hard to feel appreciated by a narcissist."

"John looked to Sharpe as a substitute for his family, who aren't willing, or able to accept him for who he really is."

Tom said, "Does it ever feel like you're using someone's pain to get what you need?"

"I'd say Bobby's deep wounds led him to his current situation. As he works to extricate himself, the pain is bound to surface. If we can offer him a sense of agency, maybe that helps him come out the other side."

Tom said, "Allows him to say, 'I'm not him, and I don't like what he's been doing.'"

"Occasionally, we have the opportunity, if not to restore justice, but to at least help a person feel they're on the side of good."

"Now that's a great line for a book," Tom said.

Chapter 40

Tuesday Mid-morning (4 days to Christmas)

Tom knew his way around the hospital. Leamington didn't have many private rooms, but almost getting blown up seemed to rate one. That and the uniformed cop outside the door made it pretty easy to find Bobby Sharpe.

Lawrence and Tom entered and stood together in the space between the bed and the doorway.

The Leamington hospital is an older facility, and Tom thought it showed around the edges. Even so, it smelled right, and they kept it clean in ways newer places often missed. Tom was glad to see Bobby's window blind was up, the glass was clean, and the sill free of dust.

Bobby was sitting up in bed. The faded blue hospital gown was stretched tight over his belly.

Tom noticed Bobby's gold cross, a gift from his Aunt Gloria, visible over the neck of the gown.

Bobby's eyes were focused on the screen of a small purple laptop. Next to the laptop was an unopened souvenir deck of cards, featuring photos of Leamington landmarks. Maybe it was all they had in the hospital gift shop.

Sensing he had company, Bobby shut off the Poker Channel and set his earbuds on the overbed table. A thick letter-size manila envelope poked out from under his lunch tray. The return address was for a Windsor law firm.

Bobby said, "Doc gave me good odds my hearing will clear in a day or two."

Tom hoped that was true.

Barbara warned them Bobby had been deafened by the blast.

She'd left him the Chromebook, loaded with an app that converted speech to text in real time.

Bobby pointed at the laptop and said, "I need this to talk to you."

Tom said, "Barbara show you how to use it?"

He watched their words appear on the screen. He was speaker #2.

"She's a real doll," Bobby said. "Says since she helped drag my sorry... uh, she helped find me, she feels responsible for me."

Lawrence nodded.

Tom wondered how Barbara would feel about being called a doll.

Bobby pointed to Lawrence and his sling, then typed quickly. The words on the screen said, "She told me there was a raid on Sunday, and a couple of officers were hurt. Is that how you got that?"

Lawrence said, "I'm okay. Nothing broken. The sling just takes the weight off so the wound isn't stretched."

Bobby nodded, and said, "She says I need to tell you everything, and this program will record it all, and make a transcript, to send to her work computer."

Lawrence said, "She's the techie in our dynamic duo."

"Detective Barbara says you need to identify yourselves for the recording and give me the caution speech."

Bobby pulled the big envelope from under the tray.

"This is from Auntie G's lawyer, to take with you, and read later," Bobby said. "And don't worry, I know my rights, and if I needed a lawyer, I'd have one here."

Lawrence recited name, rank and badge number, and indicated Tom's presence as Bobby's pastor. He also read the formal caution; from a card he kept in his badge wallet.

Bobby said, “So, you know how I make my living.”

Lawrence nodded.

Tom said, “On Sunday, Catherine mentioned poker on television.”

“That’s the flashy part. Week by week it’s smaller games. But, yeah, it’s about the tournaments.”

Lawrence said, “How does it work?”

“Guys ranked higher than me, they have sponsors. I’m not there. I borrow my stake, then depending on how I do, pay back what I owe, and a little more.”

Lawrence said, “So you have a backer?”

“I did. Auntie G didn’t just say she was on my side; she literally bet on me.”

Tom said, “We all need someone to believe in us.”

“You got that right. I already told some of this to the Rev... to Tom, before. But not the details.”

Lawrence said, “Start as far back as you need, and don’t worry about repeating yourself.”

Bobby interlaced his fingers, and stretched his arms out in front, cracking knuckles.

“Okee doke. Two months back, I’m lined up for a big deal in Reno. On the network and everything. Auntie G staked me for the buy-in, plus a little extra for expenses, so I bought some new track suits. And they’re like five, six large each, if you can believe it. But we’d figured between the tournament, and the side book, we’d make it all back and more.”

Lawrence said, “The side book?”

“You can bet on anything in Vegas, if you know the right people, or the wrong ones. Anyways, we laid money I’d finish in the top tier.”

“So, what went wrong?”

“I was doing pretty good, first day of play. Climbing the ladder, doing better than we’d expected. And then I got a little greedy. Figured this was a chance for a big pay day and maybe get out for a while. Auntie G and I’d been talking about maybe I’d go to cooking school, try something different.”

Lawrence said, “What did getting a little greedy mean?”

"So... I did this on my own, without talking to G. I called my guy, and got him to call his guy, and bump up the side bet. He says, 'you sure? You know the kinda guys were dealing with.' I says, 'don't worry, I got it covered.' "

Tom said, "But something happened?"

Bobby turned his head away from his visitors and towards the window, which framed the clouded grey sky.

He said, "I'm what happened... It was like I lost what little mind I had left. Played like a chump and was laughed out of the event. Well, not really. They let me keep the comped room for the weekend. But other players walked big circles to stay out of my path, like I was a black cat, or had the plague."

Lawrence said, "This ever happen to you before?"

"No, and that's the thing. Maybe I don't look like it, but I watch what I eat, keep my blood sugar up. I don't drink alcohol or do... anything else. Never have. But that night I saw double and triple, and had nausea, panic, and shitty judgment running through me in waves. I couldn't focus to track the cards, and I couldn't read anyone at the table. And I didn't have the sense to fold."

"What happened to you, Bobby?"

"Auntie G figured someone got to my water bottle. Next day, I woke up fevered, and I had the shakes for a week. And I owed a half mil to exactly the wrong people. And it's the kind of debt that grows quick."

Lawrence said, "Val Kazinski talked to you on Thursday at Caesar's."

Bobby said, "Tom, she's the one who sent me the tie with the deadmans' hand on it. Her way of sending a message."

Tom said, "What'd she say to you at the casino?"

"I feel bad about your aunt. You need to find a new gig."

Lawrence said, "What do you think she meant?"

"That day I heard it as a threat, like we killed her and you're next, so pay up. But that makes no sense."

Lawrence said, "Why?"

"They knew Gloria was my bank. She's the only reason they took my bet."

"Okay," Lawrence said. "Anything else about that? If not, I'd like to hear what happened yesterday."

"No, that's all. I went to the church early Monday morning to meet with Robert Sharpe, Senior."

"Your father," Lawrence said.

Tom watched Bobby fold into himself, like he'd been gut-punched.

"I don't really call him that. Haven't for most of my life."

Tom said, "I get that, Bobby. I've got one of those."

"His assistant came at me at Sylvie's visitation. I only went because I figured Robert would be there. I wanted to ask again if I could speak at Gloria's service."

Tom said, "How'd that go?"

"I didn't get near him. His assistant cornered me, said it wouldn't do to make a scene. If I wanted to talk to The Member, he'd set something up, and text me the details."

"That's harsh," Lawrence said.

"That's his way," Bobby said. "Play by his rules, or you don't have a chance with his Member-ship."

"So I got the text on Sunday, telling me to be at the church Monday morning at 7:30 am."

Lawrence said, "And you went?"

"I went early, because I figured this was my shot."

Lawrence nodded.

Bobby said, "I go in through the front door, cause that's the one I know is always open. I still know the place by heart, from all those times I went there with G, so no need to hit the lights. I was walking around in the sanctuary, picking up the feel of the place, then I thought I'd check out the spot. You know Rev, the one I told you about."

"Under the north balcony," Tom said. "That's where they found you."

"Yeah, and it's good I went in there, and even better they found me. I almost cashed in whatever chips I got left."

Lawrence said, "We're glad you're still with us."

Bobby read the screen, then covered his eyes for a moment.

"So I'm in there, and whaddya know... My emergency deck's where I left it, a hundred years ago. A pack of red Bicycle cards I kept in there, to pass the time while Auntie G was busy planning the Easter parade or whatever."

"So I opened the box, and just sat on the floor, holding the cards. I always feel better with cards in my hands."

"I heard a door open, and some footsteps, and I figure it's my... it's Robert coming in. But I feel sort of stupid, and something in me doesn't want him to know about my spot. I crack the door just a little, and before I take a peek, I hear his voice. He's on his phone, and he already sounds pissed off, sorry Reverend Tom, and he hasn't even seen me yet. So I told myself to wait."

Lawrence said, "Any idea who he was talking to?"

"Whoever it was, he kept calling him brother, which was weird, since Robert and Gloria only had one, Uncle George, and he died before I was born."

"But the kicker was... Robert said to this guy, 'Even if he does sign the papers, I won't let him embarrass me at the service.' So I know I wasted my time coming, so I decide, I'm going to waste his. See how long he waits for me to show up."

Tom said, "What happened next?"

"He's still yelling into his phone. Things he shouldn't be saying in church. I forgot how much I hated his yelling voice, so I'm trying to block it out, like I'm a little kid all over again. But I heard something like, 'No, I have no idea where they could have put it, but you can look all you want, after my sister's funeral.' Then he was quiet for a few seconds, and I wondered if he'd left, and I didn't notice.

"I was thinking about getting out of there, when I heard Robert yell, 'You stupid son of a bitch!'"

"I'd heard that a lot from him, so again, I didn't really want to hear anything else. But I did. He said, 'It's set to blow when? Are you out of your mind? I'm in the church right now!'"

"Next thing I heard was stomping, like someone running up the centre aisle. My aunt would have lost it if she saw someone running in church. Then I heard a door slam, and then nothing."

Lawrence said, "Nothing?"

Bobby said, "Not a thing. If darkness was a sound, it was like that. And I can't remember seeing anything either, until I'm being dragged out of my little cubby- and I see people's mouths moving, but I can't hear a damn thing... sorry, Tom!"

Chapter 41

Tuesday (4 days to Christmas)

Gloria Sharpe
1 Sun Parlour Drive,
Sun Parlour, Ontario
Friday, December 9

My dearest Bobby;

You have so much going on right now. I hate the idea of adding to your stress, or distress, but the situation with your father (I know you don't like to call him that!) has come to a head, and there are things you need to know. He's going to be after you to sign some papers. We both know how he is about getting his way.

I was thinking about the last time we were all together. It was five years ago, in that oak-panelled room at the back of the Old Train Station restaurant. He'd relished telling us they'd opened just for him. I felt bad that the staff had to work late on Christmas Eve.

He insisted I was too sentimental, that they were being well compensated. Everything for him comes down to who and what you can buy.

He stood, one hand around a highball glass, the other tucked in his vest like he'd risen to speak in the House of Commons. I wondered if he meant to offer a toast. Instead, he downed his eighteen-year-old scotch in one fast gulp, thunked the glass on the table and handed each of us an envelope from his constituency office. Do you remember what he said?

"I wish you both all the best, but you need to know this is the last of it."

Before you arrived that evening, he declared he'd ordered a stop to the transfers into the Sharpe Family Trust, which I use to support the church. I reminded him that our father, your grandfather Sharpe, had pledged its doors would always be open, the heat on, and a welcome offered to those in need.

I hated the way he scoffed at the most honourable aspect of our family legacy, then lectured me about how times had changed. What truly infuriated me was the way he spoke about you.

You already know my opinion that he hasn't been much of a father since your mother died. I despise the face he created for the world, of the long-suffering single parent, dividing his time between raising you, running the business, and serving the common good.

You were a few minutes late that night. You told me later you'd been having a good run at the table, and when you did cash in, you were up over $7,000. You said it was Christmas luck.

Before you arrived, Robert said, "This is typical. He's probably pissing away more of my money at the Casino. He blew through his trust in record time, with almost nothing to show for it. His so-called career causes me no end of embarrassment. I have no option but to turn off the money tap and force him to grow the hell up."

(As you know, Bobby, I am not a fan of vulgar language. I quote his words here only to illustrate the true character of the man we are dealing with.)

I told him he was being heartless and short-sighted. Couldn't he see the good the church was doing in Sun Parlour, and how happy you were, pursuing your dream? Was there really any difference between your kind of gambling, and the company's dalliances in the futures market?

He seemed surprised I knew what he'd been doing.

It was as if he'd forgotten I was finishing my business degree when he was just starting his own. Ever the politician, he said he hoped we could agree to disagree. That was when the server opened the door, and you walked in, smiling ear to ear because of your big win. I've always loved your big goofy grin.

You stayed with me at the house that night, and we had a lovely Christmas. I set a place for Robert in case he chose to join us for brunch. He did not, and I hadn't heard from him again for the last five years.

Just a few days ago I answered a call from his Ottawa office.

His personal assistant said, "The Member will be on the line in a moment, but while you wait, can we confirm a meeting at the church in Sun Parlour for 7:30 p.m., Tuesday, December 13? The Member assumes you'd rather he not visit your home. For expediency, we have messengered some documents to you, which The Member requires you to sign, and return to him when you meet next week."

I've read the documents and asked my attorneys to review them. I'm including notarized copies, and their notes with this letter.

Robert still needs us. Or at the very least, one of us. He plans to restructure the family corporation, to allow a partnership with some shady people. The less you know about them, the better.

I'm telling you this now, because I believe your father (sorry!), Robert, pulled the wool over your eyes. When his lawyers released your trust money, they rushed you through signing all those forms. They avoided telling you that you still hold voting shares.

Your portion of the company's returns, paid as dividends on your shares, are being held in trust. (I've used mine to do what Robert refused to do, support the church. For my own reasons, I've never told the leaders of the congregation.)

All of this has kept you at more than arm's length from the company, except in the case of his proposed changes to the letters patent. He needs at least one of us to agree. It won't be me, and I sincerely hope you will resist his efforts to gain your support.

There's something else.

It's cloaked in weaselly lawyer language, but the gist of it is that control of the company is vested in Robert Sharpe Senior until his death, declared incompetence, or a documented incident of "conduct unbecoming". My attorneys tell me it something like a morals clause. If he was to be caught in any of his extra-legal shenanigans, he could lose control of the company and its assets.

I mention this now, because I intend to tell him when we meet next week, that I'm aware that he's crossed significant lines, and brought shame on us all.

You know, of course, that your grandfather made his initial fortune as a smuggler, during Prohibition. Ours was not the only family in this county that bought their way to respectability, and I have devoted my adult life to making amends.

In an effort to recover his losses in other areas, Robert has become involved with modern-day counterparts to the rumrunners, and it's a very ugly business.

I told him on the phone that I have no intention of signing off on his ill-considered plan, and there is nothing he can say or do to alter my position. When I meet with him next week, I will lay down the law and insist that unless he ends the arrangements with his shady friends, I will expose him and invoke the clause to remove him.

I hope for once he will do what is right.

One last thing, my dear. I have reason to believe that despite his dramatic declaration to have cut all ties, he's kept an eye on you, or more likely, had someone watching you. He knows about what happened at the last tournament. I expect he'll try to buy your vote, by offering to bail you out.

Trust that I'm doing what I can to sort things out on your behalf.

All my love,

Your Aunt Gloria

Chapter 42

Wednesday Morning (3 days to Christmas)

Annika thumbed up the volume control on the Range Rover's steering wheel. Jose Feliciano was singing Feliz Navidad.

She looked over her shoulder at Marta and Estella.

Barbara said, "I heard him in an interview a few years ago. He said was homesick when he wrote that song, wishing he could be with his family."

Estrella said, "I feel that in his voice. He's saying he'd like to wish them a Merry Christmas but can't because he's too far away. Marta and the baby are my family now. She had no one, and my people, they don't want me. Where I come from, there is much hate, still, for people like us."

From the third-row seat Hope said, "I'm sorry."

Barbara said, "You've been through so much."

Estrella said, "You have all been so kind."

Jose' Feliciano was replaced by Bob Dylan singing, "Do you hear what I hear?"

Annika laughed.

"This may be the worst version I've ever heard."

Marta whispered something to Estrella.

"She says Whitney Houston is much better."

Barbara said, "I think so too."

"Crap!" Annika said. "Everyone hold tight!"

Hope looked first in the rear-view mirror, then turned her head to see it live and up close.

A big black truck was bearing down on them, fast.

She stared, scared and confused, as it roared, picked up even more speed, and rammed the Range Rover.

A jarring thud shook the vehicle.

Hope said, "Annika, did Paul show you the..."

Annika said, "He did, and I'm on it."

She thumbed another steering wheel control, and the big in-dash screen displayed a view of the big ugly SUV close on their tail. Red and blue lights strobed from its front dash.

Annika said, "This is more aggressive than what happened to Tom on Thursday."

Barbara said, "I just called Michael."

"Tom didn't mention police lights," Annika said. "Barbara, do you think these guys are law enforcement?"

"Doubtful."

Barbara spoke into her phone.

"Superintendent... yeah, that's right... we're coming up on the transportation museum. Just a second."

She looked at Annika.

Barbara said, "Don't pull into that first driveway. Slow down, act like you're maybe going to pull into the second entrance. Up where the old cruiser is parked. Michael says help is very close. We just have to drag this out a little."

Hope felt their speed drop as Annika touched the brake and heard the tick-ticking when she flipped on the turn signal.

Barbara said, "That's some serious Batmobile stuff, with the rear-view camera."

Annika said, "Paul normally keeps this car on hand for a friend. Tom hasn't said much about her, except that she's dangerous, but in a good way."

"Sounds like someone I should meet," Barbara said. "Estrella, everyone okay back there? The baby? La nina?"

"Si... yes, we're good. She's still sleeping, gracias a Dios! What's happening?"

Barbara said, "It's okay. We had a plan in place for this. Hope, you good?"

Hope said, "Yeah, I'm fine."

Barbara was on the phone with Michael Powers.

"No sir. No visible markings, no front tag. Shiny new black Escalade."

Annika said, "They're staying on us. What does he want us to do?"

Just as Annika spoke, another black Escalade roared by and veered into our path, a few car lengths ahead. The driver tapped the pedal long enough to show brake lights.

Annika said, "What do I do? They've boxed us in."

Barbara said, "We've run up the clock best we can. It's time to stop. I like it here. The shoulder is narrow, and angles down towards that deep ditch. It'll mes with their footing."

Annika braked, and steered on to the shoulder, close to the edge of the ditch. Reverse lights glowed from the vehicle ahead as it backed in tight to their front bumper. The chase vehicle pulled in tight behind them and continued to flash red and blue emergency lights.

Across the ditch to the right Hope saw a really old cop car. It had to be part of the museum. There were mannequins posed in the driver and passenger seats.

Hope tuned in to details like how badly the old timey peaked caps fit their heads, so she wouldn't have to think about what was happening.

Annika put the Range Rover in park and left the engine running. She lowered the volume on the radio, but Hope could still hear Bob Dylan sing, "Pray for peace, people everywhere..."

Hope thought peace would be a good thing.

Barbara said, "Help is less than a minute out."

Two large men in black suits exited from the second row of doors on either side of the Escalade ahead of us.

The way Annika parked meant that the guy on Barbara's side was half-stepping in the snow-filled ditch.

Annika said, “Driver stayed in the vehicle.”

Barbara said, “I see two in the car behind us, but they’re staying put. No visible weapons.”

A man appeared at the window on Annika’s side. He wore dark Ray-Ban sunglasses and the earpiece with the coiled wire down his collar, from all the spy movies. His twin was at Barbara’s window, forced to stand a little lower, because of the ditch.

Barbara said, “Still no weapons in sight. Don’t lower your window. Keep the motor running. We need 30 more seconds. Lower my window when I nod. I’ll talk to sunglasses on this side.”

Ray-Ban #1 gestured for Annika to turn off the vehicle and lower the window.

She shook her head and pointed toward Barbara.

Annika said, “Guy on my side has empty hands. Yours?”

"So far, so good," Barbara said. "You can lower my window now."

She displayed her open badge wallet with one hand and leveled her side-arm, a Glock M17 pistol with the other. Both were at eye level for the guy standing in the snow. As her window rolled down, she said, “Detective Sergeant Palmieri, OPP. Stand down before this gets messy.”

Ray-Ban #2 shook his head.

“Those women are in Canada illegally.”

Barbara said, “I repeat, stand down. We are not screwing around.”

Sirens in the near distance won out over Bob Dylan’s gravelly “he will bring us goodness and light...”

Ray-Ban #2 said, “There are five of us, and one of you, Detective Sergeant.”

Barbara said, “Do you hear what I hear? That song, high above the trees?”

Sunglasses did not respond. The wail of sirens grew even louder as multiple vehicles approached at high speed, then cut out, replaced by the screech of braking tires, and the sound of multiple cruiser doors opening.

Annika turned off the engine and the radio. In the sudden quiet, Barbara said, “Who are you guys?”

Sunglasses said, “That’s way above your pay grade.”

Barbara said, "I highly doubt it's above my boss's."

The man at Barbara's window smirked, and said, "Oh yeah? Who do you work for?"

Barbara said, "The guy I work for has the Tactics and Response Unit on speed dial. They're the ones with automatic rifles trained on you and your friends, watching for the slightest provocation. Raise your hands above your head and step away from this vehicle. Now."

The big man behind the dark sunglasses looked left and right, nodded his head, and raised his arms. His hands were pulled behind him by a grim-looking officer in ranger green tactical clothing, who bound his wrists with a zip restraint.

From her back row seat Hope heard Barbara's sunglass man say, "Ow."

She watched as more tactical officers repeated these actions with the Ray-Ban man on Annika's side of the Range Rover, and those they removed from the two black Cadillacs.

Hope heard Barbara say, "Separate bags for all the sunglasses, and the earbuds. We'll need those, their radios, cellphones, and anything in their pockets. You guys know the drill."

The big GI-Joe looking TRU officer removed Ray-Ban's eyewear, and said, "Absolutely, Sarge. We need to ensure their personal safety while they are in our custody."

Barbara raised her phone and said, "Smile for the facial recognition database."

Annika said, "How did Michael get them here so fast?"

"He had them on stand-by for us, while they were also gearing up for another operation. They set up their staging area one concession road over, because this looked like the most likely spot on our route, if something were going to happen."

Annika said, 'It's good to have friends."

Barbara said, "Michael's still on the line. I'm putting him on speaker."

Michael said, "Everybody good there?"

Annika looked back, and then said, "Yeah, we're all good."

"Okay. Barbara, after you get everyone settled back at the Quiet Centre, I'll need you in Leamington. You'll take the lead on the paperwork, and on processing these guys. Our TRU friends have another engagement."

Barbara said, "Happy to, boss. We'll be on our way soon as they can move the vehicle ahead of us."

"Leamington's sending people out for the Cadillacs, and to transport the prisoners."

Annika said, "Thanks for having our backs."

She started the Range Rover and turned up the radio.

Andrea Bocelli sang a Spanish version of O Holy Night.

From the middle row, Estrella joined in, her pure clear voice rising above Bocelli's.

Chapter 43

Late Wednesday evening (3 days to Christmas)

"Do you want to go to a hockey game tomorrow night? The firefighters gave me Spitfires tickets. Hope already said yes."

Annika said, "She said you'd be asking. I'd love to."

Tom and Annika were in the Aerie, the glassed-in observation dome at the top of the brick silo at the Quiet Centre. Their club chairs were angled so they could see each other's faces and also look out over Lake Erie.

Tom said, "I think it'll be fun, and we could all use a break from... well, everything."

They'd switched off the dome's interior lights to sit in the soft glow from the scattered stars, and the waning crescent moon.

This would have been a good night for the smugglers who once plied their trade in the narrow stretch of water between Ontario and the United States. Invisible in the darkness were the tiny islands of the Lake Erie archipelago, legendary locally as places of refuge and subterfuge.

Annika slid her chair a little closer to Tom's. Tom thought her blonde hair took on a silvery sheen in the star light.

"It's been a lot, but I'm still glad to be here."

Tom said, "With all that's happened..."

Annika said, "We're all good. I'd rather be with you and Hope than be hearing about it all over long distance."

Tom laid his hand over hers.

"But today could have gone very badly."

"But it didn't," Annika said, "And we're all safe, and... we're here. I like that room with the big fireplace, but this is my favourite part of the retreat centre."

"It's a good spot," Tom said. "I'm glad I finally got to bring you up to see it."

Any background sound was masked by the white noise of the heater fan keeping the Aerie warm and the big windows clear on a cold December night.

The relative quiet was broken by Barbara Palmieri's voice from behind them.

"It's also great for overwatch."

Barbara climbed the last step of the circular stairs up to the Aerie.

She said, "From up here we can see anyone, anything that might approach the Quiet Centre."

She was faced away from the water, surveying the grounds through a night vision device.

Tom said, "Paul thought you'd appreciate it. He also said he'd be happy to take the watch from midnight on."

Barbara flipped the high-tech goggles up and away from her eyes and turned to look at Tom and Annika.

She wore a body armour vest over a long sleeve black turtleneck, which matched the tactical pants, and high-top duty boots. Her long auburn hair was pulled away from her face in a tight ponytail, and her detective's badge was clipped to her belt.

"I just talked to Paul before walking the tunnel from the main house. This set up is like something from a comic book."

Annika said, "Or a James Bond movie."

"Hope, and the new family are all resting," Barbara said. "Lawrence's gone back to the motel, and we have a uniformed officer in a cruiser in the driveway. We anticipate an uneventful night, but..."

"We'll keep watch," Tom said.

Barbara said, "I told Paul he can relieve me at four a.m. You can take over at eight. By then, Michael should have an update for us."

With one finger Barbara lowered the night vision goggles.

"If you two want to head down, get some rest, I can keep an eye on things from up here."

Chapter 44

Late Thursday morning (2 days to Christmas)

Tom said, "You're not coming in for a coffee, chat with some folks?"

Jesse stopped the black Chrysler 300 a car length ahead of the rear entrance to the Aird and Bower Funeral Home. Behind them, the parking lot was filling up with cars that had been at the cemetery for Gloria Sharpe's burial. Jesse turned down the stereo, to spare any approaching mourners from having to hear Elvis rocking out on "Viva Las Vegas", but he left the big sedan in drive.

"I... have someone I need to check on," Jesse said, "But you go ahead."

With the church out of commission, Jesse and Mrs. Bower had arranged to host the reception at the funeral home.

"Almost everyone you know is going to be... oh. Are you talking about Johnny Friendly... John? How is he?"

"It's hard to stop calling him that, I know. He's having a tough time. He lived for Sharpe- and distanced himself from anything, anybody else."

"You're a good guy Jesse. He's going to need a friend."

"Yeah, I think so. Thanks Tom. And thanks for what you did for Bobby, reading what he said about his aunt. That part about her being the only one really there for him after his mother died really got me."

"I'm not sure his father appreciated it."

"The Member had his turn, and then some. That was a truth Bobby needed told, and you helped him."

"Thanks."

"And you seemed so calm and cool, the casual observer wouldn't have known your house almost got blown up."

"What did Elvis say, just taking care of business?"

"You did that, Tom. But I wondered early on, when you were saying God is with us in the places we'd rather not be. You froze. I gave it a beat, and you recovered, but I thought I'd have to come up, bring you a water or something."

"Sorry about that. There was someone in the crowd I wasn't ready to see."

Tom had spotted Brad Kazinski, the neighbourhood crime boss from Oakville, seated directly behind Robert Sharpe, Senior.

It made sense Kazinski would be there to support his old friend, especially since the arrest of their other fraternity brother, Troy Donaldson, on a long list of indictable offenses.

Brad's dark suit fit the occasion, but his slate grey shirt and tie, and lifeless black eyes lent an air that Tom felt was more menace than shared grief. Tom's perception was shadowed by the memory of threats Kazinski made against him and his daughter, but it seemed to him that Brad never blinked.

Tom had reminded himself to breathe, then turned his gaze to Bobby Sharpe, who sat with Marco and Liza Testardo, and Catherine from the Wagon Wheel. He was holding the script Tom had given him, of the funeral service, which included Bobby's own words about his aunt.

Bobby gave him a nod, like he was prompting the dealer for another card, and Tom had found what he needed to keep going.

Jesse said, "You recovered well."

He stretched his right arm to pat Tom's shoulder.

"I think our little hiccups let the crowd know we're human."

"Thanks Jesse. I meant to say how well the Blue Christmas went. That piece you said about your father, was very touching.'

"Talk about a hiccup... I had to pretend to tune my guitar, just to give my throat a break. I was literally choking up."

"Me too, Jesse, but in a good way. I better get in there before all the egg salad sandwiches are gone."

"You know they won't touch anything until after you say grace."

Chapter 45

Mid-afternoon Thursday (3 days to Christmas)

"Excuse me."

Tom's words puffed a little cloud into the cold air between him and the very large, well-dressed man who was blocking his way.

Two and a half hours earlier, Jesse had dropped Tom off at the funeral reception for Gloria Sharpe.

That event wasn't quite over, but Tom felt close to being done. It must have shown.

Mrs. Bower found Tom in the hall, retrieving his coat, and pointed him towards the rear exit, and the chance to slip out without getting caught in one last conversation.

"It'll lock behind you."

Tom couldn't move, so he had time to note the man's tailored car coat, cut from black cashmere, over a well-fitted black suit.

Tom heard the lock click.

Cashmere man stood behind Tom. The open door of a large, black SUV jutted out, barring the way forward

Diving under the open car door was out, and Tom couldn't pull it shut, without backing up against the very large man.

The cashmere coat was unbuttoned. Tom saw the shoulder holster, and the handgun. Which were also black. They matched the collared shirt and silk tie.

Tom shifted on his feet. Salt crystals crunched under the leather soles of his shoes. He hadn't bothered with overshoes, since his car was just a block away, behind the church.

He thought about his phone, which he never carried during a funeral. He'd left it in the centre console of the Range Rover.

Tom opened his mouth but was saved from inventing something to say.

"Ms. Kazinski would like to speak with you."

The man in the cashmere coat pointed into the SUV.

Two rows of bench seats faced each other.

The nearest row was empty, except for a bright red sports bag, which looked quite festive against the white leather upholstery.

Val Kazinski was seated on the opposite side. Her coat, and her short spiky hair were the exact shade of the sports bag. Blood red.

"It's getting cold with the door open."

Tom remembered Val's husky voice, and watching Bobby Sharpe turn pale when she whispered in his ear.

As he stepped into the limo, he wished he was still carrying Michael's tracker.

Cashmere man closed the door as Tom settled into the seat facing Brad Kazinski's aunt.

"This won't take long."

He'd read in Barbara's file this woman was known as Big Val, or Bloody Val, which he hoped was about her hair.

"What do you want?"

"To give you that bag on the seat beside you and clear the air."

"Why?"

"This is the second time my nephew has fished in your pond."

Tom felt the SUV begin to move. Val must have seen the question on his face.

"Marty's going to drive us around for a while. We'll end up back at your car, which needs a wash, by the way. Road salt's a killer on those British makes."

Tom was silent, then decided to be direct.

"Did Brad have anything to do with blowing up the church?"

"The guys who rigged the boiler, likely thought they did it for us. Bradley claims they got roped in by his frat boy buddy, the one who can't keep his fancy pants done up."

Tom remembered the work truck Barbara spotted on the feed from the church's parking lot camera.

"I'm just a simple country preacher."

"Hah! I like you, Rev... but I don't buy the holy country bumpkin act. Like I said, I know all about Saint Mungo's. That's a whole other layer of this cake."

"What does that mean?"

"Bradley was supposed to have learned his lesson about messing with churches."

Tom was starting to like, if not trust Big Val.

"It sounds like Troy Donaldson, who I already know is up to his... fancy pants, in some very bad business, over-reached."

"See, you're not that simple. Your cop friends must be rubbing off on you. Whoever did it should've checked if the guy ordering the job had the juice. Besides, they botched it."

"What do you mean?"

"Don't get me wrong, I'm glad they screwed up. But they tried what a small-time operator does when they want the insurance to buy a new heating system for their greenhouse."

Val gestured with her hands, like she was teaching a shop class.

"They rigged a magnet on the float-valve that controls the water return, that's supposed to keep the boiler from over-heating. When all the metal parts turn red hot they pull off the magnet and cold water rushes into the dry boiler. The water super-heats, and boom!"

She clapped her small hands to mimic the sound of an explosion.

"My guy says in the old days they'd do it with a big magnet on a string. These days it's probably an electro-magnet set up on a timer."

"So why do you say they botched the job?"

"If they'd defeated the fail-safes on the gas line, the explosion would have flattened the church, and probably your house next door."

Tom shivered.

"But why? Was Troy trying to kill Bobby?"

Tom wondered if Donaldson was involved in Gloria's death and also wanted Bobby dead.

Val said it for him.

"Like maybe Brad and Troy cooked this up to take out their buddy's only living relatives? Would that give Sharpe free rein over the family business? I wouldn't rule out my nephew plotting something like that and then setting up his old buddy to be the fall guy if the plan failed."

"Sounds like your nephew's got a different idea of friendship than I do."

"He uses people and apparently has no conscience. It makes him good at his job, but also means sometimes he goes too far, and someone has to clean up."

"Is that your job?"

"He's family. It's what we do."

"Your family... business seemed to be doing quite well in Oakville. Why the interest in Sharpe's company?"

"I can tell from your tone you have an opinion of the man. We don't like him either, but if Bradley gets a seat on his board, and shades some of our interests under Sharpe's umbrella, it changes things for us."

Tom nodded.

"It makes you look respectable."

"You probably know Sharpe's grandfather started as a rumrunner, and ended up a church elder, with a big house and streets and parks named after him."

"It's like the Canadian version of the American dream."

Big Val was smiling, so Tom pushed.

"Could there be another reason someone would want to blow up my church?"

"We think fancy pants was scared. He spent a lot of our money on security consultants. He had them looking for a woman. It's possible when she left his employ, she took certain things that represented a threat. Efforts were made to re-acquire those items."

Tom remembered Estrella saying their minivan was robbed. He also thought about the black Escalade that ran him off the road on the way home from the casino, and the team of cop lookalikes who tried to grab Marta and Estrella as they left the hospital.

"So, if they had reason to think these items were hidden in the church..."

Val said, "Maybe the hired help gets the go-ahead to pick up the former employee and her friend. Before they can make their move it's suddenly all lights and sirens. The security guys back off, watch, and wait. They gather intel and pass it along. For them it's just another contract. But maybe the boss really needs those items back."

Tom said, "Or to make sure no one else got their hands on them. The boss, Donaldson in this scenario, decides what he's looking for must be hidden in the last place the former employee was seen. They hire someone to blow up the church."

"That's a good theory."

"So Bobby had nothing to do with any of this?"

"Uh, not exactly nothing."

"What does that mean?"

"Bobby was in deep, with a Vegas bookie. My nephew bought his debt."

"So how does that work?"

"You really are an innocent, Reverend Book. I like you, so I'll lay it out for you. You know how Bobby makes his living?"

"He's a professional gambler."

"And normally, pretty good at it. But like you said about Troy Boy, Bobby over-reached. Like that guy in the story with the wax wings who flies too close to the sun."

"Icarus?"

"That's the one. Bobby was doing good at a tournament in Reno. He tries to be a high-flyer. He upped his side bet on himself, trying for the big score."

Val rubbed her hands together.

"Bradley already had eyes and ears on little Bobby, as a favour to his father. Bradley hears about the big side bet, and he buys the paper."

Val clapped her hands, like she was trapping a mosquito.

"A half mil is parking meter money in Brad's cup holder."

Tom said, "I think I see where this goes."

"Yeah, but I'll tell you anyway, because like your Icarus, it's a cautionary tale. Bobby comes down from his comped suite the next morning, all grins like a cat spitting canary feathers, and the wax starts melting, and he doesn't even know it."

Val lowered her hands, which she'd been using to illustrate a winged figure falling from the sky.

"He eats something, maybe drinks something he shouldn't. His head isn't right. His game's off, and he doesn't do so good. It happens. You fold, walk away and live to play another day."

Tom said, "Except..."

"Except for the big side bet, which he can't make good on, and which his aunt, who we know all about, maybe can't cover. So maybe Brad, or more likely one of his associates has the talk with little Bobby."

Val says this next part in a sing song voice.

"So sad, too bad, you owe us a half mil and counting. But hey, there's something you can do. There's some papers we want you to sign about your dad's company."

"But Bobby didn't sign, and his aunt was murdered, and he almost died when the boiler blew up."

"Yeah, it's a shit show. And like I've been telling you, it's not the way we like to do business."

Tom remembered Icarus was warned, not just about flying too high, but also of the dangers of going too low, getting too close to the watery depths. Was he about to do that?

"Are you saying people in your line of work don't kill?"

Val showed her teeth when she laughed.

"Hell no... that's just business. No, it's about how and where. I don't know who did Bobby's aunt, but I hate that it happened in your church.

And trying to blow the place up? Even doing it badly... whatever this was really about, and maybe it was about more than one thing, there's other ways it could've been handled."

"Like I said, we didn't like when Bradley got mixed up with your church in Oakville. We're old school. Believe it or not, we got rules. We don't mess with God's house."

Big Val pressed a button on the polished wood console beside her. The smoked glass between the chauffeur's compartment and the passenger zone slid down with a luxury whir.

"Okay, Marty. Take him back to his church. We're all done here."

Tom held up the red sports bag.

"What am I supposed to do with this?"

The bag was crafted of very soft leather, had a designer name Tom didn't know, and was a lot heavier than it looked.

"You'll figure that out. Do some good, to balance out the bad."

Tom unzipped the bag. It was packed with bricks of cash.

Tom looked at Big Val. He opened his mouth, but for the second time he had no words.

She said, "Anyone asks, that didn't come from me, and we never had this little talk."

Chapter 46

Friday evening (Christmas Eve)

Hope said, "Mary and Joseph were effectively homeless until a kind soul offered them shelter."

Annika smiled.

"That's a pretty deep thought. Maybe Tom should get you to preach tonight."

Hope was riding with Annika in her SUV. Zeke was in the K-9 carrier in the back.

"I used to help him with services all the time."

Her father had driven out to Tinsel Acres earlier with Estrella, Marta and the baby, with Lawrence and Barbara following in their unmarked car.

Annika parked near the reception building. People were going in through the open garage door to choose costumes.

Lori Gregoire gave wings and halos to those vying to be angels, and her daughters Savannah and Sadie passed towels, headbands and bathrobes to prospective shepherds.

The girls' grandmother, Mrs. Bower, was tying the sash on a silky purple robe for her cameo as the innkeeper.

Wannabe wise ones seeking robes and fancy headwear went to Penny Oltmann-Potter. A surprising number of adults were suiting up as magi.

The little girl in Hope would have loved to don a costume. Her father had led impromptu Nativity plays in the past, and they were always a lot of fun.

The parking area between the two barns was empty of cars. Most people had arrived on the shuttle buses from the church. Those who needed to drive had parked to one side of the long driveway, or behind the new barn.

Steve Tinsel-Smith had borrowed a truck with an aerial bucket so he could stretch long strings of white lights overhead from the old equipment barn to the larger new barn. They twinkled like stars and lit up the snowflakes that were floating down like fluffy white feathers.

The outside air was just crisp enough to feel like Christmas.

Zeke kept pace with Annika and Hope as they added tracks to the well-trodden snow. They headed to the brightly lit new barn.

Steve had used the aerial bucket to hang strings of lights from the rafters.

Long planks lay across hay bales to serve as pews. A stable had been built at the front, with a stall for a black and white Holstein on the left, and a pen for a few sheep on the right. There was plenty of fresh straw spread on the concrete floor.

The manger, a bench for Joseph and Mary, and a small electric fire had been set up on a riser between the cattle stall and the sheep pen.

From their seats midway up the centre aisle, Hope counted at least 150 people. That was more than she'd ever seen at worship in the church on Sharpe Street.

Patrolling barn cats tolerated the congregating humans but seemed leery of Zeke.

All three sets of barn doors were wide open. Without craning her neck, Hope was able to watch as the aerial bucket rose above the courtyard.

Hope watched her father pump his arm in the air, as if ringing an invisible bell. She'd seen him use that method many times.

Someone said, “Shh! I think it's starting.”

Sound traveled in the sheltered area between the barns. Hope heard the squeaky wheel before she saw the brown robed figure pulling the Radio Flyer wagon across the packed down snow.

Estrella wore a monk's cassock, borrowed from Paul Bennett. Her hair was covered by a hand towel with a silk tie for a headband.

Marta looked tiny in the red wagon. Hope could believe her as Mary, who'd only been thirteen when promised in marriage. She wore a sky-blue robe and had a white scarf over her hair.

Mrs. Bower got a chuckle from the crowd when she and held up a green No Vacancy sign with neon yellow lettering that suggested a Holiday Inn from the 1970's. She led the pilgrim couple into the barn and up to the stable.

They parked the Radio Flyer wagon in front of the riser, then took their seats on the bench. Marta warmed her hands over the electric fire, and a barn cat curled around Estrella's feet.

From high above the courtyard came the voice of an angel.

A spotlight shone up at Sun Parlour firefighter Lori Gregoire standing in the aerial bucket, wielding a bullhorn. Poster board wings sprung from her safety harness, and her helmet head lamp provided a halo-like glow.

"Don't be afraid, shepherds, I bring Good News!"

Sadie shouted, "You go, Mom!"

Sadie's lavender bathrobe hung open over her blue hockey jersey. She clutched a football-sized stuffed lamb.

Beside Sadie, big sister Savannah, in a lime green bathrobe, leaned into a hockey stick shepherd's crook.

"You're so embarrassing!"

Ten more junior shepherds, in various hues and patterns of robes, flocked near the bucket truck.

The angel raised her bullhorn.

"A special baby's been born in Bethlehem."

Savannah said, "How will we know this baby?"

"You'll find the baby wrapped in cloths and lying in a manger."

A door swung open on the old barn. A flight of angels tumbled out, and tromped through the snow, towards the shepherds.

The littlest angels wore white junior choir robes over winter coats and had tinsel halos wrapped around their toques.

A very tall angel wearing a bright red toque said, "Cherubs, let's sing!"

The angels began the carol. The shepherds joined in, then most of the crowd in the big barn.

"Hark the herald angels sing..."

Savannah led the shepherds and angels into the barn as the verses progressed.

Hope slipped out of her seat to meet her father backstage.

There was a room at the front end of the barn, out of sight behind the stable. That's where the sound board and live-stream gear had been set up, and where Marta and Estrella had left Alegria with Hope's father.

He came out the door pushing a stroller. Hope unclicked Alegria, snoozing in her car seat, and delivered her to the manger, where Marta and Estrella could watch over her.

By the time Hope was back to her seat, the angel with the red toque had directed the cherub chorus to settle near the cattle stall, and Savannah had her crew shepherded next to the sheep pen.

Hope's father rolled out a podium and switched on the mike.

"Mary and Joseph traveled to Bethlehem, to be counted in the Roman census. They had no place to stay, so their baby was born in a stable. Shepherds, who'd been told by angels about a special child, came to see the newborn."

Sadie, Savannah, and the rest of the little shepherds began to sing, and the congregation quickly joined in.

"Away in a manger, no crib for a bed..."

After the carol, Hope's father said, "Thank you to our innkeeper, angels and shepherds, and to Marta and Estrella, and their baby Alegria, for being our Mary, Joseph and Jesus. Alegria was just born on Sunday."

He waited until the applause subsided.

"Alegria means joy. What a perfect name for a Christmas baby."

The crowd rose to sing Joy to the World.

Estrella scooped up Alegria, who was wriggling out of her swaddling cloths.

At the end of the last verse, about the wonders of God's love, Hope's father returned to the podium.

"But what about the wise ones?"

A little voice cried out, "We're coming!"

A parade of Magi started up the centre aisle. The first six were children in bathrobes and tissue crowns, little hands gripping the white handles of colourful plastic beach pails.

Behind them were more than a dozen adults in more elaborate costumes, carrying larger buckets or shiny foil gift bags.

Hope could see her father had questions but he pushed on.

"The wise ones believed a star would lead them to a child born to be king of the Jews. They met King Herod, who asked for their help finding this rival to his power. Warned in a dream, they avoided Herod on their way home. That was very wise, because Herod planned to kill all male babies under the age of two."

The mention of Herod's evil intentions cast a momentary pall, and an eerie quiet fell over the big barn.

The first little magi, whose unruly red hair poked out at angles around his tissue paper crown, leaned over the manger.

"Hey, there's a car seat in there!"

The crowd laughed.

Hope's father said, "Before they headed home, the wise ones presented their gifts."

The redheaded junior magi flipped his purple pail and shook out a flurry of brightly coloured paper money, which fell into the Radio Flyer wagon.

The other little Magi closed in around the redhead and dumped out their treasures. Currency in many denominations was added to the growing pile.

The adult Magi approached the manger, and following the lead of the little ones, upended their larger buckets and gift bags, releasing even greater billows of tens, twenties, fifties and hundreds. The loose bills filled the wagon to overflowing.

"The Bible doesn't say how many Magi visited. We've thought three, for the number of gifts. Gold, frankincense, and myrhh. But we have a lot more than that tonight!"

While Hope's father waited for the crowd's applause to subside, Penny Oltmann-Potter slipped by him and grabbed the microphone from the podium.

Penny wore a pale-yellow robe with a light blue vest, which made Hope think of Herod as a Walmart greeter.

Her father's eyebrows crinkled the way they do when he's ticked.

Penny said, "Merry Christmas everyone!"

The crowd returned her greeting.

"I know you've all been worried about our church. While some people have seemed paralyzed, I've been reaching out to groups who share our building. I made a list..."

Penny clicked the microphone back in its stand and opened her phone.

"Our donors include AA, NA, and Alanon, the Association of Mediocre Poets, the Barely Used Clothing Exchange, Betty's Ukulele Academy, the Butterfly Festival Board, Chair Yoga..."

Folks in ordinary winter wear processed up the centre aisle, to pour out their gift bags of cash.

"...the Chess Club, the County Folk Conspiracy, Debbie's Daycare, the Food Bank, Human Rainbow and Friends, Kiddy Karate, Migrant Workers Solidarity, the New Canadian Support Group..."

Some pulled money from their wallets to drop on the pile. There were many more donors than Penny named.

"...the Not Ready for Shakespeare Players, Power Girls Gymnastics, Ralph's Tai Chi, and the Tuesday Morning Movie Watchers."

Penny said, "So many answered my pleas! We've depended too long on handouts from the Sharpe family. I hope I'm not speaking ill of the dead when I say there were times I wondered if the next payment would arrive. On the day she died, poor Gloria..."

Hope saw that her father had reached his limit. She almost cheered when he reached over the podium to grab the mike.

"Thank you to Penny, and to all who've been so generous, and not only with their money. We depend on the passion, creativity, and hard work of many."

The magi, big and small, exited down the centre aisle.

"Penny mentioned Gloria Sharpe. She made a difference in many lives, often in quiet ways that did not draw attention."

Hope's father nodded to Estrella, who passed Alegria to Marta and rose from their bench.

"When Gloria asked Estrella to sing a solo tonight she initially declined, saying she'd rather sing a duet with her friend Gloria. I wish that could have happened. It would have meant Gloria was still with us, in the flesh.

Even though they die, those we love never completely leave us. They are safely held in God's great love; they remain in memory and are with us in spirit.

The one whose birth we celebrate tonight taught there is no separation between God and us, or between heaven and earth. Everything God makes is good. Spirit and flesh are one, and this night... every night, is holy."

Dad handed Estrella the microphone.

Her voice rang out clear and true as she sang O Holy Night, in Spanish.

Chapter 47

Later Friday Evening (Christmas Eve)

After Estrella's soulful rendition of O Holy Night, Tom suggested a moment of silence. It felt right and gave him time to improvise a blessing for the deluge of donations.

Just before the service, during a loud and harsh discussion in the potting room, the board had again vetoed Penny's proposal to collect an offering.

The heat of that exchange sparked images that made it hard for Tom to find words of gratitude for the pile of cash.

The fallen tree. Shards of ornaments wet with Gloria's blood. The boiler explosion. Grey ash and shattered glass on the street. Bobby Sharpe in the hospital, mourning his aunt and grieving a father who didn't seem to have a heart for him.

Tom breathed deep. The smell of fresh straw helped. He fumbled through a prayer, then said, "Let's conclude with 'Silent Night'. While we sing, let's pass the light from one candle to another."

There were candles under the plank pews, with plastic holders to catch drips and shield the flame. They'd been stored in the church hall and had been untouched by the ashy residue of the boiler explosion.

Tom went down the aisle offering his flame to people at the end of each row, who passed it along.

Steve Tinsel-Smith dimmed the lights in the barn and those over the courtyard.

Tom felt joy when he saw the faces glowing. He gestured towards the open doors.

"Let's meet under the stars."

Kelly Halligan followed the crowd outside. His video camera was the main feed for the live-stream of the service.

Tom wondered if the Deputy Fire Chief breathed a little easier since there'd been no mishaps involving flames and hay bales.

Tom walked out to the bucket truck and stood beside Lori Gregoire. She'd descended from the sky, but still wore her safety harness, helmet and wings. She handed him the bullhorn.

"Look around at all the shining faces. Even after we blow out our candles, we can bring light to the world. Like the shepherds, we each carry the story of what happened in the stable. Bless you all. Merry Christmas and safe travels home!"

Lori blew out her candle.

"They aren't losing any time getting out of here."

Worshippers headed for the reception building, where shuttle buses waited.

Shelley was outside the open garage door to collect costumes or tell parents they could drop off their kids' nativity gear in the new year.

Tom said, "Folks still have things to do tonight, and tired little ones to put to bed."

"Speaking of which, I'd better catch up with Savannah and Sadie."

"Thanks for being our angel, and for talking with me about the night we found Gloria."

Lori's helmet lamp halo was still glowing.

She said, "It was good to talk, Tom, and I'm glad if it helped. And tonight was good. Savannah actually wanted to come to a church thing."

Lori's poster board wings flapped with each step as she strode away.

Tom returned a wave from Hope, who was already across the courtyard. She and Barbara were helping Marta and Estrella make their way with Alegria to the Range Rover.

Before heading out to the farm, they'd all had Mexican breakfast for supper, gathered around one of the sturdy tables in the Quiet Centre's dining room, which Paul called the refectory.

In a monastery, the refectory is where meals are taken. Paul had continued the monastic theme with a house rule that prohibited talking business while they ate.

The meal was chilaquiles, prepared by Lawrence and Barbara, supervised by Marta, with translation by Estrella.

Tom waited until everyone had scraped the last bits off their plates with tortilla chips, and Marta and Estrella headed upstairs with Annika to sort out their costumes for the Nativity play.

Tom shared his gut feeling about a member of the church board.

"I'd be happy to be proved wrong."

Marta and Estrella had left baby Alegria with Paul, to his total delight. He held her against his chest, and spoke quiet words about her namesake, Santa Maria de Guadalupe.

Lawrence put Paul's plate on top of his own and reached across the table for Barbara's.

"We talked the other day about trusting your feelings and treating them as a form of data."

Barbara laid her cutlery on her plate and passed it to Lawrence.

She said, "Sounds like a chapter for your book."

Lawrence looked at Barbara.

"You know about that? Tom, did you..."

"I didn't say a word."

Barbara grinned.

"You're not that hard to figure out, Lawrence Kitchen, and I am a trained detective."

Hope added her plate to the pile in front of Lawrence.

"Dad, you started to say something."

"When we were after the killer at Saint Mungo's, I saw that some people hide their true selves, at least for a while, but most of us can't keep it up, especially when provoked."

Paul Bennett paused his conversation with Alegria.

"From what I recall, you two made a good team. After a timely nudge the killer revealed themselves."

Lawrence said, "Barbara, the trained detective, also played a role."

"I was a bit player. You texted me, and I walked in on cue."

Tom said, "There is... antagonism between a few of them, and strong feelings about Gloria. I don't think it'll take much."

Hope said, "Dad, I'm a little scared of you right now."

Paul looked up from the baby, and said, "Your father's capacity to observe keenly, and anticipate threats may have developed out of fear, but I believe that for the most part, he's motivated by love."

Hope said, "It sounds like you're saying he'll only use the force for good."

Paul chuckled.

"Something like that, little padawan."

Lawrence said, "There are dramatic exceptions, but often, a person who's done something terrible doesn't sit well with it, or they've twisted themselves up to justify their actions. When you find the part of them that's cracking under the strain, and give a little push, sometimes they start to untwist, and show themselves."

Hope said, "What if all this deep, dark psychology doesn't work?"

Tom said, "There's a plan B. I've already asked Annika to help."

As the Christmas Eve service ended, Steve turned up all the lights, like at the theatre when the movie's over.

Tom was walking back into the barn, through the door closest to the stable, when he felt the buzz in his pocket.

Annika texted, "With Kelly now."

Tom replied, "Is he all done?"

Kelly brought his video camera over to the bus lines, to offer people waiting to board the chance to send greetings to those watching at home.

"Yes."

"Are you headed to the cars?"

At Tom's suggestion, Steve had directed the board members to park behind the new barn.

"Almost there."

Tom met Lawrence behind the stable, and they headed for the potting room, which had been used for sound and video.

Lawrence said, "How are they doing?"

"They're on their way."

Tom had asked the board members to meet after the service. He hadn't expected they'd need to count and bag a mound of loose bills that overflowed the Radio Flyer wagon.

Raised voices came from behind the potting room door.

Lawrence held up his phone.

"Michael has a cruiser at the end of the road, in case we need it. Let's see how this goes."

Tom opened the door. The room fell silent.

Shelley was at the sink, trying to open a kitchen-sized trash bag. It matched one that bulged with cash, on the lower shelf of the rolling cart for the sound and video gear.

Jesse and Marco sat at a table, sorting currency into piles. Jesse was doing twenties, and Marco the fifties and hundreds.

They'd been in that small room all evening. Marco kept Jesse company while he ran the soundboard and the live stream.

Liza Testardo stood behind Marco, still wearing the white robe and red toque she'd donned to guide the little cherubs. She didn't seem so angelic with her hands at her hips, and fury in her eyes.

Jesse met Tom's eyes, then nodded at Liza and Penny, as if to say 'it's already happening'.

Tom tried for a light and friendly tone.

"As the minister, I usually stay away from the money."

Penny leaned over the Radio Flyer wagon, hands squeezed tight around a ball of cash.

Her red cheeks, and the flame in her eyes, rivalled the stable's electric fire.

"You! What do you want now?"

Her hands opened, and crumpled bills fell in a flutter. A few missed the wagon.

Penny unfolded, to face Tom full on. She was a foot shorter but radiated indignation.

Tom felt the urge to run or assume a fight stance. He went over to Shelley at the sink and helped her open the trash bag.

Lawrence remained in the doorway.

Penny chased him with words.

"You couldn't let me have the spotlight. You had to steal the microphone!"

Liza Testardo stepped around Marco and closed in on Penny.

"Actually, you hijacked the mike to blow your own horn."

Penny said, "I felt it was important to acknowledge the generosity..."

Liza cut in.

"It was all to make you look good. You manipulated those people..."

"They wanted to help this church in its time of desperate need!"

Liza said, "And God bless them."

She paused, stepped back from Penny, and went to her husband.

"If they mailed a cheque, or sent a transfer, I'd send them a hand-written thank you with their receipt."

Liza stabbed a finger at the wagonload of cash.

"But I can't record their donations, because you went for the big movie moment."

"Everyone saw the amazing response I had, when you were all sitting on your..."

Liza cut her off.

"You went behind our backs, and staged your spectacle even though we said no."

Tom felt his phone buzz. He showed Annika's text to Lawrence.

"Zeke caught a trace. Penny's car. Kelly used his key fob to pop her trunk. We've got an item wrapped in a church tablecloth, shape and size of a golf club."

Lawrence whispered, "Texting Michael now."

Plan B seemed to be working, but Lawrence had warned Tom earlier that finding the murder weapon wouldn't be enough.

Tom looked up and saw that all eyes seemed to be on Penny.

He texted Annika, "Please send Kelly over."

Marco, who'd been keeping his head down and his hands busy securing stacks of bills with elastic bands, looked up at Penny.

"Reverend Tom took back the mike when you were starting in on a woman you know nothing about. Jesse and I were watching."

Jesse spoke for the first time.

"Penny, you've been spreading malicious gossip. Gloria helped this church, and this community for decades before you came to town."

Jesse'd been leery of Tom's plan but still managed to hit the right note.

Penny scowled.

"I'm tired of hearing I'm an outsider. As if living and working here for nine years means nothing."

Jesse said, "We just had her funeral, and you've been bad-mouthing Gloria in front of people who love and respect her."

Kelly texted Tom. "I'm here, what now?"

Tom replied, "Come to the potting room. Lawrence will let you in."

Penny's scowl flipped to a strange smile.

"She had an odd way of helping. The church was down to nickels and dimes, and she died with a fortune in her purse."

Tom said, "How could you know that, Penny?"

"Reverend Tom, you know I'm very close to our deputy fire chief. Kelly told me about it when he came home."

Tom said, "I was there that night. Kelly had to leave before the officers on scene uncovered Gloria's remains. I talked to Lori tonight. They were called to a motor vehicle accident on highway 3."

"Lori has it wrong. Kelly will back me up on this."

The Deputy Fire Chief entered the room.

"I'm sorry Penny, but I can't do that."

Chapter 48

Christmas Morning Breakfast

Tom washed down a bite of breakfast sausage with a sip from his travel mug.

"If you were writing this for the Casebook of the Reflective Detective, would this the scene where the sleuth and their loyal but slightly thick sidekick gather in all the loose threads?"

Lawrence sat opposite Tom at the long folding table they had to themselves, for the moment, under an open-sided eating tent in the church parking lot.

He seemed warm enough in his navy down-filled jacket over a matching wool sweater, and a white collared shirt.

"Who's the sleuth, and who's the sidekick?"

The auxiliary OPP officers had been exuberant in their distribution of orange traffic cones, and were diligently directing traffic towards either the drive-thru lane or the parking area set aside for those eating on site. A third of the lot was taken up by dining tents, each warmed by a propane heater.

The heaters made it near enough comfortable to encourage diners to linger, even after they'd had their fill of eggs, pancakes, sausages, ham, and bacon. The congregation had a long history of offering a free Christmas morning breakfast to the community.

“Oh, you’re definitely the sleuth," Tom said. "I just kind of went where the story led.”

Lawrence used his plastic knife and fork to saw through a stack of pancakes. The knife bit into the foam plate.

“I’d say you did more than that. Last night was a solid result.”

Tom hoped Lawrence would attribute his reddened face to the heater aimed their way.

“How’d it go with Penny?”

“By the time we got her to county for processing, she demanded we record her confession. Michael called in a favour to get a criminal defense lawyer to come out on Christmas Eve.”

Tom said, “I hope it helps her, in the long run, to come to terms with what she did.”

“I think what got her there was Kelly refusing to back her lie about Gloria’s purse. His basic goodness shone a light she could no longer block out."

Tom pointed to the Deputy Chief, flipper in hand, presiding over the pancake grill.

“He and his squad were here at six a.m. to set up.”

Lori Gregoire and her husband were at a table under the same tent, packing clamshell containers into brown paper takeout bags.

Their daughters, Sadie and Savannah were carrying takeout orders to waiting cars.

“Make sure you keep the bag sideways, or you’ll spill.”

“I know,” Sadie said. “Stop acting like you’re the boss of me!”

Lawrence said, “I hope this is good for Kelly, to have something to do.”

Tom nodded towards the church building and the parsonage, both of which now had boarded-over windows. Someone had outlined the distinctive arch of the old style frames on the sheets of plywood.

"We were worried we'd have to cancel the community breakfast, until Kelly offered his squad's Plan B."

Volunteer firefighters, in full bunker gear, but with Santa hats instead of safety helmets, cleared and reset place settings. They also offered top-ups on hot beverages. It was a way of telling folks to stay as long as they wanted.

Tom was happy to see a lot of diners he'd yet to meet. Like the Blue Christmas, this event drew people who'd never be seen at the church on a Sunday morning.

Jesse King, his black hair slicked and combed in full Elvis mode, picked up a platter of pancakes hot off Kelly's griddle.

He sang “Santa Bring My Baby Back” as he strutted over to a table occupied by a group from the Community Living Group Home.

Tom said, "Thank you for backing my Plan B last night."

“But how did you know it was Penny? At supper you said you had a gut feeling, and hoped you were wrong."

"It all came together because of a dream."

Lawrence made a show of looking for paper and pen.

"That would make a great first line."

Tom smiled over his coffee mug.

"Bobby Sharpe dreamed he was playing a one-armed bandit, but the handle was too long, and he had to twist himself into an odd position to grasp it. It sparked a memory of the person we saw in the surveillance video, walking oddly as they left the church. My impression was they were walking ramrod straight."

Lawrence raised his coffee mug, in a kind of a toast.

"Good eye."

Tom said, "The coroner said Gloria’s wounds resembled someone being hit by a golf club."

Lawrence estimated the length with his outstretched arms.

"Which might well fit under a long parka."

"That video was timestamped minutes before Penny arrived late to our board meeting. Barbara said the person in the video was about five feet tall. Penny's height."

"Was there something more than her height?"

“At our board meeting Penny said how sad it was poor Gloria’s light was snuffed out.”

"That's creepy, and cheeky."

"It felt cold, and the way she called her 'poor Gloria' brought me back to my Wednesday morning conversation with Penny."

"Your unhappy wake up call? I remember."

"She kept calling Gloria poor. It felt like a dig. She also seemed to know more about how we found Gloria than she should have."

Lawrence nodded.

"The purse."

"Which as Kelly confirmed, he could not have told her about."

"Yes, to great effect."

"During his Blue Christmas show, Jesse couldn't find the candle snuffer, which we also use to light candles. I was so focused on his improvised a solution; it took me days to wonder why it was missing."

“You got there. But if our team hadn’t been rushed we could have found the snuffer before Penny came back for it. Her prints are likely on it. We could have pulled her in a lot sooner.”

“I’m guessing your report will mention that.”

“Michael’s drafting an internal memo.”

Tom dropped a paper napkin over his plate.

“Internal memo. So Sharpe won’t be held accountable? He interfered with your investigation. I think he did it mostly to give Troy Donaldson time to try to recover the evidence against him.”

“Pursuing that means admitting we succumbed to outside influence, and risks complicating the proceedings against Penny.”

“So Sharpe walks away clean?”

Lawrence shook his head.

“Michael’s having a meaningful conversation with the Honourable Member as we speak.”

“Is Barbara with him?”

“Michael sent her home. By now she’s in Barrie, having breakfast with her parents.”

“We’d planned to invite both of you to supper tonight, out at the Quiet Centre. Annika and Hope are already working on it, with help from Marta and Estrella. But I’m glad she’s with her family. I wish...”

Lawrence met Tom’s eyes.

“I appreciate it, Tom. And I’ll be glad to join you.”

“Have you reached out to your daughter?”

"I called Emily this morning. My five a.m. was seven p.m. for her. We talked for twenty minutes."

"After my wife died, Hope was very angry. A twenty-minute conversation would have involved a lot of long silences."

"Things shifted when I told her I'd been shot at."

"How'd she take that?"

"She softened. I was glad but also didn't want to milk the incident for sympathy."

"How did she..."

"Emily cried and said she wished she could hug me. But she was at a friend's and needed to get to the supper table."

"How did you leave things?"

"She asked when I'd come see her."

"You going to go?"

Lawrence held up his arm, no longer in a sling.

"I'm due some time. Emily will have eight days off around Easter."

Hope approached their table with a plate of steaming pancakes.

Tom said, "I thought you were helping..."

"There are enough hands in that kitchen. They kicked out Paul, and I figured I was next," Hope said. "I stopped in at the parsonage, to pick up the Christmas presents."

"Good idea," Tom said.

Hope took a seat next to her father and unwrapped her cutlery.

"We'll open them after supper. I hope you got Annika something good. She's already told me what she has for you."

Lawrence said, "Merry Christmas Hope."

Hope said, "You both look very serious. Talking about Penny?"

"I was telling your Dad about my daughter Emily."

"Does she know you were wounded?"

Lawrence's face told Tom he'd reached his limit.

"Lawrence says Penny confessed to killing Gloria."

Hope said, "We know they didn't get along, but that wasn't new. What was the thing?"

Tom said, "The thing?"

"Whatever it took to push her to kill her last week, and not last year."

Lawrence relaxed into safer conversational territory.

"This is my amateur psych profile. Penny envied Gloria's position, and the respect she received, even from people who nattered behind her back."

"Penny told us her family moved a lot as she was growing up. Lots of one-to-two-year stints in small towns all over Southern Ontario. Her father, Henry Potter, worked for one of the big banks as a kind of a hired gun. They would send him into local branches to solve problems, then move him on. Penny had a hard time making friends in small communities where everyone already knows everyone, except the new kid."

"Penny followed her father into the same national bank, but after a decade of bouncing from branch to branch, and a marriage that didn't end well, she detoured into a management role at the Sunny Shores Credit Union. She'd hoped to set down roots and become a part of the community."

"Penny joined the church, and the choir, and worked her way into a lot of local organizations. She kept the books and handled the finances for most of the groups that met at the church."

"We suspect Penny skimmed a little from a lot of different accounts and pooled the money in short term investments. Then she cashed them out and put back what she borrowed."

Tom said, "Was she doing that with the church's funds? Was Gloria on to her?"

"Penny said the most annoying thing about Gloria was that when she noticed what Penny was up to, Gloria tried to reform her rather than turn her in."

Tom said, "I'm guessing this would have been around the time Gloria ended the annual lump sum payments from the Sharpe Trust and switched to monthly cheques."

"Penny believed Gloria did that to rub it in her face on a monthly basis that she'd been caught. It made her feel even more the outsider. I suspect it also reinforced her desire to accumulate wealth by any means and symbolically assume Gloria's power."

Hope said, "That's pretty deep, and really sad."

Tom said, "Kelly told me the other day that Penny had been pressuring him to give her signing power on all his accounts."

"Did he give it to her?"

"No."

"Good for him. That could have been a real mess."

Hope said, "If Gloria caught her stealing years ago, why did Penny wait until now to... do what she did?"

Lawrence said, "Penny was at the church that night to ask Gloria one more time to give her the Christmas Eve solo."

Hope said, "O Holy Night. The one Estrella sang. It was breathtaking."

Lawrence opened his notebook.

"Penny said, 'I couldn't believe she did that to me. I walked away, to see if she'd call me back, but she just went back to singing. She was mocking me with every note she didn't quite hit. I picked up the candle snuffer and stopped her from finishing the song. Then I knocked over that ugly tree she insisted on putting up every year.' "

Hope said, "It's just a sad, awful story. But I'm glad you got her."

Chapter 49

Mid-afternoon Christmas Day

Tom said, "Do you think justice has been served?"

Michael turned towards Tom and lowered the long-range binoculars he'd been using to follow the progress of a freighter on Lake Erie.

He peeked at his phone.

"Marine traffic app says that's the Algoma Innovator, a bulk cargo vessel, headed for Montreal. It needs to hustle to get through before the seaway closes for the winter. From up here, without a landmark, it's hard to tell if it's even moving."

Tom said, "Are you trying to say justice moves slowly?"

"You give me a lot of credit, partner. Maybe I was just watching a big boat."

Michael still wore the OPP dress uniform he'd donned for the meeting with Robert Sharpe.

Tom wasn't sure what The Member thought, but he'd been impressed when he saw the medals against the dark blue tunic, the gold leaf trim on the peaked cap, and the crowns and pips on the shoulder boards, denoting the rank of superintendent.

They were up in the observatory, on the bluff overlooking the water, at the edge of the Quiet Centre property.

Michael said, "It is a great view."

Tom said, "Paul calls it the Aerie."

Michael set the binoculars on a table, next to a matte-black headset. He picked up that device and gave it a closer examination.

"A trained investigator might wonder why a retreat centre has better night vision gear than our tactical teams."

"Paul can probably hook you up. He knows a guy."

Michael pointed at the windows.

"Clear sight lines in every direction. By land or by water."

He removed his peaked cap and set it on the table beside the optical devices.

"I hope someday you'll tell me more about this place, and what you and Paul were mixed up with two years ago."

Tom gestured towards a pair of comfortable chairs angled for conversation, but also for the view over the lake. They each took a seat.

"I will when I can. Most of the story isn't mine to tell."

"I figured," Michael said.

"And what do you figure about justice?"

"We scored a win. Marta, Estrella and baby Alegria can live without looking over their shoulders. They'll have the legal right to stay in Canada, if they choose."

"That part feels like a win. But The Member just slinks back to Ottawa, and the Kazinskis carry on."

Michael said, "There's justice and there's justice. We've got Penny for Gloria's death, thanks to you. We've got Troy Donaldson on a list of unsavoury charges, including human trafficking, forcible confinement, and rape."

"And the mess at the church?"

"We probably won't get anywhere on the boiler explosion unless someone who knows something gets picked up and tries for a deal."

Tom said, "Even then, that won't reach the people at the top."

Michael said, "The Honourable Member won't be running the Treasury Board. It will cost him, to get the Minister's permits for Marta and Estrella."

"So you weren't just trying to help them..."

"Two birds, partner. We'd have found a way to get them clear. But pushing The Member has an added bonus. In the back room where the guys still talk through cigar smoke, they maybe don't know why Sharpe called in this favour, but they'll assume he's been compromised."

"He couldn't sell it as going above and beyond for a family in distress?"

"Two young women from Mexico, and their newborn," Michael said. "One is smuggled in without papers to work in The Member's greenhouse and is brutally assaulted by one of his oldest friends."

"An unlicensed grow-op in the middle of his home riding, with a cache of firearms, and more than a dozen undocumented workers living and working in hellish conditions."

"The guys in the club chairs can't risk backing him for anything high profile, in case it's made public."

Tom said, "Which it probably will, if Estrella gets her story out."

Michael said, "If The Member and his friends knew that, we wouldn't have got the Minister's permits. They won't be happy if she publishes, which I have to say, would warm my heart. The Member would then be well and truly cooked."

"What about the Kazinskis?"

"Like I said, we might eventually get a line on whoever they paid to sabotage the church boiler. But even if we find them, it'd be a stretch to prove they knew Bobby was in the church, and then to draw the straight line back to Brad Kazinski."

"So they carry on, business as usual?"

"Not entirely. They took a major hit. Estrella's intel led to our raid on the grow op. We seized a few trucks, which led us to a leasing company. We've learned more about their pipeline."

"This all feels enormous," Tom said. "How do you not lose hope?"

"We shut down a significant part of their operation, and seized millions in product, weapons, and cash. We've siphoned off the fuel that keeps their machine running."

"Think about that lake freighter out there. I wouldn't want to be in a small boat that was caught in its path. But if we cut off its diesel, it wouldn't be long before the engines stopped, and the whole thing was dead in the water."

Tom said, "Won't the Kazinskis just set up somewhere else?"

"That'll take time, and more money. Short term, we've slowed them down. Longer term... again, if Estrella gets her story out there, it'll help. It could put pressure on certain agencies on both sides of the border."

"We have indications they'd previously been told to go easy on the trucks that service the big greenhouses, because such a big industry can't afford time delays."

They were silent for a few minutes.

Michael picked up the binoculars and stood to look again out over the water. In the time they'd been talking, the big freighter had sailed out of sight.

Tom thought about a conversation he'd had at the church breakfast.

He'd asked Lawrence, "Knowing what you know, and with all that you see, how do you keep your heart light and your head above water?"

Lawrence laid down his fork.

"The short answer is I haven't always. A failed marriage and a daughter on the other side of the world should tell you something. A longer answer is I work at remembering why I do this job."

Tom said, "Tell me why."

"There are always going to be people who do bad things. They threaten, hurt, and kill people, take what doesn't belong to them, and throw their weight around so they can keep doing it. The rest of us, who are just trying to live our lives, raise our kids, have a mostly happy life, need to know someone's out there to stop them."

"We can't get them all, but we also can't just lie down and let the bullies, the creeps, and the apparently heartless have free rein. You heard Estrella's description of what was done to Marta and her friends."

"We need to keep on them, shine light on their actions, and work to have them held accountable. So that's what we do."

Tom walked over to Michael, who was still at the window, looking out over Lake Erie.

"I have some thoughts about Estrella, and Marta, and the money."

Michael said, ‘What money?”

“Big Val took me for a ride the other day and gave me a swanky red leather bag full of cash.”

Michael said, “I’m just hearing this now?”

“We’ve had a lot going on. She said it was to make up for her nephew’s bad behaviour, and that back in the day, churches were off limits.”

“Did she come out and say Brad was behind the explosion?”

Tom said, “She admitted it was possible.”

Tom summarized his conversation with Big Val.

“Interesting. Did she say what she wanted done with the money?”

“She did not,” Tom said. “At first I assumed it should go to rebuilding the sanctuary, but the building is very well insured.”

“You have a different idea?”

“She doesn’t want anyone to know she gave it, and I’d rather not explain a bag full of money from a crime family.”

“She’s not expecting a charitable receipt.”

“She is not.”

“If you were to hand it to your new treasurer, when you get one, they would have questions. Any bank deposit over $10,000 rings alarm bells. I’m guessing Val’s gift bag contained at least that much.”

“Oh yeah.”

“What about the actual cash?” Michael said. “Does it look legit?”

“Like it came straight off an armoured truck. Twenty bricks of ten bundles each, freshly wrapped. Each bundle has its Bank of Canada strap, with a tracking number. All shiny new hundred-dollar notes.”

Michael said, “So, two million in cash. Do you want me to run the serial numbers, see if it’s clean?”

“That’s been done.”

“Hmm. And you’ve learned to talk about bricks, bundles and straps. Who’s helping you?”

“We’re friends, Michael, and I’d trust you with my life.”

“I appreciate that, partner. And that goes both ways.”

“I’ve no doubt you’re connected with things you can’t tell me about.”

Michael shrugged.

"It comes with the job."

"It's more than your job. I have a sense of who you are, and why you do things. Even your strategic move with the Minister's permits, which serves more than one agenda. You work in a world of wheels within wheels, and sometimes those wheels roll through a lot of muck."

Michael said, "You're not wrong about that."

"But I don't need to know the details of everything you do to have confidence in your choices."

"Thank you for that... and I see where you're going with this. You're going to ask me to trust you."

"I am."

"I do trust you, Tom. And I'm still a very curious person."

"You're a detective. You probably can't help it."

Michael smiled.

"Paul's Aerie is impressive. When we walked the underground passage that connects the main house to this silo, it occurred to me that his whole setup was carefully considered."

"Paul's like that," Tom said, "He and his mother had been planning something like this for years. She helped him find the location and drew up sketches."

Michael said. "This property, and the enhancements he's made, couldn't have been cheap. Never mind the Range Rovers he keeps giving you."

"Paul never married and has always lived simply. His mother had a long career before she came over from England to live with him. She did something important with the British government."

"Uh-huh. So, what's your idea about the money from Big Val?"

"I'd like to use a chunk to help Marta and Estrella get on their feet. What if a foundation provided a kind of settlement grant, then a monthly stipend for a fixed period? Maybe until Alegria starts school?

It could help them set up a home, and cover living costs until one or both of them finds employment."

"That would be a very kind thing to do."

"The same foundation could offer Estrella a project grant, to assist the completion of her investigative project. I was thinking she could hire a production assistant, and maybe also get an intern from the journalism program at St. Clair College. It would help her go public with her story, for the reasons you mentioned, but also to provide answers to the families of the disappeared."

"It all has to be totally legit," Michael said. "Marta and Estrella need a clean paper trail, so they can open bank accounts and file taxes."

"Paul's had the foundation in place for years. It's squeaky clean, and does some amazing things, in a very... quiet way."

"Yes. Quiet. I get it," Michael said. "And I really do look forward to hearing more about the real mission of this place."

Tom put a hand on his friend's shoulder.

They both looked out over the calm water.

"Like I said, that's a story for another time."

Acknowledgements

I am part of two writing groups. One meets Mondays and Fridays at the Kingsville library. The other meets twice a month at Storyteller's Bookstore on Ottawa Street in Windsor. (Linda, who owns the store, allows us to invade her space, and when we publish, there is always room on her shelves for our books.)

Becoming active with these groups has helped turn a largely solitary pursuit into something wider, and more convivial. It's the writerly equivalent of Norm walking into Cheers, without the chilled steins.

I'm also a member of Crime Writers of Canada (CWC), and The Writer's Union of Canada. I've developed professional relationships and received mentoring through CWC. The Writer's Union has provided financial support for public readings.

The Book of Christmas Joy was born out of a conversation with my wife, while we were out at Point Pelee National Park. She said something like, "You did Easter in the first book. You should do Christmas," and we went on to talk about a church matriarch as a possible victim. We also discussed aspects of congregational life in that busy season, many of which found their way into this story.

The birthing of the final version of this book could not have happened without the kindness and patience of a team of "midwives" who read an earlier draft. Their questions and comments led to significant changes that I think have made the book better.

About the author

For thirty-five years Darrow Woods served as an ordained minister and spiritual director, a career that took him to rural, suburban and inner-city settings all over Canada. In an earlier life he worked construction, helped run a pizza joint, was a chauffeur and car washer, and had a stint as a railway brakeman. Long before that, with unnamed co-conspirators, he ran an underground newspaper in his high school.

Until he got serious about writing fiction, he used to run marathons for fun. Well, fun may be an overstatement.

These days Darrow serves as a volunteer chaplain with one of North America's largest police services. When he's not at his writing desk, he's often "loitering with intent" at police detachments, or out riding in police cruisers. (They let him sit in the front, which is better.)

Darrow's first crime novel The Book of Answers was a finalist for a Crime Writers of Canada Award of Excellence.

Darrow writes about crime fiction and other things for his Reluctant Sleuth Substack page.

https://darrowwoods.substack.com/

To arrange an in-person or virtual book club visit, contact the author by email: revdww@gmail.com

Also by

The Rev. Thomas Book Mysteries began with The Book of Answers,
available in print or digital form through Amazon, KOBO and Apple,
and in many fine bookstores, including:
Story Tellers, Juniper Books and Biblioasis in Windsor,
River Books in Amherstburg,
and the Art Society of Kingsville.

Preview First Chapter of The Book of Answers

Zeke the cadaver dog raised his big head as if he'd just thought of a question. He paused his zig-zag search pattern, to turn and face me and his handler. His loud bark sent a shock through me, even though I'd watched him open his jaws to let loose with it.

The producers of "The Ghost Toucher" claimed to be testing a theory that dogs like Zeke are guided by the spirits of the dead. They'd brought him in to sniff out the ghost of Saint Mungo's Church.

I thought it was a ploy to jazz up an otherwise boring location shoot. The generic minister type in a dark suit and clerical collar saying to the camera, "I've heard the wild rumours, of course, but haven't seen anything like what you're looking for..."

That's the line I planned to stick with if they asked. I sure wouldn't be telling them what I'd seen just before the dog barked.

Annika, the handler said, "Good dog, Zeke. You're such a good dog."

She knelt to unclip Zeke's black nylon leash from the safety orange Search and Rescue harness.

"Bones, Zeke. Find the bones!"

Annika tucked the leash in a pocket of her khaki tactical vest as she rose to stand.

She said, "That bark was his first tell Reverend Tom. He may have something."

The sable-coated German Shepherd bounded up the aisle towards the front of the Saint Mungo's sanctuary, leaving paw-prints pressed deep into the crimson carpet. He took the three steps up to the chancel platform in a powerful leap, landing under the dark oak communion table, and skidding between its legs. Zeke's nails clicked and scratched at the polished wood flooring as he scrambled for footing.

I turned to face the dog-handler, who was all my six feet and a bit more in her tactical boots. I met her eyes, which were amber.

"Annika, is he really searching for bones?"

"That's just his go-word. Zeke's trained to find bones, blood, and partial or complete human remains."

Those last words chilled me, despite Annika's bright smile, and the withering heat. The production crew had set up a bank of huge carbon-arc spots. They shone down from the rear balcony, lighting the church up like a high-end car dealership, and roasting us like convenience store hot-dogs.

All the sanctuary windows are stained glass. You'd never know that outside it was a cold and grey morning. A late winter blizzard that left folks from Arkansas to Quebec plowing and digging had also blasted Oakville. I'd been grateful to get from my car to the side door of the church without tumbling on the slick ice.

Zeke regained his traction on the hardwood floor and dashed towards an oak door set in the wall beside the organ keyboard. He nosed it open and stood peering down the back stairs.

His body vibrating, Zeke turned back towards Annika and opened his jaws for another harsh bark, which echoed through the sanctuary.

"That's his second tell," Annika explained. "He wants to get down to the basement."

Annika's long blonde hair lifted as she ran to her dog. Her thick-soled boots thudded on the hardwood floor. A holstered phone and a long black flashlight bounced against her hip.

Reaching the doorway, she squatted near Zeke and dug into a vest pocket for a treat. The German Shepherd licked it from her open palm.

"Good dog, Zeke. Bones?"

Zeke took his cue and dove down the back stairs. Annika was right behind him.

I headed toward the chancel steps, halting when I heard, “You need to let us through, Reverend Tom!”

I pivoted in time to avoid Kat Daniels, the assistant director, waving her aluminum clipboard as if she were swatting flies, and me, out of her path.

Hassan, the camera operator was close at Kat’s fashionable heels. His muscled frame made the video rig strapped to his shoulder look small. As he side-stepped to pass us, I backed out of his way until I felt the hard edge of a pew against my rear end.

Kat ran after the camera operator, shouting orders.

“Go! Go! We need this shot. Get downstairs and see what the dog’s found.”

Manufactured by Amazon.ca
Bolton, ON

51064520R00149